THE BOOK OF DEATH

— — —

RAMY TADROS

 NIGHTLIGHT BOOKS

The Book of Death

Ramy Tadros

📖Nightlight Books

Edited by Proton Writing Consultants Pty Ltd
www.WritersMarke.com | info@WritersMarke.com
PO Box A2379 | Sydney South | NSW 1235 | Australia

ISBN-13: 978-0-9875530-2-7

Disclaimer
All characters appearing in this work are fictitious. Any
resemblance to real persons, living or dead, is purely coincidental.

1

Despite the stifling atmosphere, it is the patchwork of puke and broken beer bottles carpeting the concrete path that signals summer's approach. The heat and humidity sap my energy, and even the dog succumbs to the night air's thickness. He pants and protests and drags on the leash, but I coax him into trudging on. For a reward lies ahead.

The park is as exhausted as the metropolis choking it. Yet grass and shrubs and trees somehow eke out a living among the dirt and dust and debris. The trees, gnarled and anaemic, also nurse many manmade wounds and carvings. They cling to life, though, for this is their gift and their curse.

No rains have fallen for several weeks, and dirt islands have erupted from the scorched Earth. The sucked-out remains of a worm, having failed to draw any sustenance from the desiccated soil, crown one of the islands. But, between the islands, life marches on: an ant colony toils. For this pheromone-based sterile sisterhood, the night poses no barriers, and it is work as usual. An ant strays from her colony and stumbles on an invisible yet gluey tripwire. She is trespassing on private property; she is trapped in an alien system. Her struggles vibrate throughout the web infrastructure, and within seconds the owner, a tactile-based recluse, glides over the silk threads of his home to claim the entangled intruder as payment. The web glistens with the moisture collected from the muggy air and trembles with the settlement of nature's contract.

Near this exchange, a weed also grapples with life—but this battle is being fought between two concrete slabs. The weed's roots are exposed; its leaves, wilted. Life-and-death struggles abound.

Mole crickets' chirps haunt the night air. And though it is a coastal park, the air smells acrid and smoky from recent fires that have incinerated an inner-city slum and many of its residents. A noxious film now coats everything in the metropolis, adding another layer of grime to the already bleak landscape. But the conflagration's cause remains unknown, and everyone suspects everyone. The people are frightened; the State is perishing.

A startled flying fox launches from a tree branch and fades into the blackness. Darkness reigns except for a faint glow rising from the city's heart in the west; from this vantage, it resembles an ember in a dying campfire. Few streetlights work. The majority—abused and neglected for years—offers no light, whereas the functioning minority emits a muted white light. They flicker and splutter in

2

protest, yet no one fixes them. Their days are numbered. Then, the darkness will be endless. Even the clouds are conspiring to keep this place shrouded in black, for the night is starless and moonless.

But the dysfunctional streetlights serve another purpose. Many are coupled with black hives: security cameras shielded by thick black domes. On each hive an imprint says, "Proudly made by Worldwide Industries & Finance Co. at the request of the Occidental Union." And even though I can hear a few hives buzzing with activity as the cameras focus on their targets, the majority remain lifeless. The all-seeing State is going blind—and no beast, no matter its strength, can survive for long without its eyes.

Apart from the hived streetlights, ragged signs also blight the landscape. They declare many objects and pastimes to be "forbidden" or "not permitted" or "carrying severe penalties", yet few people heed the warnings. The State cannot enforce the countless rules all the time, and the rulers rarely try to antagonise the masses these days.

State-owned apartment complexes skirt the park. Many of these crumbling eyesores host signs proclaiming them to be "condemned" or "scheduled for destruction" or "registered for demolition", even though they have worn these signs for years, possibly decades. Yet few people care. Swarms of vagrants call these condemned structures home. And, through the cracked windows, the squatters' fires can be seen dancing from the buildings' depths—a last flicker of life from the decaying behemoths.

Vagrants also call this park home. An unguarded pile of junk, someone's lifework, rests under a diseased coast banksia tree. But something nestled in the junk captures the dog's attention. He stops to sniff a bird's carcass, and I tug on the leash just before he reaches his prize. And, yes, it *is* a prize, for nature wastes nothing. Even a decomposing system gives birth to something else, and new life emerges from old. A tangle of maggots devours the oozing rot, while scavenger beetles tear at the firmer flesh. Although this rot embodies nature's cycle and is a microcosm of the universe, the stench of death overwhelms me and I rush the dog forwards.

Farther down the park path, I spot a group of youths occupying a graffitied gazebo. Smashed beer bottles mark their territory, and their shouts and screams warn intruders to avoid trespassing on it. So I respect the ancient law and steer a detour through the shrubs and bushes. As the dog and I pass the group, the screams become more frenzied, and this vindicates my natural instincts. Are they cries of joy or pain? It does not matter, not anymore.

The park path ends, and the beach path begins. Yet the darkness—the nothingness—lurks here, too, for the ocean appears inky in the moonless night sky. Despite this, my mood lightens as I hear the roar of the crashing waves and inhale the refreshing salt breeze. The surf's sound and smell arouse ancient images—a memory from a visit to one of the Free Islands, a place lost in a vast ocean and forgotten by the world. I picture blue waters quivering at the Sun's touch. So long ago yet still so vivid. I can even smell and taste the clean island air. The oceanic atmosphere revives me and fills me with hope—nature, on occasions, can be good. But the fantasy soon fades away, as a movement on the beach snuffs out the illusion and restores the sky and ocean to their original sooty hue.

Small fires dot the beach, and the aroma of charred wood mingles with the air. A few humans scurry across the sand, scavenging what they can from unprotected campfires. Many of these drifters will wallow on the beach for the entire spring and summer—a free summer vacation home—while peace officers will occasionally pester them to return to their assigned lodgings. But the threats, as usual these days, lack authority. For even though the State's networks have infiltrated every aspect of life, the government is effete and bankrupt. It lacks the strength and will to govern. And, in any event, bigger problems than dealing with drifters plague the peace officers.

The dog and I continue strolling along the beach path. Although sporadic bouts of shouting and shrieking arise from the beach, the metropolis to the west is gripped in an eerie silence. Once bustling, thriving, simmering; now hushed, thinned, drained. Halfway down the path, a teen waif emerges from the shadows and surprises me. His shirtless frame reveals a tattooed torso glistening with sweat and grime. Underneath this odious coating, angry red boils blanket his body. Several swellings have burst and are weeping—or, at least, they are trying to weep through the encrusted filth. Such boils have probably ripened from infected bedbug bites, a common scourge occurring every spring and summer. This spring, though, the bedbugs have been swarming every inch of the metropolis in staggering numbers, and every warm-blooded creature has been suffering frenzied nightly attacks. It is a brutal, bloody, and unstoppable feast—unstoppable because the bedbugs now resist every insecticide. And making matters worse, many persons have died from the infected bites and the untreatable multidrug-resistant *Staphylococcus aureus* bacteria brewing within the boils. Deaths have also occurred from the bedbugs themselves, as weaker people, unable to tolerate the numerous nightly assaults, succumb to the little suckers. I have even stumbled across bodies, drained of every last drop of blood, still hosting late-coming bedbugs as they try in vain to squeeze out a few more corpuscles.

Besides the boils, the waif also sports a slight hunch exaggerated by his forward-jutting shoulders. His shaved black hair is not level, and a few patches dominate the rest. Sunken amorphous eyes blacken his pasty face, and a dried-urine reek clings to the air surrounding him. It is the unmistakable stench of a festering human, which few other animals share. Assaulting my nostrils, penetrating my lungs, swamping all my senses—I want to escape the stench, but I cannot. I must confront the waif and avoid exposing my back. For although the waif is tiny and alone, he remains dangerous. They all are. One can multiply and become many within seconds. And how can one man and his dog—although he is a hefty wolflike mongrel in his prime—resist an armed mob?

"Oi, mate," the waif says, "gotta smoke?" He then snorts and spits out a phlegm wad that splashes near my foot.

"Sorry, kid, I don't smoke," I reply. "It's illegal and—"

"Illegal? Ha! Nothin's illegal. It's all good. And don't tell me nothin', mate. No one tells me what to do. Me do what me want, when me want. Got it?"

"Hmm, kid, I think you'd better—"

"That's a big ugly dog ya got there," the waif interrupts, while scratching furiously at several boils on his neck. "A really, *really* ugly dog. Friggen hell—really big, too! What is it?"

"*It? He* is not an *it. He* is not an object, like a rock. *He* lives and feels and thinks, just like you and me. *He* is a—"

"Whateva. Evil lookin' too. What's *its* name?"

Sensing the hostility, the dog growls and tugs on the leash as he inches towards the waif.

"Calm down, Anup," I say to my dog, while patting his luxurious coat. "That's it. Good boy, Anup. Good boy. Come on, let's go."

Then, ignoring the waif, we turn to leave.

"Hey, ya prick!" the waif shouts. "Me jus' wanna smoke. Jus' one! Ya greedy bastard!"

I snap around and face the waif. Although I know I should avoid any confrontation, especially with the State's Spawn, his smugness and disrespect infuriate me. The decay of civility has mirrored the decay of the city. Or is it the other way around?

"*Prick?*" I say. "Nice manners you've got there, you dirty runt. The State must be proud of the way it has raised you. Brilliant job! But as I tried to tell you before you so rudely interrupted me, I haven't got any cigarettes. Now, *get lost* before you really make me and my dog mad."

On cue, Anup snarls and pulls on the leash. Despite his usually loving nature, he loathes the State's Spawn—something about their smell and demeanour. And he shares

7

a horrific history with them—a cruelty they inflicted on him as a puppy.

But the waif fails to grasp my threat, and says, "Yeh? Well, then, then, why ya lookin' so well off? Ha? It's not fair—ya gotta share. Ya know, like they teach us. Yeh. *It's not fair—ya gotta share.* Okay? So whaddya got in ya pockets?"

"*It's not fair—you've got to share*?" I repeat, while sniggering. "You're joking, right? Is that the latest slogan the State's got you parroting? Is that the garbage they're teaching you nowadays?"

"C'mon, mate. Me hungry. Anythin' at all!"

"Then get the State to feed you," I answer. "It raises you and gives you handouts, rations, and everything you need—oh, yes, and all the beer you can drink. And you know this perfectly well. So go wait in line at the Temple of the People, like me and everyone else. Got it?"

"So ya got nothin' for me?"

"That's right—nothing."

"Nothin' at all?"

"Nothing."

"Come on—*one* smoke!" he says, before a coughing spasm consumes him.

He spits out another phlegm wad. This time, though, it splatters under a working streetlight, and I see blood tainting the sputum. Because of my background, I know what this probably means: tuberculosis, an ancient plague that humanity almost conquered. But now the bacteria are multidrug resistant, reverting the disease to its prior incurable-worldwide-killer status. And even though tuberculosis is unlikely to infect a healthy adult like me, I take no chances and step back from the boy.

"Look, kid," I say, feeling sympathy for the dying teenager, "I've already told you that I don't smoke and that it's illegal. So how can I have a cigarette? And if you don't believe me, then have a look." I empty my pockets and show him that I have nothing—absolutely nothing. No cigarettes, no anything. "Okay? Now, I've emptied my pockets and shown you that I have nothing in them. So I have nothing at all with me. *Nothing.* I'm like you—I have nothing. Nothing."

Eavesdropping on the exchange, another teen waif slinks out of the nearby shadows. Her reek is even more disgusting than the boy's. It is an overpowering presence.

"Hey, Mo, let's go," she says to him. "This arsehole ain't got nothin'. Better pickin's on the beach. C'mon."

And, with that, the waifs steal away towards the beach, the reek trailing them.

I breathe freely now that the stench has gone. But the meeting has left me unsettled, and I am drenched in sweat from the heat, humidity, and excitement. Even though roaming the streets at night presents a gamble, I refuse to surrender my final freedom. If it is too hot to walk during the day, as it was today, then I will risk walking at night. I have sacrificed enough freedoms.

Anup and I resume our walk. On reaching the end of the beach path, however, we find a tween–teen group loitering at the exit. This time we have no choice. If we want to continue along the coastal path, we must pass this group. Yet it would be safer to risk an encounter with them than deviate from the path, head inland, and tempt the inhabitants of the sinister side streets. As I ponder what to do, a quarrel flares up between one of the boys and one of the girls. The girl, screeching and swearing, clenches a bottle and strikes the boy's head. The boy, blood gushing out of his head wound, teeters backwards but regains his balance and then lunges at his comrade-turned-assailant. Their friends cheer and jeer, yet no one tries to interfere.

I stare at the ground and recall a proverb: "He that pries into every cloud, may be stricken with a thunderbolt." Having no wish to be stricken with anything, I decide to mind my own business and end the walk early.

~~~~~

Anup and I are about to enter the park and head for home, when we bump into two Occidental Union Peace Officers. Their badges announce Constable Dewey and Constable Wilson.

"Officers, please! I say. "There's a bloody fight at the other end of the beach!"

"Yes, we know," answers Constable Wilson. "It's been logged into the system. I am now going to scan you and your dog for identification purposes."

Constable Wilson pulls out a tablet computer from her police duty belt and points the tablet in my direction. It emits a beep, as the information from the microchip implanted in my nape is transmitted to the tablet. She peers at the tablet's screen for a few seconds and then points the gadget in Anup's direction. It beeps again.

"Okay, you and your dog are clear. All is in order. Your certificates are up to date, and you have no outstanding fines, fees, dues, rates, tolls, tithes, taxes, tributes, imposts, levies, charges, duties, excises, customs, contributions, or payments due," she says, still staring at the tablet's screen. "By the way, do you know that new regulations will be enforced next year, and that your dog will be required to wear a State-compliant muzzle? Heavy fines apply for noncompliance."

"Officers," I say, "there's a boy bleeding badly and a girl being bashed right now!"

"Yes, we heard you the first time, sir. It's been logged, and we are waiting for backup," replies Constable Dewey, who seems apathetic—almost drowsy. He then pulls out his tablet and, in a droning voice, reads aloud the message on its screen: "State-compliant muzzles may be purchased from your local Temple of the People. If you cannot afford a State-compliant muzzle, you may apply for funding assistance at your local Temple of the People. However, first, you will need to fill out a DMR0002212 form at Occidental Union Central, along with providing the relevant certified documentation. You will need to procure this documentation from your CommunityAssist caseworker, who may require you to provide signed documents from other authorised personnel such as a CommunityAssist-licensed general practitioner or a CommunityAssist-licensed social worker, in order to facilitate the process. If you need further assistance, please visit the YourOccident website or call or visit your local Temple of the People."

I sneer at the State's inanity. People are killing each other, and these officers are lecturing me about a State-compliant muzzle. What else can I do but play along with their tired and ridiculous system?

Though the State's decline has been long and slow, the end feels tantalisingly near—and yet the end has felt tantalisingly near for the last couple of decades. Always near, but never here. Perhaps this is part of the State's game, its illusion: to keep the people mired in perpetual crises, while all the time being in control. Previous governments have always used crises—the war on this, the war on that—to silence democratic discussions and enhance government power. This State has probably mastered the art of crafting crises.

How I long for the entire system to fail. How I yearn for the old mess to be expunged: the stupid regulations that expand on equally stupid yet older regulations. The layer upon layer of absurdity and inefficiency. The accumulated bureaucratic contaminants. The idiocy. I ache for a fresh start, for a fire to sweep through the spent forest, clearing the debris and old unproductive growth and giving new saplings—that is, fresh ideas and fertile beings—a chance to sprout in the rejuvenated system. The State's collapse will come; this is nature's universal guarantee. So why cling to the farcical and artificially prolong the pain? Let nature complete the deed.

"Well, officer, thank you for the information," I say, addressing Constable Dewey, "but the entire process of getting a State-compliant muzzle sounds like it will take more than one year to complete—if I'm lucky. And there's less than one year before the new muzzling regulation is enforced. How does this work?"

"The government gave you plenty of warning through various media outlets and official announcements," replies Constable Wilson on behalf of a bored Constable Dewey who is gazing at a faraway movement, a radiance approaching from the west. She continues, "You should have made your arrangements by now. *Ignorantia legis neminem excusat*. And just in case you don't know what that means, it's Latin for *ignorance of the law excuses no one*."

It is perhaps the dead language that rouses Constable Dewey, because he springs to life and says, "Besides, you can always purchase a State-compliant muzzle from a private business. That can be done immediately and online." He then glances at his tablet and adds, "You can purchase a State-compliant muzzle from Worldwide Industries & Finance."

"Sorry, officer, was that Worldwide Industries & Finance?"

"Yes, that is correct: Worldwide Industries & Finance."

"Fancy that!" I say. "Just in case you forgot, officer, there is no other legal private business to buy any goods from. The only choice is Worldwide Industries & Finance. That's the only private business left. So why even bother acting as if there were more than one private business?"

A crowd carrying torches appears in the distance, to the west. They are marching this way. Constable Dewey glances at the distant throng and alerts his partner, who mumbles something into her radio.

He then addresses my question and says, "*So why even bother acting?* Are you trying to be clever with me?"

"No," I reply, "I just want to know if the government gets its muzzles from Worldwide Industries & Finance?"

Constable Dewey looks annoyed. "Yes, I guess that's correct. I'm not entirely sure, but it makes sense that if you can buy a muzzle only from Worldwide Industries & Finance, and if Worldwide is the only legal business, then Worldwide is also the business that is supplying the government."

"Sounds like a good business model," I say, "a good monopoly for the company *and* the government. Plenty of freedom of choice for me, the consumer."

Both officers seem confused, their tablet computers unable to help them respond to my sarcasm.

"And what *exactly* do you mean by your comment, sir?" asks Constable Wilson, pursing her lips.

"Nothing, just, just thinking aloud—that's all," I reply. "Forget it. Anyway, officer, what's the purpose of all this?"

"*Public interest criteria.* It's about safety, security, and the public interest: to protect *you* and *your* interests," she says, regurgitating a platitude drummed into every public servant.

"*My* interests? *My* safety? *My* security?" I ask with a cheeky grin.

"Yes, *your* interests, *your* safety, *your* security," she snaps back. "What part of *public interest criteria* don't you understand? Everything is done for the people's safety and security—to protect you, the public."

I sneer at the officer and say, "I see. You don't want me to hurt myself. All these rules and regulations are designed to keep me safe and happy—a happy little Vegemite. So tell me, then: why muzzle this dog? How is muzzling this dog a part of—what was it you said?—the *public interest criteria*? Hmm?"

She begins to answer my question, but I interrupt: "What about those kids killing each other at the end of the beach, officer? Don't you think dealing with them is more in the public interest criteria than muzzling this leashed dog?"

"Look, sir," she says while sighing, "I don't make the laws; I just do as I'm told and enforce the laws. If you've got a problem, complain in writing to an Occidental Union Administrator or go visit your local Temple of the People. However, I can tell you that this law is for your protection and the public order. It is in the public's interest. There have been plenty of dog attacks recently."

"Yeah, and there have been many more attacks by humans—on humans," I say. "In fact, there's one happening right now, at the other end of the beach! If you ask me, it's the people—especially, the State's Spawn, the *SS*—who need muzzling, not the dogs. This dog protects me from them! I can't even take a damn walk these days without being threatened or attacked. So what are you going to do about that? Huh?"

The several-hundred-strong crowd draws nearer to us, and chants and yelling can now be heard. For the first time tonight, the officers look edgy. Or is that fear in their eyes?

"As we told you earlier, you can visit the YourOccident website or call or visit your local Temple of the People for more information," replies Constable Dewey, deciding to focus on me instead of the advancing mob. "Besides that, however, I've got nothing more to say to you, except that your tone of voice is threatening and I'm going to issue you with an official warning, which will be recorded against your name."

He taps his tablet's screen and then says, "You've now been issued with an official warning for threatening an Occidental Union Peace Officer. In addition, this infringement will appear as a permanent mark on your record."

"*What the*—"

"Don't you dare interrupt me while I'm talking!" he yells, while toying with his taser. "Now, where was I? Oh, yes, and an associated fine of OW$10,500,000 (Occidental Worldwide dollars) will be deducted automatically from your next series of Occidental Union paycheques or living allowances. If, for whatever reason, you do not receive Occidental Union paycheques or living allowances, you will be required to complete the equivalent of one thousand and forty hours of community work. Finally, if you require more information with regard to paying this fine, please visit your local Temple of the People or talk to your CommunityAssist caseworker. In addition, you can find more information at the YourOccident website or on your infringement notice, which has already been sent to the e-mail address registered to your microchip."

Constable Wilson gazes at her tablet and takes over from her partner. She then says, "Additionally, you will be required to undertake an online education course: Empathy and Interpersonal Communication Skills—An Evidence-

Based Approach. After completing this course, you will need to attend an interview with a YourEducation Officer and undertake a psychosocial assessment with a YourPsychologist, who may then recommend ongoing treatment with a YourPsychiatrist. She or he or it or they will then assess whether you require further education, treatment, medication, and psychosocial counselling, or not. This is all done for your wellbeing, happiness, and self-actualisation. Again, all this information is included in your infringement notice, which has already been sent to the e-mail address registered to your microchip."

"Are you kidding me?" I say, stunned at the situation's silliness. "What exactly have I done wrong?"

Always aware of my body language, Anup snarls at the officers—yet I refrain from discouraging his unique style of interpersonal communication.

Constable Dewey apprehensively eyes Anup before saying, "Sir, I am going to ask you to lower your voice and calm down, or I will be forced to arrest you. Your behaviour *right now* is why you're being re-educated and rehabilitated. Am I being perfectly clear?"

"This is hilarious! *I'm* the bad guy who needs punishing? You've got to be joking."

"Final warning, *sir*," he says, as he pulls out his handcuffs.

I decide to stop talking, before the constable acts on his threat. In any event, the officers now face a bigger problem than a quarrelsome man and his unmuzzled pooch. For the advancing rabble is only a couple of hundred metres away, and I can already hear the people's rallying call: "*Hum ho, hum ho, to bonobo discrimination we say no! Ho hum, ho hum, death to bigots and sexist scum!*"

Despite the slogan's pleasing melody and rhythm, an underlying rage fuels the chants. This is no friendly protest; this is a whipped-up mob. And as they approach, I notice that many protesters are also wearing black masks and wielding metal poles.

Constable Dewey grabs his partner, who is talking on the radio, and they flee. Anup and I try to follow the officers, but before we can escape, a man and a woman splinter off from the protest's main branch and home in on us. Both are wearing the Occidental Union's standard sartorial handouts: black pants and a black shirt. The man also carries a placard that says, "Worldwide Workers Union ... *Equal rights for bonobos!*" A sketch of a red fist separates the trade union's name from the bonobo-rights slogan below it. But why would a trade union be interested in bonobo rights? It is a bizarre alliance that shows just how far trade unions have drifted away from their original role of improving workplace conditions.

"Do you support bonobo rights—equal rights for the only matriarchal ape?" asks the heavily studded woman, as she points her thumb at me.

"That's an interesting question," I reply, trying to be polite, "but it's also a fatuous question."

Both protesters look perplexed.

"Huh?" grunts the tall bald man, gawking and revealing brown pug-like teeth. Although nasty gnashers afflict the majority of the population, his teeth are particularly revolting.

"It's a *pointless* question," I say, trying to avoid staring at his teeth, "because bonobos have been extinct in the wild for more than one hundred and seventy years. And I know for a fact that the last bonobo died in captivity, in a zoo, almost one hundred years ago. So bonobos are extinct. They're all dead. Gone forever. And to harp on about the 'rights' of something that's extinct is absolutely absurd. It's ridiculous. Surely, there are more urgent and practical matters to protest about?"

The studded girl looks furious. "What do you mean *ridiculous*? And what do you mean *extinct*? Are you the Nazi scum that killed them?"

"No," I reply, "how could I have killed a bonobo, if the last one died in a zoo, almost one hundred years ago?"

"Oh, sorry, I missed that part," she answers.

"You men, you're all the same filth," says the pug-toothed man, rejecting my answer. "Kill, rape, steal, hoard, exploit, discriminate, use and abuse. You do whatever your greedy little dicks tell you to do. And, of course, you had to go and mass murder the only matriarchal ape—the only peaceful and egalitarian ape—because you hate its female-led society. Shame! Shame! You filthy sexist Nazi scum! Shame! Shame!"

"And what are you?" I ask, sniggering at his inanity. "Aren't you a man also?"

"In the strictest sense, I am *not* a man like you," he responds. "I've deconstructed the traditional culturally constructed idea of maleness, or masculinity, and reconstructed a gender-neutral mentality. I've transcended the primitiveness of traditional male–female role limitations

19

and restrictions, and I've erected a new genderless construct in its place. So I'm nothing like you. I am the *new man*—or, to be more accurate, I am the *new being*."

"Sounds like moral vanity and a muddled moronic ideology to me," I say. "So you are right: in the strictest sense, you are *not* a man like me."

"Hey, mate," protests the man, "I'm not one of the *SS*, grabbing food and beer handouts and then slumbering all day like a sated sloth. So don't talk to me as if I'm one of them. I've got a PhD in primatology from the Occidental Union University. And, for your information, I have never heard anything about bonobos being extinct. Yet I should be the first to know."

"Well, then," I reply, "your PhD from the Occidental Union University isn't worth much, because it is a fact that bonobos are extinct. The last wild population was wiped out around the year 2040 by hunting and deforestation. You can check this fact online or ask a real primatologist. I would be happy to give you a few contacts."

The man grunts something, as a coughing spasm cripples him. I wait for him to finish, before changing the topic and asking, "Anyway, what was your research thesis on?"

"It was on deconstructing the false boundaries erected between each so-called ape, including man. You see, there is no such thing as 'chimpanzee' or 'bonobo' or 'gorilla' or 'orang-utan' or 'human'. These are all just cultural creations, arbitrary classifications aimed at dividing and disuniting. We are all one—united. One family. Bigots and capitalists created the concept of 'species' in order to allow man to exploit and kill what he deemed inferior. My thesis helped demonstrate, once and for all, that the term 'species' is an illusion, a cultural construct. There is no such thing as a 'species'. So there is no such thing as a 'bonobo'. It is a false human-constructed category. And if these are artificial boundaries, then bonobos and humans are one and the same. It's simple logic. Hence, bonobos must have the same human rights—equal rights—that we have."

"Ah, I see," I say, while using all my willpower to suppress laughing at the moronic state of the academy and the Occidental Union University. "So we are all the same—no differences? I guess everything in the world is just an illusion, including the obvious physical differences. My mind, eyes, and senses are just playing naughty tricks on me. And because of all these illusions, I suppose only 'academic experts' can tell us the truth about reality and how we ought to live our lives. I suppose only the 'enlightened intelligentsia' should make informed decisions for the good of society."

"Yes, exactly!" replies the man, missing my sarcasm. "We have to deconstruct our traditional culturally constructed biases, and then we have to reconstruct, and progress, our new society according to the only existing noble truth: equality and social justice for every single living creature in the universe. This is our ultimate purpose: interconnectedness, universal equality, and social justice. Only then will utopia blossom. And this is why we need social experts. It is their job to transform the old society— the old system based on superstitions and inequalities and bigoted traditions—into a new society based on relativism and enlightenment and equality. We need to abandon the absolutist postcolonial there-is-such-a-thing-as-objective-truth narrative and embrace *relativism* in all its forms. For there is no absolute truth, no objective reality. Culture constructs reality. You view the world through your cultural narrative. Consequently, our Occidental social experts need to deconstruct the old and reconstruct the new cultural narrative. Only then will this new expert-constructed culture based on relativism allow us to attain true enlightenment and universal oneness and tolerance."

"Sounds wonderful," I say glibly, as the pair bask in their own relativism-inspired vacuous moral vanity. "But listen carefully, Tweedledum and Tweedledummer, because there are two major flaws in your argument. First, an absolute reality *does* exist, even if you doubt it. And, yes, you're free to question and doubt the objective world—the truth. You are free to believe that everything is relative. But the problem is that your words and beliefs don't match your actions. For you *do* experience an objective world, and you *do* respond to this reality in a *non*relativism-based way. Take this heavy concrete block, for example. Now drop it on your foot, and then tell me the intense pain and broken bones are just a culturally narrated response, an illusion based on relativism. Or try walking through that brick wall over there. An objective world *does* exist. Of course, you can spout cultural-relativism nonsense—but I guarantee that you *act* in a different way from the relativism you espouse. Your words and actions fail to mesh with each other. You *behave* knowing that an objective world exists—that certain things are absolutely real and not relative—even though you *say* that all reality is subject to relativism. Now, the second flaw with your argument is that it is self-refuting. If you insist on relativism being 'true', then you must make your own claim the *exception* to your own rule. For you are claiming that your statement—relativism—is true; you are declaring it as a *fact*. Yet, at the same time, you are claiming that *all* 'truths' are relative and that no objective truths exist. So how can your truth-claim be true according to its own internal logic, which denies objective truth-claims? Therefore, your argument defeats itself, and your claim is absurd."

By their blank stares, I deduce that neither the man nor the woman has grasped the meaning of what I have just said.

"Anyway, good luck with your work," I say, growing bored with their company and searching for an exit point.

But the man misses the hint, ignores my apathetic body language, and continues the conversation.

"Yeah, but I'm unemployed," he replies.

"Oh, that's no good," I say, trying to subdue my irritation with the situation. "How long have you been unemployed?"

"Well, I finished my PhD last year. I was forty-three years of age. And I haven't found any work since."

"You mean to say you've been studying all your life? You've never worked a day?"

"That's correct, but—"

The woman interrupts him and says, "I finished my PhD eight years ago, and I haven't found any work either. I'm forty-nine now."

Although most of the population is unemployed or studying at the Occidental Union University well into middle age, even old age, I am always stunned when I hear someone mention it.

"And what was your PhD thesis on?" I ask the woman.

"It was on Sci–Coll ideology, which is the Occidental Union's ideology, and why the individual cannot exist apart from the group. Essentially, I helped demonstrate that because humans are a social species, it is the group that counts, not the individual. Individualism is an illusion; the collective is reality. Individualism fosters the worst traits in people, whereas collectivism brings out the best. So I helped prove that the Occidental Union's practice and belief in Sci–Coll, in the triumph of the collective over the individual, is morally correct and scientifically sound."

"So you're saying the individual doesn't matter?"

"That's correct," she responds. "Without the group, there would be no society and no progress. So individuals must conform to the group or be forced to conform, because this is for the *greater good* of the group. The collective is progress; progress is science; science is a product of the collective. Do see how society progresses? Do you see the circle of progression? Do you understand?"

"I see," I say. "The individual can be sacrificed for the greater good—for the greatest good of the greatest number. It's the oldest argument in the book. But even though such a philosophy might appear superficially benevolent, it can, in practice, be a deeply dangerous doctrine. Because if people were to base their actions only on the social or greater good, then this would lead to the abuse of

24

individuals, minorities, and their rights. And history shows that people will justify all sorts of evils—against individuals and minorities—in the name of the social good or the greater good. Consider, say, Nazi Germany in the 1930s and 1940s. Adolf Hitler and his Nazi Party murdered millions of innocent Jews and confiscated—or 'nationalised'—their private property in the name of the 'greater good'. So he stole everything from the politically demonised minority and redistributed it all to the politically entitled majority. His whole ideology was based on a grandiose idea: that the individual must sacrifice himself for the people and the State—and the propaganda worked."

"What a silly and hyperbolic example," the woman says, while clucking. "The Occidental Union is far more enlightened than that primitive form of dressed-up utilitarianism."

"Really?" I reply. "Okay, then, take the following recent example, which happened here in the Occidental Union. Five patients were being treated in Occidental Teaching Hospital 748B. Each patient was waiting for a specific organ transplant. One patient needed a liver transplant; another, a heart; another, a kidney; another, a pancreas; another, a lung. Now, a healthy woman walked into the hospital, and the hospital staff declared her to be a perfect donor–recipient match for all five patients. According to Sci–Coll utilitarianism and the concept of the greater good, this woman was then legally sliced and her organs redistributed among the five patients. And what was Sci–Coll's moral justification for butchering this innocent and healthy woman? By sacrificing her own life, she was saving *five* lives. So the trade-off was one for five—and this sacrifice represented the greatest social good. Yet does this constitute 'moral' behaviour? Would any sane person want to live in such a society, where the greatest social good trumps all other concerns, including the individual's rights?"

"It sounds like you are arguing for individualism," the man interrupts.

"I'm not arguing for individualism; I'm arguing for *individual rights*. And there exists a huge difference between the two. Individual rights—natural rights to my body and my personal property, including equal rights to seek legal restitution for damages to my person and my personal property—must form the foundation of any decent society. These individual rights erect the only real barrier to complete State control. But where are our individual rights in the Occidental Union? They've all been eroded because of the devious greater-good argument."

The man and woman look confused, so I try to refine my argument.

"To be precise," I say, "we ought to ask the following question: *whose* greater good? What, exactly, is this mysterious group or collective that an individual must prostrate himself before? The truth, once we define our abstract term, is this: an individual is harmed not for some vague concept of the 'greater good'; rather, an individual is milked or mistreated to benefit another person or specific other persons. And certain people—politicians, mainly—hide behind the superficial argument of the 'social good' to camouflage a selfish agenda designed to advance their own needs or desires. Yet when the State parasitises my toil and steals my property, then it is enriching *specific* individuals in government—this is not some abstract 'collective' or 'greater good'. By appropriating my personal stuff, the State is also benefiting other *concrete* beneficiaries, such as the State's Spawn or *SS*. The State provides them with food, clothing, shelter, education, healthcare, transport—everything they need for survival. And they, in return, become absolutely dependent on the State and its handouts. So they reciprocate by voting for whatever makes the State stronger. They end up supporting the State in all its grabs for power and property, because they will also receive a part of the confiscated booty. So, for the 'greater good', the State is harming me to benefit *specific* persons x, y, z—just like the poor woman in the Occidental Teaching Hospital was butchered to help five specific persons. Yet where is my benefit in all this? And where is the woman's? Am I, or the woman, not part of the 'greater good', too?"

"You sound like a person stuck in the primitive stage of individualism," the woman says, completely ignoring or misunderstanding my arguments. "This is perfectly fine. You're just not on our higher level, and you will never be able to understand anything we say." She then shakes her head in disgust. "It's your type of selfishness that has got society into the mess it's in. *Gemeinnutz geht vor Eigennutz,* which means *the common good supersedes the private good.* Shame! Shame! You Nazi scum!"

Yet the woman misses the irony in accusing me of being Nazi scum, because *Gemeinnutz geht vor Eigennutz* was originally a Nazi slogan endorsing the tyranny and benefit

27

of the "collective" at the expense of the individual and his life, liberty, and property—which is exactly my point.

Both protesters then start squawking, "Shame! Shame!"

In the meantime, I shake my head in frustration rather than disgust, while waiting for them to simmer down.

"Behaving like that is very mature for someone with a PhD," I say sarcastically. "Silence me by bullying me and screaming at me, which is the sort of puerile behaviour I expect from everyone now."

"Hey, at least we have PhDs," says the man, sniffling and trying to subdue a fresh coughing attack. "You're a no-one, a nothing. So there's no reason to listen to any of your free-market individual-rights liberal nonsense."

"By the way," I reply, "I've got a PhD also. Every second person has a PhD now. Anyone can get a PhD from the Occidental Union University. But what good is it? Is there a market or a demand for us? No. The market is saturated with them; worse, the majority of PhDs are junk. Something is only worth something, if someone else wants it. And that desired something usually has a practical value. So if no one wants to employ a PhD graduate, then the PhD is worthless—even if *you* think it is worth something. Besides, no job market exists anymore, because there are no employers except for the *one* corrupt State, the *one* corrupt business, and the *one* corrupt trade union. And if there are no employers, then there are no jobs. It's that simple. A person is even forbidden from starting his or her own legal private business. Ha! Lots of freedoms and opportunities! So when you argue against me, you are arguing against common sense and your own welfare."

"You're a capitalist pig!" the woman screeches, as she wags her finger at me.

"If by that you mean I'm a realist, then thank you for the compliment," I say, while grinning. "I live in the real world of individuals and markets and competing self-interests, not some platonic fantasy the academy has conjured up to advance the State's agenda—and its own."

Both protesters look deflated after having exhausted, without any success, their ad hominem and ridicule-based attacks.

Meanwhile, Anup is growing restless. He whimpers and nudges my leg, which is his way of saying, *I'm bored—please let's go.*

But before I can excuse myself from the pair's company, the man asks, "So what do you do, then?"

"I, like you and most of the population, am also officially unemployed," I answer, having failed once again to exit the forced conversation. "But I love to keep busy, so I unofficially run my own hobby. Yes, let's call it an unofficial hobby."

"Which is?"

"I make electronic products that actually work and that don't break down after one day's use. You know what I'm talking about: the garbage sold by Worldwide Industries & Finance. You buy something from them, and it never works. Yet try getting a refund and some justice—it doesn't happen, thanks to the company's worldwide business monopoly and the complete support it receives from the Occidental State and Worldwide Workers Trade Union."

The woman seems genuinely intrigued by what I am saying. "So how do you make these goods?" she asks.

"I salvage what I can from rubbish and discarded technology. The stuff is everywhere, on every street and in every building. Then, I reassemble the titbits into functional technology. For example, I make a nifty tablet computer that you can wrap around your forearm or that you can fold and put in your pocket. You charge it by placing it in the sunlight for a couple of hours. After charging, it will run for a few days, depending on how much you use it. It's cheap, effective, durable, and free to charge, and it works when you need it to work. Oh, it's also waterproof. So how's that for ingenuity?"

"I'm impressed!" says the man, smiling. Any earlier animosity has now vanished.

"Thank you," I say, returning the grin. "By the way, here's my contact card, if you need to trade or buy electronic goods that work. You'll notice that there is just an e-mail address on the card. This is for my protection, because if the State finds out—well, you know the rest."

The man snatches my contact card and says, "I'll definitely try your products. Anything is better than the crap Worldwide sells. And you don't have to worry about us mentioning your unofficial hobby to anyone."

"Fantastic. I look forward to hearing from you."

An awkward silence follows, without even a cough or a sniffle from the man. After several moments, the woman then glances at the man, who nods his head.

"Hey," the woman says nervously, "the real reason we approached you at first is because we both find you cute—

and, well, we were wondering if you would like to have sex with us tonight."

"Oh, hmmm," I mumble, searching for a reasonable excuse to reject their invitation without offending them. "That's very flattering, but I have been assigned Progenitor Duty by the Occidental Union. You know, 'my duty to the community' and all that stuff. Perhaps when my Progenitor Duty is complete, we can meet up. But thank you, again, for the invitation."

There are many reasons why I abstain from collective sex. First, I hate collective sex, even though everyone does it and even though it is the State's expert declaration on natural relations. I have even been branded as a "disgusting pervert" and a "filthy radical" for going against what the herd practises and for saying I would prefer one-on-one sex. Yet anyone familiar with man's biology, evolution, and history, instead of what the State preaches, would know that monogamy and serial monogamy are the human standard, not group sex. But the State is clever. It understands the power of sex and how it can be used to shape thinking. The State knows that sex poses an obstacle to supreme State authority. For once a person becomes sexually attracted to another person—"falls in love"—then individuality tends to strengthen. The collective fades into the background, whereas "I" and the object of "my" desire become the focus of "my" life. So one-on-one sex and loving monogamous relationships erect a block to complete authoritarian rule.

Throughout history, however, various States have tried to enhance their might by poisoning this two-person nucleus and thereby eradicating individuality. In Ancient

31

Greece, for instance, a few city-states enforced *institutionalised pederasty*: the State-sanctioned and State-enforced culture of ripping a prepubescent boy away from his mother and sexually partnering him to an adult male. The Minoan State, in particular, exemplified this institutionalised policy. Why? Because the practice served its purpose: it weakened male–female couplings, warped the individual's mind, sapped the nuclear family of its strength, and increased everyone's dependence on and allegiance to the city-state—to the "collective".

So the Occidental Union, learning from history and science, and inspired by Aldous Huxley's *Brave New World* and Yevgeny Zamyatin's *We*, lighted on the idea of collective sex to tear down individuality—that ingrained biological barrier to State power. For if a State cannot eliminate sexual attraction and the strong sense of individuality that emerges from it, then perhaps a State can collectivise sexual attraction and change the emergent "I" into "we". Collective sex—where everyone engages with everyone and shares everyone—would allow people to express their sexual desires, while strengthening the collective mentality *and* weakening individuality and natural partnerships. And with this brilliant insight, the Occidental Union began a programme of reprogramming mankind to overcome this final hurdle. The State was edging closer to complete control over the masses.

Yet a second reason exists for abstaining from collective sex: promiscuous sexual intercourse is a dangerous activity. It can be lethal. Despite some early successes against pathogens in the twentieth and twenty-first centuries, old and new diseases are today devastating the population, and the majority of pathogens are completely resistant to every drug and treatment. Even gonorrhoea, a sexually transmitted infection that was easily cured with a course of antibiotics, now resists all treatments. To make matters worse, few new treatments and technologies have emerged since the first half of the twenty-first century. Man is losing the war against pathogens—something unthinkable during the dawn of evidence-based medicine.

"No worries," replies the woman, the disappointment sounding in her voice and showing on her face. "Maybe we can all have sex together after your Progenitor Duty—we can even invite heaps of others! A big juicy gangbang! Anyway, we've got your e-mail, so we'll be hunting you down later."

The couple wink at me, as they retreat to the safety of their pack.

I tug at Anup's leash, and we hurry home.

~~~~~

Almost home. We reach the end of the park—the scene of an earlier exchange, of a devoured ant. The ant colony is excited; the scent of war charges the air. Reinforcements are beckoned, and the soldier caste arrives. Fearsome mandibles, huge armoured heads, angry pulsating stings— these ants are bred for war, for killing, for destruction. The alarming scent of their fallen sister infuriates them, and they begin tearing at the base of the spider's web, where their fallen sister's pheromones are strongest. But the spider, feeling the web quiver and acting on instinct, crawls down from the safety of his home and pounces on the first soldier he finds. He punctures her body with his fangs and injects a deadly cocktail that paralyses her, while liquefying her viscera for later siphoning and nourishment. He then drags the soldier to the centre of the web and wraps her in a silken cocoon to seal in the freshness. Yet the battle has just begun.

More soldiers stream in—a seething black mob, tearing at every silken strand attached to the ground and shaking the entire web. The spider hesitates. These are not the good vibrations of a struggling prey; these are the bad vibrations of a calculating predator. Though his instincts tell him to run for safety, they are wrong. It is a bluff. For the ants cannot harm him, even with all their numbers. He is safe as long as he stays on his property, the system that has served him and his ancestors well for millions of years.

The shaking becomes more violent, and the spider decides to abandon his home. But his first step into the alien system is his last. He lands in a soldier's mandibles and is instantly crushed to death. Other sisters join the frenzy and slice him into shreds—a fine meal for the royal larvae.

The web glistens with the moisture collected from the muggy air and trembles, for a final time, with the settlement of nature's contract.

~~~~~

2

Anup refuses to drink any tapwater. I know he is thirsty, though, because he is circling the water bowl and staring at me with warm pleading eyes.

"What's the matter, boy? Why aren't you drinking?"

He whimpers and wags his tail, while licking my hands and wrists.

"Yes, yes, and I love you, too," I say, as I rub his ears and scratch his back. The massage soothes his itchy flea-bitten back, and he sways with delight. No matter what I try, the fleas refuse to die, because they have grown resistant to just about every chemical. So, on most days, I am forced to sift the tiny bugs out of his coat with a flea comb.

"Okay, Nups, I'll get rid of the tapwater and give you something else. Wait here, good boy."

I dump the untouched tapwater and fill Anup's bowl with bottled water instead. He immediately licks and slurps and empties the entire bowl, so I refill it with more bottled water. After taking a few final mouthfuls, he ambles into the living room and jumps into an armchair. Content with his morning's work, he finds a comfortable position and dozes off.

I then fill a cup with some tapwater and inspect it. Although the water looks clean and clear, it exhibits a subtle yet distinct odour—an odour I have detected previously on a handful of occasions. Just one month ago, to be exact, the tapwater emitted the same odour. And on that day, like today, Anup refused to drink it. I also recall two other odd facts about every previous tainted-tapwater day. First, the people of the metropolis would always behave in a strange, scatty, and subdued manner—as if they were drugged from the tapwater. And, second, the timing: the tapwater would always smell odd the day *after* civil unrest. And lately, the metropolis has been experiencing ceaseless civil unrest. A slum has been torched and reduced to ashes. Food and energy shortages abound. Mobs are seizing control of the streets. Peace officers—terrified and powerless—are vanishing. And the unseasonal heat and humidity are bringing everything to a boil.

So, on days like today, I follow Anup's lead and refrain from drinking the tapwater, despite lacking hard proof that the State is spiking it. Still, such an action would mesh well with the State's ideology: dragoon the people into submission in the slyest and most cost-effective way possible. And mood-altering drugs dispensed through the drinking water would fulfil such requirements. Medicating the masses is cheap, simple, and effective—certainly cheaper and simpler (and more effective?) than maintaining a free civil society, with moral individuals, healthy families, stable civil institutions, and an efficient and accountable government. And because Worldwide Industries & Finance Co. owns every chemical-testing laboratory in the Occidental Union, the State can hide any evidence of a mass drugging. One State, one company, one corruption. Best of all, who would believe the State would act in such a wicked way? Only a "rebel" would spout such nonsense.

The wind pushes against the living-room window, and I gaze out at grey buildings blending into grey skies. It looks like it will finally rain. Perhaps this will quench the parched lands and wash away the torched slum's ashes, which are coating the entire metropolis. The rains may even cool the masses.

I open the window, and an air gust floods into the room, filling it with new life. The refreshing wind washes over me. A baptism by air. I shut my eyes, and my spirit floats away on the gentle air current. Yet the breeze recedes almost as quickly as it fills the room. I open my eyes. The window's steel bars welcome me back to reality and trap my spirit before it can escape with the wind. Shackled, once more, to the Occidental Union. I shall never be free.

The apartment consists of a kitchen, a living room, two bedrooms, and a bathroom with a laundry. Countless books, electronic junk, and rusted gym equipment clutter the living-room floor; three stained armchairs and a weathered timber table complete the décor. Two doorways allow access to the apartment: one from the ground-floor hallway and the other from the communal garden. This suits Anup, since he can enter and exit the communal garden whenever he wishes. As for its title, one might call "communal garden" a misnomer. For it is not communal, nor is it a garden. Rather, the "garden" comprises a dirt patch secluded and walled off from the street. And because Anup scares the other lodgers from trespassing on his dirt patch, the "communal" part should be omitted altogether. "Private" might make more sense, if dogs were to embrace property law. But they do not. So, resorting to the natural law, the garden is Anup's *territory*—and I encourage him to protect what belongs to him. For this is nature's design, the most basic right of any living creature.

But man, not nature, has designed the apartment's two bedrooms. I, "Progenitor A", sleep in one bedroom, whereas she, "Progenitor B", sleeps in the other bedroom. "Progenitor A" is the official title stamped on my Occidental Union Reproduction Licence; "Progenitor B", the official title stamped on hers. We are not married, though, because the State has banned marriage. The Occidental Union Population Board has, instead, temporarily matched us together, using our superior statistical and biological profiles, for the purpose of reproducing. The State has also reversed my vasectomy (administered to all male babies at birth to prevent unauthorised reproduction as adults), thereby allowing me to impregnate Progenitor B. But after one year without any pregnancy or baby, the State is probably becoming restless with our unfulfilled duties. It assigned us this "luxury" apartment, while expecting exceptional progeny in return. More accurately, the Occidental State desperately needs *any* progeny because of the plummeting fertility rates and crashing population size.

After the industrialism-triggered population growth explosion of the nineteenth, twentieth, and twenty-first centuries, Gaia—the Earth viewed as a self-regulating organism, or one superorganism—entered a phase of readjustment. For plagues of humans had overrun the planet, polluted the environment, and choked the life out of every ecosystem. And, in reaction, the Great Heat began—a worldwide atmospheric fever fanned by manmade pollution and carbon dioxide production. This Great Heat then simmered the oceans and scorched much of the lush land. The result: the bulk of ocean algae and land vegetation died. And, with this extermination, the life engines of Earth faltered, which reduced the planet's carrying capacity for all life, particularly human life. As a consequence, the Great Population Crash followed.

So even though population control might have been a good idea, it came a few centuries too late. The damage has already been wreaked on the environment and cannot be reversed in the short term. Today, with human numbers dwindled *and* dwindling, and with Gaia limiting our species' havoc in her own special way, no need exists for such a costly and cumbersome population programme. The Occidental State has, nevertheless, an ulterior motive behind population control. For it is not about licensing reproduction: it is about *eugenics* and breeding "superhumans". The State wants to forge man in its chosen image.

However, controlled reproduction—eugenics disguised in the greater-good garb—is the State's plan, not mine, and it should know by now that nothing goes according to plan in life. Did people learn nothing from the vileness of twentieth-century eugenics rooted in misguided scientism? Or was George Santayana, in *The Life of Reason*, correct when he wrote, "Those who cannot remember the past are condemned to repeat it"? For instance, in the pursuit of the collective good based on twisted science, more than sixty thousand women were forcibly sterilised in Sweden between 1936 and 1976. Proponents and the government argued that such procedures would improve the population's "genetic stock", while reducing the burden of "inferior genes" and their subsequent inferior individuals on the rest of society. Meanwhile, in the United States, more than sixty-five thousand people were sterilised between 1907 and the 1960s; in the words of a 1907 Indiana statute, the procedures were carried out "to prevent procreation of confirmed criminals, idiots, imbeciles, and rapists". A sterilisation ideology founded on eugenics and social Darwinism also spread throughout Europe during the same period—except in countries where the Catholic Church was established. For the Church opposed eugenics and forced sterilisation in all its forms and disguised ideologies. Then, in the 1930s and 1940s, came the tragedies of German National Socialism and its eugenic policies that saw the mass butchery of countless innocent "undesirables" and "deviants" and other people from "inferior races". This massacre included the genocide of roughly six million Jews. And it was all executed in the name of scientific progress and the greatest good—that is, to produce the perfect new man and the perfect new civilisation.

And here we are today: the Occidental Union has institutionalised the forced sterilisation of all new-born males and the controlled reproduction of society. A State-run eugenics programme based on unsound scientism and greatest-good collectivism. Yet many Occidental and Worldwide scientists are just as guilty as the Occidental Union Administrators, because the scientists failed to use caution in interpreting their scientific results. They extended their scientific claims into other fields, where science should not have the only—or final—say, if any.

Progenitor B's bedroom door opens and my statistically perfect mate, Bulla, dressed in the Occidental Union's black pants and black shirt, enters the living room. She is roughly ten years younger than me and in her childbearing prime. Since Bulla is a Female Progenitor, the Occidental Union has lavished plenty of resources on her compared with the rest of the population. And it shows. Although plain, she radiates health. And her skin is clear and smooth, except for a couple of bedbug bites.

Bulla, like the majority of children today, was born and raised in an Occidental Union Public Nursery, one of the many experiments in State-planned social restructuring. This programme in communal childrearing started after State-sponsored double-blind placebo-controlled research showed that "children reared progressively and communally, in a public nursery run by State experts and specialists, are happier, more social, more empathetic, and more intellectually advanced than their traditional family-raised counterparts." Another academic study said, "Children are no longer the 'property' of their caregivers; children now have full rights under the protection of the State. They are free from antiquated laws that degraded children by reducing them to be a 'good', a piece of 'property' to be exploited by capricious and unskilled caregivers. This progression, in liberating the children from parental exploitation, mirrors the preceding legislation banning marriage, which liberated women from being traded as a 'chattel' and from being treated like a property contract to be exploited at the whim of the male owner. Soon, all people will be born free and equal under a new paradigm, a new collective awakening. The legendary Age of Saturn, the age of international collectivism, is about to dawn, heralding humankind's first worldwide utopia."

So after battling for centuries to abolish the independence of individuals and families, the State has finally triumphed and replaced parent and husband as the sole caregiver. The State is the official family. And its children, those brought up in one of the countless Occidental Union Public Nurseries, are colloquially termed the "State's Spawn", the *SS*, because they are the State's products.

Without the State, without its handouts, without its constant care, the *SS* would fail to survive. And without the *SS*, without their support, without their mob violence and terror and brutality, the State would fail to survive. So the two groups have formed a symbiotic relationship designed to sustain the status quo and terrify everybody caught between them into submission.

"Good mornin'," Bulla says, still yawning.

"And a good morning to you, Bulla," I reply.

"I didn' hear ya arrive last noight. What toime did ya come home?"

"It was late. I had a few problems with crazy people and the police."

"Didn' I tell ya to stop walkin' at noight, even with the mutt? Aye? It's just too dangerous, matey. So what happened this time?"

"Same old, same old," I reply, "children killing each other and police doing nothing except handing out ridiculous fines over ridiculous laws. You know the routine."

"Are ya hurt?"

"No, I'm fine. Thank you for asking, Bulla."

"*Thank ya for asking*?" she repeats incredulously. "Hey, even though we're just mates, ya do know how much ya mean to me—don' ya? We've shared the same dump for a year. We know each other's dirt—'n', well, you're closa to me than anyone else. I don' have a traditional-like family. You're it."

"And I feel the same way about you," I reply courteously rather than honestly. "You are, uh—I guess you are pretty much the only person I trust."

"The only person ya trust? I'm the only person you actually talk to without thinkin', 'She's out to get me.' Ya nut-job bastard!"

Bulla then surveys the area for Anup and spots him dozing in an armchair.

43

"Allo, 'n' is our big boy okaye? Aye? Is he?" she says, as she pats and coddles Anup. He wriggles ecstatically at her touch.

"What do you think? Of course, he's fine," I answer on Anup's behalf. "Most people may be crazy, but they're not crazy enough to go near that beast."

"He's not a beast; he's a beau'ful boiye."

"According to your eyes, perhaps."

"Are ya jealous of Anup?" she asks.

"Now, why would I be jealous of Anup?"

"Cause," she replies with a mischievous grin, "I'm rubbin' his chest 'n' belly but not yours."

Her clumsy coquetry surprises me. Despite Bulla being content initially with a platonic relationship, her behaviour the last few weeks hints at dissatisfaction. Something has changed, and she obviously desires more than a friendship. But I am not interested in Bulla. Nor do I want to produce a human "product", a future SS for the Occidental Union and its machinations. For if I had been given a choice in whether I wanted to be born or not, I would have chosen *not* to be born. So, then, how could I justify bringing new life into this barren world, when I would avoid choosing the curse of life for myself? Either way, I would never surrender my child to the State. And despite what the Occidental Union Population Board's algorithms spit out, Bulla and I are not a statistically perfect biological match. We are a perfect *mis*match.

"Hey, by the way," I say, thwarting her advance, "don't drink any tapwater today."

Her demeanour instantly changes. "Oh, here ya go again. It's toime for the tapwata paranoia."

"It is not paranoia. It is real."

"Real?" she says, while rolling her eyes. "What gov'ment would spike the tapwata supply? Aye?"

"Are you joking?" I reply angrily. "I know you must be joking, because we've had long chats about States and the way they treat their citizens. Chairman Mao, Joseph Stalin, Adolf Hitler—how about those lovely leaders and their governments to start with? How many tens of millions of innocent people did they collectively butcher in the name of the State, in the name of their ideology? Or what about the hundreds of murderous Islamic theocracies that plagued humanity's past? Iran, Somalia, Afghanistan, and Saudi Arabia weren't known for their respect of minorities or women or individual rights or equal legal rights. And the Turkish Ottoman Empire combined the worst aspects of statehood and Islamic religious extremism to butcher roughly one and a half million Armenian civilians between 1915 and 1923, in what was later coined the *Armenian Genocide*. Succeeding Turkish governments never even apologised for the genocide—and every single leadership denied that their country ever carried out a crime against humanity. Hmm? Shall I continue, Bulla? There are thousands of other examples. So please don't spout garbage and claim that a government wouldn't spike the tapwater to control the people. Governments have done much, much worse than that."

"That's all in the past, that is," Bulla says, while playing with a blemish on her forearm.

45

"Bulla, are you being obstinately naive? Seriously, you think it can't happen today? Oh, yes, that's right—our authorities are too kind and caring. Yeah, real humanitarians. They're simply interested in our safety and social welfare—and we have to believe this, because it's what they announce every day. So let's give them more control and more power, since they will only use these extra powers for good—for our social good. Oh, yes, government is never interested in expanding its might for its own benefit—never. Ha! If you believe such garbage, then you are stupid or gullible or both."

Bulla is ignoring me, but this tirade is more about me than her. I need to talk to someone, anyone, and vent my frustrations with life. Even if she were failing to grasp anything, I would still continue talking—talking to myself, talking to no one in particular. For the Occidental Union has whittled me down to this.

My two lower-left molars ache continuously. Parasites are invading my body—internally and externally. I lack friends and family. I struggle every day to secure State handouts. I rummage in putrid garbage for discarded parts to make basic technological goods.

Life is hell.

My only remaining freedom: words, ideas, imagination. For the State already owns my body. But can the State rob me of my private inner world, too? If it were able to achieve this, as it has done with the *SS* and so many others, then I should be the living dead, a cog in the State machine. And with my last independent thought, just before the State were to appropriate my mind and soul, I would suicide. My final act of rebellion. My final free act.

"Bulla," I go on, unperturbed, "the State has even rewritten our Constitution, which was designed to *limit* the government's power and curb its growth. Now, the Constitution does exactly the opposite of what it was originally created to do. The new Constitution shackles the individual and the people, while unchaining the State. No individual rights, or rights to liberty and person and property, are mentioned in the new Constitution—just the muddy and exploitable idea of 'collective rights as determined by the State in order to progress equality, safety, and efficiency'. To add further insult, the State has also eliminated the final series of checks and balances on its own expansion. Where once government was splintered into three independent branches—the legislature, the executive, and the judiciary, each with its own responsibilities—today all three have been merged into the one State body. Total State authority. Complete State power. A totalitarian monopoly."

"Well, I don't think life is so bad," she answers. "It ain't bad at all, matey. You bitch too much. We get fed, roised, taken care of. Ed'cation is free. The roof ov'a our heads is free. So much is free, 'n' the gov'ment don't ask for nothin' in return."

"You are right, Bulla. The State does provide us with some basic needs—but it strips away all our freedoms in return. It erects a prison cell around each individual—a prison cell constructed of rules and regulations and mind-control programmes, with the government acting as the warden. The people forfeit their freedoms, and the State, in return, might be kind enough to provide equal yet basic goods and services to each inmate citizen: simple meals, spartan accommodation, minimal healthcare, and a limited State education followed by a regulated State job. *Equality* in every *material* aspect. A homogenised and regulated mass of clones. But how does this differ from a jail, where the criminal inmates lose their freedoms in exchange for basic goods and services provided by the State? Material equality exists in jail—but losing one's liberty is the price to pay. No, Bulla, *this* Occidental prison is too real to dismiss. The State tells us what to do, how to do it, and when to do it. And if we don't obey, then it unleashes its terror—its mobs, the *SS*—and suffocates us with more rules and regulations and mind-control programmes. We are the prisoners, and the State is the prison. The State and the *SS* are our warders. Yet if you are happy being a prisoner and having your basic requirements met while surrendering *all* your freedoms in the name of the greater good and enforced equality, security, and efficiency, then, yes, the Occidental Union and its prison society is wonderful. But this *is* a prison—and I'll take freedom, including its personal responsibilities and unpredictable outcomes, any time over servitude and imprisonment."

"A prison?" Bulla inquires sarcastically. "Ha! What a drama queen ya are! Ya bitch too much 'n' make the State look like a monsta, when it's our friend 'n' protecta. It roised me 'n' made me what I'm todoiy. It *does* care about us, even if ya think otherwoise. Matey, your problem is that ya read too much on that Internet crap and in all 'em books.

You're brainwashed. Ya doiydream 'bout the ol' system, a system o' greed 'n' exploitation that almost destroiyed the world. The ol' system was the real evil, 'n' the Occidental Union 'n' its Sci–Coll way a thinkin' saved us from that evil."

I shake my head in despair. I can argue and provide evidence all day long, but nothing will change her mind. Even though Bulla may, at times, be more refined than the rest of the State's Spawn, she is just as indoctrinated as the others. She still views the world through the State's eyes, its lies, and its ideology. She cannot, however, be blamed for failing to see clearly, because she has belonged to the State and its ideologues from birth.

But it might be impossible to change Bulla's way of thinking and eliminate the Occidental Union's mind-altering infection from her system. To illustrate, consider *Toxoplasma gondii*, a protozoan parasite that infects many mammals, including humans, mice, rats, and cats. For *T. gondii* to complete its lifecycle, it must find and parasitise a cat, which is its primary host. As a consequence, the parasite has evolved a nifty mind-altering trick. When it infects rats or mice, it changes their brain chemistry and behaviour. It causes infected rodents to find the scent of cat urine irresistible. So instead of fleeing from their natural enemy, the infected rodents actively seek out cat urine, thereby embracing their *cat*astrophe. After the cat devours the home-delivered rodent meal, the parasite can then complete its lifecycle inside the cat. Perfect rodent 'indoctrination', from the parasite's perspective.

Similarly, the State's lifelong inculcation of its people mirrors the parasite's mind-altering trick with the rodents. Although the people should fear the all-powerful State more than anything else in the world, the ideology-infected people instead find the concept of the all-powerful State perversely attractive. So the people freely grant the State more powers and embrace their own doom. Perfect indoctrination, from the parasite's—the State's—perspective.

"You just don't know any better, Bulla," I say. "You think that living in this hellhole is acceptable, because you grew up in it and haven't seen anything else. You are unable to compare this misery with anything else, so you believe this misery is a good life—the only life. And, besides, you haven't seen how the Occidental Union gets all your 'free' handouts. I have. Remember, if you're eating for free, then someone else has suffered on your behalf. Nothing is free. Have you never wondered where all the State handouts come from? Hmm?"

"Couldn't care less," she replies, before attending to her forearm's blemish once again.

I ignore her spoiled-child apathy and continue with my speech: "The food and goods, which you enjoy for 'free' from the Occidental State, come from the labour of the people of the Free Islands. They toil so you can live without working. Our government has been using the previously confiscated private property of billions of Occidental Union citizens to buy food and goods from businesses located in the Free Islands. The Occidental State then hands out these 'free' goods to the Occidental population. This means, the

Occidental Union is a net importer of everything. So the Occidental Union and its defunct socialist 'democracy' is a net *consumer*—not a producer. It produces nothing, since its economic system is a complete failure. The Occidental State just parasitises the labour and consumes the wealth of others. But you know what else, Bulla?"

"Wha'?" she murmurs, without even glancing in my direction.

"The Occidental State ran out of confiscated private property, including the confiscated precious metals of citizens, decades ago. We've been living off Occidental State debt and the goodwill of the people of the Free Islands. They have been feeding and clothing and housing us— without any 'concrete' payment in return—for decades. And this is why the Occidental Union has never declared war against the Free Islands: if the Occidental Union were to wage war against the Free Islands, then the Occidental Union would be unable to feed and take care of its own people. The Occidental Union would perish. However, the entire Occidental charade is coming to an end, because the Free Islands have said *enough is enough*. They have announced that there will be no more charity and no further foreign aid to the Occidental Union."

"And so ya keep remindin' me. How 'bout shuttin' ya trap for a change?"

"Sorry, Bulla, but I've shut my mouth for too long—and I'm no longer scared. I will speak out against the Occidental Union whenever and wherever I can. You, unfortunately, don't realise how bad things are, because you've never experienced another way of living. You've never seen a better world. Yet I've seen a better world: a world free from the Occidental Union. When I was working as a scientist at Worldwide Industries & Finance, the company sent me to the Free Islands on a short business trip. And while there, I learnt about another system of living. I witnessed things you cannot imagine, Bulla. And once you have seen these things, then you will say that we are slaves living in fear and filth—that the Occidental Union is the epitome of evil."

Bulla looks irritated, almost furious, as if she were enduring the fantasies of a ranting fool.

"Well, I know our gov'ment ain't perfec'," she says, "but I just think the idea of it spikin' our tapwata is ridic'lous—simply ridic'lous."

"Okay, so why does the water smell odd today? Huh? And why does the dog refuse to drink the water when it smells funny? Huh? And why does this peculiar odour appear only when society is on the edge, when the people are about to riot? Hmm? And why do the people in the streets act strangely—why are they docile and lifeless?—on the days when the tapwater smells tainted?"

"*Act strangely? Why are they docile and lifeless?*" she repeats condescendingly. "I jus' don't see it. Moiybe—"

"But I *do* see it," I interrupt. "I *am* aware of the subtle signs. I know what to look for. You do not."

Bulla turns her back on me and stares out the window. Her silhouette in the faint grey light betrays her fragility—and a sudden sadness overwhelms me. I pity her. She cannot handle the truth. Few people can. The majority choose—or have imposed on them—a suitable narrative or worldview. A narrative that helps them pass their lives in certainty and stability. A narrative that requires little thought and assimilation. A narrative that allows them to get on with their everyday struggle for survival.

But the narrative—in possibly all cases—is false. And this presents an unsettling idea: what does the truth matter, if one can successfully live a lie? If there are many different narratives and worldviews that let one survive and thrive, then what use is the overarching narrative that gives meaning and purpose to each person's life? I am religious; I am irreligious. I am a theist; I am an atheist. I am a realist; I am a relativist. I am an individualist; I am a collectivist. I am an evolutionist; I am a creationist. I am a monist; I am a dualist. I am a naturalist; I am a supernaturalist. If all these narratives have no measurable effect on a person's daily activities and survival rate, then does the narrative matter? If people can believe in any narrative, no matter how ridiculous or lacking in evidence, and they can still eat and work and breed, then does any narrative have any value? In other words, does the truth—the ultimate truth—matter? Does it matter to beings, to life, here on this delicate planet floating in the darkness and coldness of an empty and uncaring cosmos?

Yet searching for the truth distinguishes humanity from the millions of other species. We are conscious, curious, questioning creatures who are always asking *why*. And only humans philosophise and seek a worldview, a narrative—*the truth*. So perhaps the truth does matter. Perhaps humanity's quest for the truth makes us unique in the universe. And perhaps the ancients understood this and, as a consequence, declared that man was made in the image of God.

Still, it bothers me. For why does the truth—or the lie—seem so superfluous to life, living, and the struggle for survival? What does such a proposal suggest? That truth and meaning and purpose are emergent illusions? That they neither shape nor influence life? That all ideas and narratives, even consciousness itself, amount to nothing in the end? That matter—cause and effect—is all that counts?

I take a final look at Bulla; an instinct tells me I shall never see her again. Then, something instantly crushes my spirit. But what?

Is it the frail, fleeting, and tragic nature of all life? Of all existence? Or is it my inability to change anything or save anyone? And what exactly would I be saving life from? From itself? From nature? From God? From *it*, whatever *it* is?

But what is *it* that has crushed my spirit so suddenly?

Nihilism?

Emptiness?

Nothingness?

I have my answer.

~~~~~

Even though it is still morning, darkness envelops the building's communal hallway. At the far end, a lone grimy window blocks most of the sunlight from flooding into the corridor; above me, a fluorescent light flickers pathetically. A sharp odour fills the air. Garbage coats most of the floor, and human waste clings to the walls. When the plumbing fails, which is often, the apartment dwellers urinate and defecate in the hallways. What do they care? They are all transients. No one owns any private property, so no one cares for anything. Economists have even coined a phrase to describe this well-known phenomenon: the tragedy of the commons. These are people without property or family, without roots or connections, without culture or identity, without memory or history, without knowledge or understanding, without freedom or responsibility, without wisdom or a soul, without duties or experiences. Transients living a brutish and impoverished existence. And once they trash their shelter, they move to another location—and the cycle continues.

But one animal's waste is another's nursery: rodents and cockroaches flourish in the filth. Hundreds, perhaps thousands, of cockroaches scurry for cover with each step I take. And from under a soiled shredded mattress, a giant water rat peers at me with lifeless eyes. It has caught lunch: a scrawny kitten is struggling for its life. Yet as I spring towards the rat, it snatches the kitten and bolts into an opening in the wall. Hushed activity. A desperate meow. Then silence. I can do nothing for the kitten, now.

An apartment door opens and my neighbour enters the hallway. She glimpses me and immediately stares at the floor. I also refrain from greeting her, though we have bumped into each other several times during the past month. She lives alone, another transient, a stranger who will disappear sooner rather than later. The young woman rushes to the end of the hallway and knocks on an apartment's door. An older man opens the door, and she vanishes into his apartment. Although the State describes prostitution as "an eradicated symptom of the diseased old system that was based on exploitation", the trafficking of women, even children, is alive and thriving. Sexual favours are traded for food, protection, basic goods—anything. A desperate being will do everything to survive. And the loss of individual and property rights has particularly hurt the most vulnerable people in the Occidental Union.

Strolling past several apartments, I hear strange and threatening noises emanating from within. What are they? Human? Nonhuman? There is no speech, just scratching and scuttling like a community of human-insects.

I pass an apartment missing its door, and I peer inside the room. It is usually empty but not today. A man has ensconced himself in a pile of sullied rags and is sleeping in the middle of the room. Trash and shattered furniture surround him. He seems satisfied—a warm place to sleep and a roof over his head. What more does a man need apart from these material basics? Still, few other higher mammals would nestle in filth, in their own waste.

In the opposite corner of the same room, a naked woman is squatting down while gazing directly at the wall in front of her. Cruel curled dirty-brown claw-nails, roughly ten centimetres long, extend from each of her fingers, and dirt-encrusted creases mark every inch of her pasty skin. I can even spot assorted parasites bustling about in her hair. Yet despite the crawling bloodsuckers, she remains motionless, mesmerised by the stains on the wall. Is this her usual behaviour? Or is the contaminated tapwater subduing her? Either way, my roommate is correct: it would be hard, based only on the people's behaviour, to determine whether the State is drugging the water or not. Because even without being drugged, the Occidental population is weird enough.

I cannot endure anymore, however. The dirt, the dark, the stench—everything about this hallway assaults my senses, and I hurry to escape the building.

A fresh breeze greets me, as I stagger out of my apartment complex. I take several deep breaths to clear my lungs of the hallway's lingering foulness. Although the ocean air lacks the previous days' smokiness, I can still detect a hint of the burnt-slum odour.

In each direction, the overcast sky teases the metropolis with the promise of rain. No Sun scorches the land today, and this provides some relief after the brutal temperatures of the last few days. Overall, a comfortable spring day. Yet the streets are empty—except for the rubble and garbage strewn all over the place. According to clips and pictures on the Internet, the metropolis used to teem with life. A typical morning would see squares and marketplaces crowded with shoppers, caffè latte sippers, and people on their way to work. Today, however, nothing: no shoppers, no sippers, no workers. All the shops in the neighbourhood have been abandoned or boarded up. Even the pigeons have deserted this area. An unnatural silence haunts the metropolis. I am the only creature stirring on the street.

A damaged sign dangles from the wall of a decaying building. The metal placard is imprinted with the Occidental Union's emblem, a red fist on a black background. Below the faded image, there is a slogan from a decades-old government campaign designed to educate the public. It says, "Scientists, Bureaucrats, Legislators—

Experts Planning the Perfect Society." Next to the placard, a cynic has graffitied a retort: "Scientists, bureaucrats, legislators—the new unholy trinity that has usurped the old Holy Trinity, the new parasitical priest caste that has drained us dry." At least some people still have a sense of humour.

I grab a lump of broken masonry and hurl it with all my might at the metal placard. The missile hits its target with a clank and pockmarks the word "Planning". Bullseye. I gather several more masonry chunks from the endless debris and cracked pavement, and fling one after the other at the ridiculous sign. Each missile slams into the metal placard with a penetrating boom, so I pause to scan the surrounding buildings for unwanted attention. Despite the racket, no one appears and I resume the pelting. After bombarding the sign for a minute, I stop to survey the destruction. It is dented beyond recognition, and not one single word can be read. I smile at my handiwork. The State may have its powers, but so does the individual. And what took the State and its supporters decades to manufacture, I, a single man, destroyed in a minute. Such is the nature of all power, collective or not. It always disappears—and often instantly.

Hiking westwards, I stumble across a Temple of the People. Although numerous Temples dot the metropolis, each building displays an identical design to espouse the cause of equality. Every Temple consists of three metallic black sides. So the building looks like a giant equilateral triangle, when viewed from above. At each corner of the Temple, a hundred-metre-tall metallic black tower pierces the sky. And each tower's tip is moulded into a metallic red fist—the inspiration for the design arising from the Occidental Union's emblem. As a result, every Temple in the metropolis boasts three giant fists, symbolising people power through the Occidental Union. And since thousands of Temples pepper the metropolis, the collective visual impact can be stunning. Viewed from an elevated vantage point during the day, the metropolis landscape resembles a mob with thousands of shimmering angry red fists raised towards the heavens in united defiance.

Vivid imagery and simple slogans—such methods have always succeeded in wooing and manipulating the hoi polloi.

Apart from the symbolism and rousing architecture, the Temples of the People serve as community and solidarity centres, where people can gather to relax, party, socialise, self-actualise, or do whatever they want. A section of each Temple is also reserved for more mundane government administration purposes. Today, for instance, the Temple standing before me has been transformed into a food distribution centre. Two queues, each with several-hundred people dressed in the State-issued black garb, wind their way through the streets like ant trails. According to two signs, the people in the first line are waiting for "Food & Beer Rations", whereas those in the second are lined up for "Household Rations". Even though neither queue is moving, the people appear dull rather than rowdy—a sign the tapwater may, in fact, be drugged.

Several armed peace officers meander through the crowds, and roughly one hundred public servants lounge about the Temple. Yet despite the sleepy atmosphere, a commotion erupts among a handful of the frontline distributors.

"I ain't distributin' out anymore food, today," a pinkish piggish woman squeals, "cause I've done me fair share o' work." She then points to a tall attractive woman and says, "She's done less work than me, she 'as. Yeah, 'er 'ighness, over there, should 'and out the rations instead o' me. Or does 'er 'ighness not want to dirty 'er royal 'ands?"

A man, probably a supervisor, rolls off a couch and saunters towards the piggish woman.

"Okay," he says, "what's going on here? What's the problem now?"

The piggish woman answers, "As I've been sayin', I've done me too much work, more than me fair share. And 'er 'ighness, over there, 'as 'anded out less rations than me, but she's lyin' around doin' nothin'. The lazy sod!"

"However," the supervisor replies while indicating the tall attractive woman, "she's finished her day's quota."

"Oh, ain't that just typical?" the piggish woman cries out, as she shakes her finger at the supervisor. "Take 'er 'ighness's side. Aye? Take the pretty girl's side. I know you 'ave a thin' for 'er. I know you're on 'er side cause you wanna shag 'er. You dirty ol' geeza, you! Well, I ain't doin' no more work, I ain't. Get someone else to 'and this crap out."

"And what about you?" the supervisor asks the public servant in charge of distributing the household rations. "Why aren't you handing out any supplies?"

"Because, mate, if she ain't workin', I ain't workin', mate," the man answers. "Mate, that's how it works round here, mate. Kinoath! Mate, I'm no idiot who's gonna work more than anyone else, mate."

A woman, probably the supervisor's manager, awakens from her slumber and ambles towards the kerfuffle.

"So what is the issue at hand, here?" she asks the supervisor after yawning. "What is terminating the momentum of the distribution of rations to each eligible recipient of State-owned goods and consumables?"

Acknowledging the manager, he responds, "Well, this worker says she isn't going to work anymore today, since she has done more work than that other worker lying down over there. And the worker in charge of the household rations refuses to work, because the worker in charge of the food isn't working."

"Is this true?" the manager interrogates the piggish woman.

"I've 'xplained this many a times already, I 'ave," the piggish woman replies, "and I'm tired of 'xplainin' it. Yeah, I've done me more work than 'er 'ighness over there, I 'ave. And I ain't gonna work no more today, I ain't. And me supervisor 'ere, 'e wants to shag 'er 'ighness—and so 'es takin' 'er side and all!"

A man, probably the departmental head and the manager's superior, hears the hubbub and staggers to his feet.

"Oi! What's all this noise about?" he questions the manager. "Aye? Why is no one distributing any rations?"

"It appears, sir, that an insurmountable situation has arisen here," she says. "This worker claims an injustice and an inequality in working conditions have occurred on these here premises. This worker additionally states that she will be distributing no further rations today, as she has distributed more than her fair share compared to her fellow workers. In addition, the worker in charge of the household rations refuses to work, as he is not going to work when no one else is working."

The departmental head scratches his ear and then says, "Yes, we seem to have a major problem developing right here, right now. Additionally, if these claims are true, then this issue will have to be handled by the relevant Occidental Union representatives. This woman's claims may even constitute a breach of workers' rights legislation."

"So what should we do?" the manager asks the departmental head.

"I will have to ask the Honour, the Honourable Occidental Union Administrator. Give me one second while I go talk to the Honour, the Honourable Occidental Union Administrator."

The departmental head dismisses the manager and then strolls over to the Occidental Union Administrator, who is dozing in a chair.

This is my first glimpse of an Occidental Union Administrator, since they rarely venture out of the Occidental Union capital. From this distance, the Administrator looks androgynous—a crop-haired effete-featured porcelain-skinned ectomorph dressed in black robes, which are stamped with a red fist on the front and an empty white circle on the back. Weirder yet, a giant brown slug, about fifteen centimetres long and five centimetres wide, is latched on to the Administrator's nape. What fresh hell is the Occidental Union about to unleash on its people?

"Your Honour, I need your advice," the departmental head says, while eyeing with revulsion the slug sucking on the Administrator's nape. "Your Honour, there is an escalation in tensions between two workers, and, well, neither worker wants to work. I think, your Honour, we may have to file several reports, because there may be a breach of workers' rights legislation. One worker is also complaining about a supervisor's sexual-based favouritism towards another worker. So, your Honour, there may be another breach of legislation. Also, judging by the number of queued people, there is no way that we have enough food rations for everyone. Therefore, you can see the mess we're in. Please, your Honour, what should I do?"

The Occidental Union Administrator opens one eye, and in a creepy gender-neutral voice groans, "Our work never ends—all the time, problem after problem." It then stands up and begins to gesticulate wildly. "When will you idiots learn to act like functional human beings? Huh? When will you behave and do as you are commanded? Huh? Is it so much to ask? Huh? We do everything for you morons. We even provide you with public service jobs. And what do you give in return? You give nothing in return—not even three hours' work per week! Useless imbeciles, the whole bunch of you! Lazy, stupid, pathetic, good-for-nothing human garbage!"

The Administrator ends its tirade and then strokes the slimy slug. It undulates and oozes a viscous mossy-green mucus in response; moments later, the host-Administrator squirms with ecstasy.

After a minute, the Administrator calmly says, "So now we have to fill out countless forms and file paperwork and create subcommittees to investigate these incidents and then report to an Occidental Union Supreme Committee. This is just wonderful."

However, the slug's sedating chemical infusion soon wears off, and the Administrator seizes a chair and smashes it against the wall. Terror grips all the public servants, and several recede into the depths of the Temple for safety.

"Well, that's it for today," the Administrator barks at the departmental head. "We've had enough of your collective stupidity. This Temple of the People is now closed for the day. Shut it all down! Lock up the remaining rations! No food and no beer for anyone else! All finished for the day! Do you understand us? Or do we now have to shut down everything ourselves? *Go*!"

The departmental head scurries away and begins ordering his inferiors to close the Temple of the People.

Overhearing these orders, though, a man at the front of the food queue says, "But, ya Honour, I need food! I'm hungry. Ya Honour, jus' ledus tayke our rations. We'll even hand 'em out ourselves. Please, ya Honour, it's easy—the food is jus' sittin' there. Please, ledme help. I'll even give out the food, if ya Honour tells me what to do."

"Quite impossible!" the Administrator yells. "It is far more complicated than just handing out the rations. No, no, no. There are rules and regulations to be followed. There are training and certification requirements to be completed, before you can hand out the rations. No, no, no! It is far more involved than you can imagine. You are neither qualified nor certified to hand out rations. Ha! How hilarious you ignorant commoners are. Imagine that! This untrained man thinks he can just start handing out the rations. How farcical! What would you dependants do without us? Without Sci–Coll and the Occidental Union? You would all starve and kill each other within a few days."

But the queued throng dislikes what it is hearing, and the people begin shouting a rallying call: "Give us our food and beer, or we will stay right here!" This is followed by, "Hell no! We won't go!" The protest fails to build momentum, however, and fizzles out after a few minutes. The crowd then disperses quietly. On any other day, riots would have erupted.

I leave the Temple of the People and continue walking inland. After a couple of kilometres, I hear the childlike caws of a murder of crows and decide to investigate. How refreshing to find other creatures, besides humans, living in the metropolis's heart. Yet my enthusiasm soon fades away, for the unfolding drama is anything but the celebration of life.

Hundreds of crows are huddled together on a ledge protruding from an Occidental Union Public Nursery. A sign fastened to the Public Nursery says, "Celebrating the Liberation and Emancipation of the Child from the Tyranny of Father, Family, and Tradition; Embracing the

Rights and Progress of each Child under the Expert and Loving Guidance of the State."

Although the Nursery's architectural design is almost identical to the Temple's, all Public Nurseries lack the three fist-shaped towers. This Nursery also looks deserted, and two of its walls are crumbling, thereby helping it to blend in perfectly with its surroundings. For everything in this neighbourhood is decaying or dying, except for the excited crows.

Despite missing it at first glance, I finally spot—and smell—the focus of the crows' fascination. Two dark masses rest behind a spindly bush, which is growing next to the Nursery's main entrance. On closer inspection, I discover two abandoned boys—both writhing in agony, their gaping festering wounds crawling with The Nightmare. This must be one of the most painful ways to die, and for these unlucky children there is nothing anyone can do.

The Nightmare terrifies everyone. It is one of those things that sounds like it could only exist in a nightmare—yet it is real. Too real. And even though it was once limited to specific regions in the tropics, it has now spread to many parts of the world, thanks to the Occidental Union's open-border-and-no-quarantine policies. The Nightmare starts with a nick or a tiny wound on a human or another warm-blooded animal. This wound attracts a fly called the screw-worm fly, which then deposits and glues hundreds of eggs on to the wound's side. Once the maggots hatch, they bore into the wound and feast on *healthy* flesh and tissue. Hence, the fly's name: screw-worm fly. The wound expands and putrefies as the screw-worm maggots gorge and grow; meanwhile, the rot's stink lures other flies, which add new offspring to the feeding frenzy. And the feeding–breeding cycle continues, until the wretched victim is devoured alive. It is a slow and agonising death: a nightmare.

Both boys are barely breathing. One boy opens his eyes but says nothing. He just stares at me, his face distorted with pure dread. He is too weak to do anything else. Wriggling maggots have consumed most of his flesh and muscles. The white ricegrain-shaped creatures are even crawling out through his nostrils and mouth. Hundreds of thousands of hungry little monsters on and inside the child.

"I am so sorry, child," I say to the boy. What else can I utter in the face of such horror and pointless torture?

Sensing my presence, the other boy moans. But I can hardly hear him above the buzzing flies and cawing crows. With great effort, he turns his head in my direction. His eyes have been eaten away—a squirming mass of maggots replacing them. I look away and retch.

What can I do? How can I help these dying boys who have been discarded by everyone, including the State? No one can save them now, not even the State Emergency Services—which have, moreover, stopped responding to emergencies. So what am I supposed to do? I unwrap my tablet computer from around my forearm and log the incident with the emergency services. Although this act lacks any meaning, I am powerless to do anything else. In the meantime, I talk comforting nonsense to the boys, while waiting for the State's unlikely help. But no one responds. The boy without eyes dies first, and then the other follows him. One instant alive, the next dead. From animate to inanimate. Nothing special or spectacular about the transition. Gone and forgotten in a flash.

And I rush away from the gruesome scene, before the screw-worm flies target me.

~~~~~

I trek inland for a further hour, before arriving at the entrance of a no-go zone. No State exists from this point onwards; instead, a patriarchal and traditional religious group rules these streets. And even though the State has condemned these Coptic Orthodox Christians as terrorists, I know from past experience that it is a lie and I will be safe.

The State calls it the war against religion—but the war against the Copts is just another war in the State's endless list of unending wars. In this war, however, the State is battling against another form of collectivism. For the State cannot permit a competing collective ideology to flourish. Room exists for only one collective ideology: the State's collective ideology, Sci–Coll. Room exists for only one religion: the religion of State worship, which in its essence is the religion of man worship—because man is State, and State is man. To allow a stronger collective ideology than statism to spread and infect the public mentality would guarantee the State's failure. And religion has always represented a dangerous alternative to State collectivism. Whereas the State ideologues promise a *temporary* utopia on Earth, religions promise an *eternal* utopia after death. And whereas the State draws its authority from *human* experts, religions gain their authority from *God*, a supposedly perfect power beyond this universe. So which promise would the people find more seductive? Which promise would better win the hearts and minds of the majority? Which promise would more effectively gather and mould the people into a single organised body with a collective morality? A collective identity? A collective consciousness?

Although the Occidental Union dislikes all religions, it particularly loathes Christianity as it represents, in the State's eyes, the final link with the old system. According to the Worldwide Workers Union, "Christianity is a system of repression and exploitation—a system where privileged, elite, rich, white males claim divine authority in order to abuse, oppress, and subjugate women, children, homosexuals, minorities, the poor, and all other races and religions and cultures. Christians seek to maintain the capitalist status quo and ensure the workers remain without capital or property or freedom. The religion is designed to keep entrenched white males, the bourgeoisie, in power, while reducing the proletariat to slavery and poverty through laissez-faire capitalism. However, the most abhorrent aspect of Christianity is that it forces people to behave unnaturally and denies them their human right to live life freely, as they choose. Christianity, at the hands of the white wealthy elite, is used to coerce the proletariat into acting and thinking in a correctly prescribed and codified manner. Christianity inculcates in the working masses an attitude of submission to tradition, authority, and revelation. Christianity even dictates how, when, and with whom a person should have sexual intercourse. The religion is nothing but mass mind control of the most primitive and totalitarian kind. Christianity produces the vilest form of slavery."

And once the State eliminates the Copts, then the last organised Christians in the Occidental Union—the last remnants of the old system—will be terminated.

The Occidental Union will never assault the Copts with its armed forces, though. For the Occidental Union observes human rights and is a signatory to the Occidental Union & Free Islands Declaration of Human Rights. An armed attack against the Copts would probably provoke the Free Islands into retaliating. The Occidental State will, instead, use subtler and more devious methods to whittle down this final bastion of Christianity. The State will legislate against them. It will isolate them economically. It will ban their businesses from trading with the general population. It will impose sanctions on them and try to cripple them. It will weaken their families, communities, and social structures. It will encourage the media to spread vile propaganda about them. It will pressure the academy into demonising them—from an objective perspective, of course. It will trick the masses into envying and hating the Copts. It will unleash its mobs, the State's Spawn, to do its bidding.

But the State will never dirty its hands. It will always remain righteous, hiding behind its pseudomorality and calls to "social justice": Christians deserve to be punished for the so-called sins of their ancestors.

So I enter the Coptic territory. A huge Coptic cross welcomes me, and polished street signs declare, "You are entering a Copt-controlled zone." Though many bullet-scared buildings line the streets, several structures have been reduced to rubble, no doubt from old clashes with enemies fired up by the State. But at least I can stop worrying about the Occidental Union watching me with its cameras: every black hive has been wrecked or removed, ensuring the statelessness of this zone.

After taking several steps into the territory, five armed guards suddenly jump out from a side structure and encircle me. They are dressed in black paramilitary uniforms with black riot-police helmets hiding their faces, so I am unable to see their eyes and judge their intentions. Yet their intentions soon become clear, as they point their assault rifles in my face.

"Halt! Who are you, and why are you visiting our community?" asks the lead guard, a giant who towers over me. Although his accent exhibits a strong exotic flavour, he pronounces every syllable cleanly and crisply—a marvel in these times.

"I've come to trade money for information," I reply, while raising my hands in surrender. "If you want, please feel free to scan me for identification purposes."

The leader nods and motions to another guard, who points his handheld scanner at my neck and scans my implanted microchip. A third guard then pats me down for weapons.

"Okay, sir, this man is clean," the guard says, as he finishes checking my clothes for weapons.

"Occidental State fiat currency is no good here," the leader says. "Brother, I suggest you turn around and depart this area."

"But I don't have any Occidental Worldwide dollars," I reply. "I've brought one-troy-ounce gold and silver coins from the Free Islands. These coins are used as legal tender there."

"Silver and gold coins from the Free Islands are *definitely* good, here," he says. "We use them for trade. Unlike the State's ever devaluing junk money, Free Island coins maintain their value. We even trade with the Free Islands, when we can sneak past the Occidental State. So the Free Island's currency is always useful. But tell me, brother— why do you come here rather than trade at another market?"

"Because what I need I can't find anywhere else."

"And what is it you seek, brother?"

"Information," I reply.

"Information about what?" he asks, lowering his weapon.

"Information about the government—about our tapwater. I'm even willing to trade gold or silver coins for this information."

The lead guard ponders my request for a few seconds before answering, "We do not even drink the government's filthy tapwater. We rely on a creek that flows through our community—thanks be to God! So why do you believe you will find your answers here, brother?"

"I believe I will find the answers here, because I used to work with someone who lives here. And I know he can help me."

"Hmm, interesting. And who is this person you speak of?"

"Dr Tawfik. Dr Ghali Tawfik," I reply. "He used to work for Worldwide Industries & Finance, but I am unsure whether he still works there or not."

The guards start chattering among each other in what sounds like two different tongues: the first, I think, is Arabic, whereas the second is a mystery. In any event, I understand nothing.

After several minutes the lead guard says, "Okay, brother, you may enter our community. But because of your unique request and because no one here knows you, one of my guards will escort you to Dr Tawfik's place—and then, at the completion of your meeting, that guard will escort you *immediately* out of our community. You may talk to Dr Tawfik only—no one else. And the guard must be present with you at all times, even while you are with Dr Tawfik. If you break any of our rules, you will be escorted *immediately* out. Brother, have I made myself clear?"

"Perfectly clear, sir," I respond. "I am grateful for your time and help. And thank you for allowing me, a complete stranger, to enter your community. You are very kind."

To express my gratitude, I offer the leader a silver coin, but he refuses it.

"Thank you, brother," he says, "but I do not want your money. Just say 'thanks be to God', if you discover what you are searching for and I shall be pleased."

The leader then snaps his fingers at one of his guards, who steps forwards and frisks me a second time for weapons. After satisfying his curiosity, the guard gestures me to accompany him.

As I turn to leave, however, the leader asks me, "*Enta Ebty*?"

"Sorry?" I reply, my brows furrowed. "I don't understand what you just said."

"You resemble us—dark skin and similar features—even though the name registered on your microchip identification is not Coptic. Nevertheless, you look like you may have some Coptic blood in you, perhaps mixed with some Ethiopian blood. Many Ethiopian Orthodox people live here with us, since we share similar cultures and our religions are basically identical."

"As far as I know, I am neither Coptic nor Ethiopian," I say. "But in this world anything is possible, I guess."

"Hmm, interesting, you are a Public Nursery child, a State's Spawn?" the leader asks.

"*No*! Definitely not!" I cry out.

The leader bows his head and says, "Sorry, brother, I mean you no offence at all. My sincerest apologies."

"That's okay—no offence taken," I respond, though annoyed at being confused for an *SS*.

Not convinced with my answer, the leader continues with his original inquiries. "So, brother, if I were to say to you *Christos Anesti*, you would not know how to respond?"

"Sorry, but I really have no idea what you're talking about."

"That is fine, brother," the lead guard says. "May God help you find what you seek."

"Goodbye, sir, and once again thank you very much for all your help," I reply, as the leader disappears with his guards into a nearby apartment block.

One guard, my escort, remains behind. He beckons me to follow, as he ducks into a tiny guard's hut. Inside the hut, my escort slips off his full-face helmet. His skin is dark and smooth, the lines of old age a distant worry. Black eyes, strong features, short black hair—all these qualities he shares with me.

"Come on. Let us go," the escort says, while snatching a backpack from a cupboard.

He then heads towards the hut's far end, where a shaft descends into the Earth's depths. We enter the shaft and shuffle down several uneven rock-carved steps. The passageway leads to a shoulder-width rocky tunnel. It is cool and damp inside the tunnel. On the walls hang lit oil lamps, their light barely beating back the blackness. The flickering flames reveal Coptic crosses carved into the walls at regular intervals. Shadows instantly appear and disappear. An earthy yet familiar odour lingers in the air. I can also detect a fainter yet unfamiliar aroma. Our footsteps echo weakly throughout the silent subterranean passageway. The dimness hypnotises me, leaving me giddy. I feel strangely safe, as if I were in a dream. So serene, so surreal.

Feeling unbalanced, I place one palm on each side of the tunnel. The cold rough texture of the rocky surface reaches deep into my being. The experience re-anchors me to reality. The physical harshness brings my wandering soul back to its rightful resting place.

I hear a voice in the distance; no, it is nearby. It is the escort. He is talking to me, but his voice is muffled. The tunnel is playing tricks on me.

"Sorry, what did you say?" I ask, snapping out of the trance.

"Whale oil," he repeats.

"What about whale oil?"

"The lamps—they use whale oil. There is a beach, not far from here, where whales beach themselves and die. We do not know why they do it, but hundreds of them beach themselves early spring, every year. Anyway, their death is our blessing, because we remove the oil from their blubber and use their meat for fishing. We also turn the whale meat into animal feed for our goats and chickens. Therefore, whales supply a big part of our livelihood."

"That's fascinating," I say. "I didn't know people still used whales for oil and industry. I thought whale products died out centuries ago."

"We have to live somehow—thanks be to God!" he says, while raising his hands. "Without the whales our community, our little city, would suffer or perhaps even collapse—God forbid. Most of the homes use whale oil for lighting, cooking, and heating, though we never eat the whale meat. We also trade the whale meat and oil for other goods."

"You use whale oil for lighting and heating your homes and buildings?" I query my escort.

"Yes, it is free and effective, and we have it in plentiful supply. For all our other energy needs, we use solar-generated electricity."

My escort then points ahead. In the distance, a pale yet steady white light bathes the tunnel.

"We are almost at the end," he says. "Once we exit the tunnel, please, you must avoid staring at the residents. In the past, we have had big problems with strangers who turned out to be very bad people. And many residents are now suspicious of strangers."

"Perfectly understandable. I promise to be respectful"

I exit the tunnel, and my eyes take a few seconds to adapt to the bright sunlight. When they do adjust, I find myself standing in a shoulder-width lane. Intricate hand-woven rugs adorn the buildings' walls on either side of me, and colourful fabrics sway from the rooftops overhead, the fluttering cloths breaking up the sunlight before it washes the worn cobblestone paving. As far as I can gaze, countless side lanes branch off this alley, each one weaving and winding its way through thousands of ancient buildings. I have entered a maze city.

Life flourishes in every nook of this labyrinth. Passers-by stir to the beat of buskers banging on their *tablas*, while bartering and chattering women draped in *kaftans* choke every tiny shop. In deeper darker corners of smaller seedier side lines, men garbed in *galaleeb* lounge around in cosy cafés, sipping Turkish coffee or fresh mint tea. A few men are also smoking *shishas*, and the aroma of apple-scented tobacco flavours the air. And everywhere I glance, children are playing and screaming while darting from shop to shop,

77

café to café. This is the stuff of old movies and faded memories. How has this pocket of life managed to survive—to bloom—in the Occidental nothingness and darkness? The contrast between my barren colourless world and this one is startling. And even though the surrounding bustle invigorates me, I also feel drained and envious—for the universe has cheated me out of enjoying a similar life.

"Hurry, hurry!" the escort cries out, while grabbing my arm. "We need to keep moving."

I follow closely my escort as he dashes from one lane to another, but soon one alley starts to resemble the other and each building begins to merge with the next. Without my guide, I would be unable to find my way out of this Coptic labyrinth. Yet I am enjoying the adventure. Numerous artisans, from silversmiths to leatherworkers, crowd each lane and display their exquisite goods to potential buyers. Meanwhile, on every building's corner, telephone-booth-sized shopfronts tease me with offerings of syrupy sweets, fresh-squeezed juices, and aromatic chargrilled meats, while street vendors tempt me with tasty morsels of *shawerma*, *fool*, and *tameya*, each wrapped in steaming fresh-baked flatbread. The exotic aromas linger in my nostrils, and my mouth waters in a Pavlovian response. Memories flash back. During my time at Worldwide Industries, the company sent me on a scientific trip to the Free Islands, and there I tasted real food for the first time in my life. Green crispy vegetables. Bright juicy-sweet fruits. Fresh delicate seafood. Flavoursome meats. But, in the pursuit of the perfectly planned and balanced diet, the Occidental State distributes only vat-grown vitamin-enriched food handouts. The same homogenised cardboard-flavoured mush every meal, every day. Even the State's alcohol handouts are bland. A throat-corroding vodka knock-off.

I gaze around me and try to absorb all the community's folksy sensations. The primaeval smells, sights, and sounds transport me to another place, another time, another culture. Yet despite the continuous sensuous feast, one particularly quaint feature enchants me: the countless chapels and grottos dotting the lanes. And just like the Coptic food, these religious symbols evoke strong emotions in me, though of a different nature. Clanging cymbals and monotonous chanting emanate from many chapels: "*Zoksapatri ke iyou-ke agi you epnevmaty ... Kenin ke aa-ee ke-is-touce e-on-ace ton e-non. Amen ... Zoksapatri ke iyou-ke agi you epnevmaty ... Kenin ke aa-ee ke-is-touce e-on-ace ton e-non. Amen.*"

My mind begins to drift away with the ancient and arcane incantations. I squeeze my eyes shut, and a gentler world kindles my consciousness. Yet words fail to describe this realm. Warm sensations flooding my being, filling me with hope and peace and oneness. Unable to pin *it* down. I just feel something, a boundless thing arousing yet dousing every cell in my body. A paradox. It conflicts with all my training, education, and indoctrination. But it exists—it is real for me—for I am experiencing it. And my experiences connect me with the physical sphere, that world residing outside my mind. How else can I know reality but through my experiences? And how can I explain the experiences of hope, peace, and oneness using just the reductive language of science? For physical descriptions relying only on concepts such as neurotransmitters, hormones, and molecules completely miss the emergent bigger picture, the person-experienced reality of hope, peace, and oneness. Do we try to explain a volcanic eruption by reducing it to quarks, the supposed fundamental building block of the cosmos? Of course not. Likewise, to *explain* experiences, needs, and desires, we must invoke agents—thinking, feeling, desiring, purposeful, meaningful, acting beings— and their motivations. And reducing an agent, a person, to nothing more than physics misses the entire story and explains nothing. At this moment, nothing matters but my experience of *it*. It is real and personal. It is—

"Hello? Brother? Brother!" my escort says, his voice shattering my experience. "We cannot stop. We must continue walking. Dr Tawfik awaits us, and we still have a fifteen-minute journey."

"Okay," I mumble, while trying to clear my head. And, for an instant, I recall an earlier encounter today with *it*— but that nihilistic encounter fostered the opposite sensation: dread.

My escort hastens the pace as we snake through ever narrowing passages. On the way we bump into several priests, each draped in heavy black robes and flaunting a thick beard—the equivalent of a lion's mane. For just as a lion rules a pride, these men rule these streets. And as for the priests' black robes, they remind me of the Occidental Union Administrator's garments; perhaps the State received its sartorial inspiration from these priests. Besides an entourage of stern-looking men, an incense-like scent also trails the priests, no doubt a consequence of the many hours spent praying in incense-infused chapels. No priest greets my escort, though. Nor does he acknowledge a single priest. A conflict seems to be brewing within this community.

After wandering through countless lanes, we finally stop at a staircase leading to a second-floor residence.

"Up there is Dr Tawfik's home," the escort says, while indicating a second-storey door. "Wait here because I need to talk to him first."

He then sprints up the staircase, and a minute later beckons me to join him. I climb the stairs and immediately recognise my old colleague, Dr Ghali Tawfik.

"Doctor!" I say. "It's been so long. So good to see you! How are you, my friend?"

"Hello, hello, my fine sir," he replies, while kissing me once on each cheek. A hint of frankincense clings to the air around him. "It is a pleasure, indeed, to see you again. You have not aged one day since, since—how long has it been?"

"I think almost seven years," I reply. "Can you believe it? Seven years! And you are looking as healthy as ever. What's your secret? Did you discover the fountain of youth, after I was fired from Worldwide Industries & Finance?"

The doctor starts to laugh, but the episode ends in a coughing fit.

"Please, forgive my bad manners, my fine sir," he murmurs, as the paroxysm peters out. "Come in, please." He then points to the escort and says, "*You*, however, are not welcome in my home. You can wait at the door."

I enter the doctor's home, while my guide remains at the doorway. Fine tapestries decorate the walls, and a schizophrenically patterned rug carpets the entire room. An ornate silver chandelier dangles from the centre of the ceiling. The chandelier boasts several arms, each carrying dozens of lit candles that bathe everything in a soft radiance. Without the candlelight, the room would be dark, for arabesque wooden shutters cover the windows and limit the entry of natural light. Towards the far end, a large Coptic cross and several Coptic icons furnish an alcove overlooking the back alley. Tracing its roots to the Ancient Egyptian tradition of Isis suckling a baby Horus, an icon of the Virgin Mary nursing a baby Jesus dominates the religious paintings. Above them hangs an incense holder, and frankincense smoke, sweet and heavenly, wafts throughout the home.

"Please, please, take a seat," the doctor says, pointing at a regal-looking armchair. Yet looks can be deceiving, because the armchair is hard and uncomfortable—unfit for royalty.

Three children, giggling and squealing, dash into the room. "*Ya katakeet!*" the doctor shrieks, while herding them into his outstretched arms. "Grandchildren, I want you to say hello to this nice gentleman."

"Hello, sir," they say in unison, as they surround and hug me.

"And a hello to you!" I reply, genuinely surprised and delighted with their gentleness.

The children then sprint past the escort guarding the entrance, stumble down the stairs, and vanish into the laneways.

"I forgot that children can be such gentle and lovely creatures," I say to the doctor. "Your grandchildren are beautiful—wonderful."

"Thank you, my fine sir, for your kind words," the doctor replies. "Yes, my grandchildren are a gift from God—true blessings. Though, it takes plenty of love, patience, and discipline to raise them. Do not think they just popped out that way!"

"I know. I've seen the opposite of your grandchildren; I'm used to the monsters the State raises. That's why I said, *I forgot that children can be such lovely creatures.*"

The doctor shakes his head: "Ah, yes, the State's Spawn—they terrify me. You cannot reason with the *SS*. You look into their eyes and you glimpse a darkness that envies, resents, and despises you—a darkness that wants to devour you. Creating these dependent monsters was a brilliant move by the State. Through them, the Occidental State maintains its power and keeps us living in constant terror. And the more terrified we are, the more we need the State—and, as a result, we then grant the State even more power in order to protect us from the *SS*. A vicious circle. Who would have predicted the State would use the rhetoric of Sci–Coll to enhance its powers democratically, while also reducing individual freedom democratically? Now, the State and the *SS* are the majority, and together they have total power. No more democracy, thanks to democracy. How is that for a paradox?"

"Doctor, I'm not sure what you mean," I answer.

"Okay, okay, my fine sir," he says, while rummaging in a nearby set of oil-stained drawers. "I keep a collection of printed articles—important documents and other historical news items. Ah! Here it is. Although this news piece is one hundred years old, it does explain exactly what I mean about democracy destroying democracy:

The Free Island Times, *"The Occidental Union embraces Sci–Coll as the only legitimate political party", 19 November 2112——— Let us see what democracy delivered in the 2112 Occidental Union One-Party Referendum, where the people were asked to vote on the following proposition: should the Occidental Union move to a one-party system, with all political parties to be banned except for Sci–Coll?*

The results shocked many political commentators. Only 21 per cent of registered voters turned out to vote, and 97 per cent voted in favour of the proposition. So democracy eliminated every political party except for Sci–Coll, and democracy delivered a one-party tyranny. Yet this result should be welcomed, because the majority voted for it. If the majority speaks, if the majority elects, then all is well. For the majority must be right. But what majority? A measly 21 per cent?

But if we scan various news sources, we discover that democracy can be bought. In this "democratic" referendum, Sci–Coll bought the SS's and poor people's votes—constituting the majority of the Occidental Union's population—with welfare handouts, including free food, free clothing, free transport, free housing, free education, free medical care, and even free beer. So political handouts and political promises bought the referendum result.

According to The Occidental Telegraph, *however, Sci–Coll and its supporters—the State's Spawn and trade union members of the Worldwide Workers Union—did more than just buy votes. They also bullied minorities into submission and forced them into abstaining from voting in various elections and referendums: "A campaign of terror and violence by the State's Spawn and members of the Worldwide Workers Union left most office workers too scared to vote in the 2112 Occidental Union One-Party Referendum. A few days before the vote, millions of armed SS and trade union members protested across the Occidental Union. Many blocked access to businesses and shut down entire business districts, whereas others bashed and murdered employers and employees. SS hackers also crippled online businesses and banks. Graffiti sprayed on office buildings read, 'Down with the old system! Death to capitalism! Long live Sci–Coll and the Worldwide Workers Union!'"*

So democratic voting can be bought with political handouts, and democratic voting can be blocked by the mobs. In The Rise and Fall of Society, *Frank Chodorov writes that we can trace these political ploys to ancient times: "[I]n every age, political power has lent itself to purposes that are uneconomic and antisocial, that it has never hesitated to purchase support with confiscated property [taxpayers' money]. For the ancients it may be said that they conducted the business in a forthright manner, unadorned with moralisms; the Caesars did not invoke an ideology to cover up the real objective of 'bread and circuses'. [This phrase refers to an Ancient Roman motto: 'Keep the people fed and entertained (with bread and circuses), and you can take away all their freedoms.'] Today, political preferment and the augmentation of political power are accomplished in the same way—with subsidies of all sorts, paid for by taxpayers—but the business is conducted under a panoply of rectitude. Our politicians do not purchase votes, they advocate 'social' programs. It comes to the same thing."*

In the previous passage, Chodorov also emphasises how modern politicians buy votes. They camouflage the practice by advocating "social programs" or demanding social justice or claiming the social good; that is, they invoke an ideology to hide their real objective of "bread and circuses". Democracy is not perfect in theory or in practice.

It was Plato, (c. 428–348 BC) in his famous Republic *(VIII, 562–A), who gave us the aphorism "Democracy passes into despotism." For the Occidental Union, this took one democratic referendum.*

"And I thought I was well read," I say to the doctor. "I had no idea about the 2112 Occidental Union One-Party Referendum or about how Sci–Coll gained totalitarian power. But these events occurred one hundred years ago, so I think I can be forgiven for my ignorance."

"Those who fail to learn their history are bound to repeat its mistakes, my fine sir," the doctor responds. "Yes, I can forgive you; however, you harm yourself, if you ignore history or accept a revised version of it. Nevertheless, I definitely do not blame you for the sins of your society. And we shall have plenty of time to discuss these matters later. But, now, it is almost time for lunch. Please, you must be famished after trudging through the labyrinth that we call *home, sweet home*. I have a scrumptious meal ready—enough food for a village! And I insist you sup with me. To refuse this request would be an insult."

"My good doctor, I cannot refuse such a tasty offer. And, yes, I am absolutely famished. I haven't eaten homemade food in years. All my food comes processed and prepackaged, courtesy of Worldwide Industries & Finance and the Occidental Union. So I am longing for real food with flavour."

"Excellent! Excellent!" the doctor says, while clapping his hands. "But before the meal, what would you like to drink? I have Turkish coffee, mint tea, fresh-squeezed lemon juice. Or perhaps you would prefer another type of fresh-squeezed juice—orange or sugar cane?"

"What will you be drinking?" I ask.

"I shall be drinking mint tea," the doctor replies. "It is made with fresh mint from my rooftop garden and green tea leaves imported all the way from the Free Islands. Delicious and refreshing and good for the soul!"

"Well, then, a mint tea for me, too. It sounds irresistible."

The doctor waddles into the kitchen and begins preparing the mint tea. After a few minutes, he returns carrying a silver tray, which is supporting a pot of steaming mint tea and two gold-etched tea glasses. He places the tray and its contents on a finely patterned arabesque table and pours some tea into the glasses. The mint leaves floating in the amber liquid resemble tiny verdant islands submerged in a honey-yellow sea.

"The tea is already sweetened with white sugar," he says. "Go ahead, drink it and tell me what you think."

I cup my hands around the hot tea glass and take a sip. The warm sweet liquid revitalises me as it trickles down my throat.

"I can really taste the mint," I say. "It's crisp, clean, and invigorating. It is more like a tisane rather than a tea. Absolutely delightful! Thank you, doctor."

"My pleasure," he says, flashing a wrinkled tired grin. "There are two things I cannot live without: coffee and fresh mint tea. Take them away and you steal a good part of my life. Although I love my family, I equally love my sensual delights!"

The doctor shuts his eyes and sips his mint tea. He is savouring the experience, forgetting the world and all its disasters. Life is good.

After a blissful minute, he opens his eyes and says, "Now, I am sure you did not come all this way for fresh mint tea, no matter how good it is. So what is on your mind?"

"Unfortunately, you are right, doctor. But before anything else, if you don't mind me asking, why did you yell at my escort and ban him from entering your home?"

The doctor answers, "Because he and the majority of his young male friends are breaking God's commandments. Copts never use violence to solve problems. We pray to God and ask Him to help us, as *He* sees fit. But we never pick up a gun and fire it, even if it is to protect our families and churches. *Never!* God will protect us, if we have faith in Him. Violence is never acceptable! Never! Under no circumstances! *Do you hear me? Or has gunfire made you deaf?*" he yells at the guard who is standing at the door. "Violence begets more violence. What happens when you kill a man? Is he not someone's son, someone's father, someone's sibling, someone's lover, someone's relative? And how do you think that other someone—that aggrieved person who has lost a son, father, sibling, lover, or relative—will react? Will that upset person not seek revenge? Will that person not seek blood for blood? And will not the cycle of violence and revenge escalate forever? Every living creature has been used and abused, at some point in time. And every living creature has also used and abused another living creature, at some other point in time. No living being is sinless. But it takes an act of forgiveness to break the cycle of violence and revenge. Without an act of forgiveness by one party, we are all doomed to butcher each other. The world will drown in blood, because we all bear guilt. Every single person is guilty! Do you hear me, oh soldier of evil? Your acts of violence, even if inflicted in self-defence, will only beget more violence upon our people. The only right, rational, and honourable act is forgiveness. *Forgiveness*!"

Several silent and tense moments pass, yet the statue-like escort refrains from acknowledging the doctor.

So I reply instead: "I'm sorry if I've touched on a sensitive subject, doctor. But, speaking for myself, you've made a few wise points, which I haven't considered before."

"No, do not be sorry," the doctor says, losing interest in the unresponsive escort. "And, yes, I do speak the truth about forgiveness being the only way to break the cycle of violence and revenge. It is practical advice. It is common sense, not some abstract and unusable theory. By picking up weapons, these young men have disobeyed the Church, its clergy, and our community elders. But most of all, these proud and impudent young men have defied God. And I am scared *we* shall all suffer for *their* sins. God has protected our people from genocide for thousands of years, and we have never had to resort to war or guns or violence. Now, though, these uncontrollable and conceited young men think that violence and returning fire are the only answers to life's problems. These foolish young men have cursed us

89

with their bloodshed—yet they still refuse to drop their weapons. They refuse to believe in the power of peace and prayer. They refuse to believe in God—that *He* will defend the faithful. That only *He* can save us."

"Again, doctor," I say timidly. "I really didn't mean to upset you or cause tension. Perhaps—"

"I take it you met the escort's other foolish friends, all dressed in their black paramilitary gear? They think they are soldiers. Ha! More like toy soldiers! They even look exactly like the *SS*, the very enemy they have sworn to defeat. Who is friend, and who is foe? Materially and ideologically, both groups are now identical. Ignorant, inexperienced, know-it-all idiots! Our young men are fools who will bring death upon our peaceful community. Please, my fine sir, you must not think badly of our Coptic community. These young men do not represent us—and they definitely do not represent the Church. If you must know, they have been excommunicated for their ongoing disobedience against God's laws, our laws."

"Believe me, good doctor, I do not think badly of your Coptic community. Honestly, I don't. On the contrary, I think your community is special. But I really don't want to get involved in your private affairs. Please, doctor, may I change the subject and instead talk to you about the purpose of my visit?"

The doctor swallows the rest of his mint tea and then pours some more into the glass. His breathing calms, and his body relaxes.

"I am sorry if I have made you uncomfortable with my public display of disapproval," he says, while tapping thrice his right palm over his heart, in an ancient Coptic sign of peace. "Forgive me, my fine sir. Please, continue with your questions."

"No need to ask for forgiveness, doctor. And I'm not uncomfortable. How can I be uncomfortable in such an inviting home, drinking such soothing tea?"

A smile replaces the doctor's frown, suggesting all is now well.

"Okay," I continue, "first, do you still work at Worldwide Industries & Finance?"

"No, I do not. I was fired a few years ago. Why do you ask?"

"Just making sure, doctor, because I don't want to put you in a difficult situation. I want to talk freely."

"Of course, we can talk freely," he says with open arms. "I think you know my thoughts and feelings about—about this world that humanity has shaped. About the totalitarian evil controlling most of the Earth's lands."

"Yes, good doctor, I do know how you feel about these subjects. I remember the long talks we used to have when we worked together. This is why I came to visit you: because I trust you. And if anyone were to know the answers to my questions, then I believe it would be you."

"I pray I can help you, my fine sir. Please, what is troubling you? What is the problem?" The doctor looks genuinely curious.

But before continuing, I gulp down the last of my tea. The doctor then refills my glass and urges me on.

91

"Doctor, do you know anything about the State drugging our tapwater?" I ask, while closely studying his face. His eyes narrow for an instant.

"Look, the State is now desperate," he answers. "Everything was initially going well for it—but, in the last few decades, it has all started to fall apart. The State is broke and exhausted, and it can barely control the Occidental population. The State is even losing power over its mobs, the *SS*. But to answer your question, yes, I am aware that on rare occasions the State does add an anxiolytic-like drug to the public water supply."

"I knew it!" I say, my excitement building. "That's exactly what I've been telling my roommate. And she thought I was being paranoid." I recline smugly in my hard chair. "Refresh my memory, doctor, because it has been a long time. An anxiolytic reduces anxiety and calms people down? Yes?"

"Correct, my fine sir. Your memory serves you well. Anxiolytics reduce anxiety and sedate a person. I am unsure exactly which drug the State is using, but at Worldwide Industries & Finance I was helping to develop a new cheap and effective anxiolytic-like drug for the Occidental State. A drug with a wide margin of safety, so as to reduce side effects and accidental deaths. Perhaps this is the experimental drug the State is using in the water. For the majority of persons who drink an average amount of tapwater, the effects of the drug should be mild to moderate sedation—barely noticeable. At the other extreme, however, there will always be a few persons who are sensitive or allergic to the drug or who drink too much tapwater and therefore receive a drug overdose. So side effects, even a few deaths, are unavoidable consequences of drugging a water supply. But I guess the State would ignore these costs, because the benefits—that is, partially calming and controlling a population that is now considered dangerous—would outweigh any costs. And given the State's bankruptcy, drugging the tapwater would probably be the cheapest crowd-control option."

"Typical," I say, "create the problems and then try to fix them with science and technology. And even when science and technology cause new problems, then newer science and technology ought to solve the problems of the older science and technology. And so on—forever. Science and technology will always save us: this is the State's faith."

"Yes, unfortunately, you are correct, my fine sir. Do you know what the State's ideology is called?

"Of course I do, doctor. Pretty much everyone knows the State's ideology is called *Sci–Coll*."

"Correct," he replies. "But what *is* Sci–Coll? What does it stand for?"

"Actually, *that* I don't know. I speak about Sci–Coll all the time, but I really don't know what it stands for. Do you know the meaning of Sci–Coll?"

"As a matter of fact, I do know the meaning of Sci–Coll. I enjoyed a privileged position at Worldwide Industries & Finance, and I learned plenty of State secrets while I worked there. Naturally, I am not supposed to talk about such things—but who cares. I certainly do not!" The doctor chuckles. "You see, my fine sir, political parties love to play word games. They love to be abstract and vague, and they adore confusing the people. Obfuscation is their speciality. Acronyms, initialisms, abbreviations—these are the tools of their political trade, along with simple slogans to manipulate the masses. For instance, have you ever heard of *Nazism*?"

"Of course, I have," I answer. "Who hasn't heard of Nazism?"

"You would be surprised. The majority of the people today have no idea about Nazism. None! The State's education system drops these topics, including information about Nazism, because the Occidental State does not believe such topics on state oppression can help educate the people. I wonder why? Anyway, what was I saying?"

"You were talking about Nazism," I reply.

"Ah, yes, Nazism. As I was saying, Nazism is an abbreviation of the German word *Nationalsozialismus*, which in English means *National Socialism*. And a Nazi was a member of the *Nationalsozialistische Deutsche Arbeiter-Partei*, or the National Socialist German Workers' Party. So Nazism was *socialism* at a national level rather than an international one. In fact, the Nazi Party's predecessor was the German Workers' Party. Who says despotism cannot emerge from a grassroots movement of the people, by the people, for the people? History demonstrates otherwise. And the history of the twentieth century featured the brutal totalitarian regimes of socialism, whether on a national or an international level. One socialist experiment after the other ending in disaster. More than one hundred million innocent people butchered in the name of communism and Marxism, which are just other terms for socialism. And hundreds of millions more oppressed and subjugated in the religious faith-based pursuit of a socialist utopia: the ultimate 'perfection' of man and society through scientific progress and social reengineering."

"But, doctor," I say, "weren't the Nazis more interested in eugenics and genocide rather than advancing any form of socialism?"

"Look, my fine sir, all forms of Marxism or socialism share one operational practice: they concentrate all power in the State and its various bodies. So, in all these ideologies, the State commands and plans every aspect of society and the economy—property, commercial markets, and production goods included. Nazism, or National Socialism, shared this same ideology of centralised State power. But the Nazis also believed in their own biological superiority over other races. So they adopted socialism on a national level, favouring—politically entitling—certain races and groups over others. In the pursuit of utopia, Nazism married socialism *with* eugenic science—yes, *science*, or at least science as they understood (or misunderstood) it back in their time. One might say that the concept of utopia, the striving towards a mythical perfect 'destination', has inflicted more misery on mankind than any other ideology. I call such ideologies a *political religion*, because they hardly differ from a spiritual religion. Political religions, including Sci–Coll, dismiss spiritual religions and their heavens as fairy tales; however, these same political religions peddle an earthly utopia, an Earth-based heaven, which is just another fairy tale. Yet how many people who worship secular progressive politics and the church of humanity see the irony in their belief system? This, too, is a faith-based fantasy—quasi-religious mumbo jumbo."

"That's all very interesting, doctor," I say, "and I agree with you one hundred per cent. But you haven't answered my original question: what does Sci–Coll stand for?"

"Having given you all these clues, can you not figure out the meaning of Sci–Coll for yourself? Try to guess what Sci–Coll stands for."

I ponder his question for a minute, before saying, "Sci–Coll. Hmm. I think the 'Sci' part has something to do with science. Am I correct, doctor?"

"Close."

"Scientific?"

"Not quite."

"Not science and not scientific, but something to do with science. Oh! I know: *scientism*."

"Yes! Scientism! Excellent!" the doctor says. "Scientism: the belief that science, or the *scientific method*, offers the *only* way to ultimate truths in the universe. One can believe in scientism yet not be a scientist, and one can be a scientist yet not believe in scientism. Do you see the difference, my fine sir?"

"Yes, I'm aware of the crucial difference. Like you, I also love science and the scientific method, although I fear scientism and the fundamentalist belief that the scientific method is the only path to 'real' knowledge, to the ultimate truth. As you would agree, doctor, the scientific method is based on experiment, reproducibility, and clarity. A scientist, using the scientific method, measures the physical world in order to discover a physical truth. These results can then be reproduced in a similar experiment by another scientist. That's what makes the scientific method so powerful: reproducibility and predictability."

"Correct, my fine sir," the doctor says, while grinning. "Absolutely correct. Now, on the other hand, *scientism* takes the scientific method one step farther and declares that only the scientific method can give us absolute truths. So scientism seeks to reduce everything in the universe to its fundamental unit, and then measure it. This ideology deals only with quantities, not qualities. And if something—that is, a quality—cannot be reduced, measured, and reproduced in experiment, then such a quality fails to count as knowledge or truth. Such 'unreal' things are then labelled as epiphenomena or illusions. I have even heard advocates of scientism describe qualities such as love, consciousness, and personal experience as nothing more than illusory side effects of matter and energy. Because they are unmeasurable and unreproducible qualities that are 'hazy', then they are not 'real'. They are just secondary side effects—useful fictions or illusions—which arise from matter. But it is only matter, and its motion, that counts or does anything significant in the universe. The rest is a fantasy. Therefore, everything from love to friendship to poetry to literature to art to music to meaning to purpose to intention to agency to beauty to values to philosophy to spirituality to religion to all the virtues—all these qualities are nothing more than illusions, side effects, secondary phenomena that emerge from the underlying matter. And it is *only* this underlying matter that counts, that constitutes real and true knowledge."

"That's a petrifying ideology. Horrendous. Disgusting. Scientism even twists the beauty of science and the scientific method into something vile, something politically motivated, something only interested in absolute power. Scientism is the pursuit of power concealed by a veneer of pseudoscience. Whereas the scientific method gifts mankind with a powerful *means* to improve life, scientism seeks power over mankind as its *end*."

"My fine sir," the doctor says, "you have captured the true meaning of scientism in that one thought. A perfect analysis. Scientism is the disguised pursuit of power. And this ideology resurrects the same methods and language used by all political religions. Scientism even embraces an identical faith-based salvation-of-man mythology. If we examine all previous socialisms, including Nazism, we find some form of scientism fuelling every one of these quasi-religious political movements. But, my fine sir, there is one more thing."

"Yes, doctor," I respond, eager to learn more.

"By its own argument, scientism fails. For how can a person claim that the scientific method is the only source of knowledge? Can such a claim be quantified and proven true using the scientific method? No, because the claim that *scientism is the only source of knowledge* is itself a philosophical argument, not a scientific one. Yet scientism rejects philosophy and its arguments as fantasy, since the discipline is not quantifiable and does not use the scientific method. So scientism must reject its own claim to truth–knowledge, because its claim is a philosophical argument, a nonscientific argument. Therefore, scientism is self-refuting and absurd."

The doctor then grabs a second article from the oil-stained drawers:

CS Lewis, "Willing Slaves of the Welfare State", 1958———Again, the new oligarchy must more and more base its claim to plan us on its claim to knowledge ... This means they must increasingly rely on the advice of scientists, till in the end the politicians proper become merely the scientists' puppets. Technocracy is the form to which a planned society must tend. Now I dread specialists in power because they are specialists speaking outside their special subjects. Let scientists tell us about sciences. But government involves questions about the good for man, and justice, and what things are worth having at what price; and on these a scientific training gives a man's opinion no added value ... On just the same ground I dread government in the name of science. That is how tyrannies come in. In every age the men who want us under their thumb, if they have any sense, will put forward the particular pretension which the hopes and fears of that age render most potent ... It has been magic, it has been Christianity. Now it will certainly be science. Perhaps the real scientists may not think much of the tyrants' "science"—they didn't think much of Hitler's racial theories or Stalin's biology. But they can be muzzled ... We must give full weight to the claim that nothing but science, and science globally applied, and therefore unprecedented Government controls, can produce full bellies and medical care for the whole human race: nothing, in short, but a world Welfare State. It is a full admission of these truths which impresses upon me the extreme peril of humanity at present ... Let us not be deceived by phrases about "Man taking charge of his own destiny". All that can really happen is that some men will take charge of the destiny of the others. They will be simply men; none perfect; some greedy, cruel and dishonest. The more completely we are planned the more powerful they will be. Have we discovered some new reason why, this time, power should not corrupt as it has done before?

After I finish reading the article, the doctor says, "So I think we have exhausted the 'Sci' part of Sci–Coll. Now, what about the 'Coll' part?"

"Okay, well, the Party's ideology resembles twentieth-century socialism in its pursuit of utopia through science and social engineering. And the Occidental State commands and plans—administers—every aspect of society and the economy, including property, distribution, commercial markets, and production goods. So it is socialist, or collective, in nature. Therefore, 'Coll' stands for *collective*."

"No, my fine sir, but you are almost there."

"Collectivism!" I shout confidently. "It stands for *collectivism*."

"Exactly! The Party's name is Sci–Coll: Scientism–Collectivism. And Scientism–Collectivism is our State's ideology, because it is a one-party State that is controlled by Sci–Coll."

I repeat the doctor's words: "Scientism–Collectivism."

"Of course, if a State wishes to scientifically plan every aspect of a society, then it can only achieve this collectively," the doctor says. "No other system will work. Collectivism must form the foundation of the social, legal, economic, and political spheres. The idea of the individual must dissolve, while the collective takes concrete form. Individuals must start to think using 'we' instead of 'I'. Even the law must change from individual rights to that murky concept of State-defined collective rights. And eventually the law must vanish altogether, as political parties must vanish, as even the State must vanish—until we are left with just a group of Administrators administering every aspect of life and society. A totalitarian Administration unlike anything this planet has ever experienced. Imagine, however, my fine sir, if citizens were free to choose their own paths. To do what they desire. To have families. To work as they wish. To own property and production goods. To trade as they want. Such a society would resist bending to the Administration's will. Administrators would fail in their quest to administer billions of free-moving particles, billions of free-moving individuals. And such a populace would have the resources, independence, and freedom to repel the State. Therefore, a scientifically and centrally administered society can succeed only if a State were to mesh collectivism with scientism."

"Doctor," I say, "things are worse than this. Although Sci–Coll idolises scientism and collectivism, as you mentioned, I believe the Administration has even diminished the scientific method. They've politicised science to fit it to their ideology. For science is funded by groups, and science is carried out by groups—by humans with hidden agendas. And the State views science as a way of delegitimising other worldviews. So, through Worldwide Industries, the State is wielding science as a weapon to annihilate all other forms of knowledge about the universe, including personal experience, which is the fundamental way of interacting with and grasping the world."

"Correct, my fine sir," the doctor replies. "Other worldviews and knowledge exist, such as knowledge developed through personal experience or *independent* exploring, experimenting, and pondering. And these worldviews can richly enhance our lives: these alternative worldviews can give truer accounts of the world than scientific studies. For instance, your earlier observation contrasting my lovely grandchildren with the depraved *SS* would be considered garbage according to Sci–Coll, because the State's scientific research suggests the opposite. Their research claims that Occidental Union Public Nurseries mould 'better' children than parent-raised children. But your observation about my grandchildren reflects *your* experiences in this world. Your statement contains truth—according to your personal and independent observations. Yet which statement would I place more faith in: your anecdotal claim or the State's so-called evidence-based research? Well, when I look at the world, I know your observation is a better reflection of reality, even though your statement is not based on the scientific method. Sci–Coll would declare the opposite, however. Imagine a world where your *personal experiences* are called illusions, but studies arising from a *scientific collective* are called facts. This is our world: diminish the individual and his experiences, while enhancing the collective and its so-called scientific knowledge. So the individual trusting his senses and independent thinking is wrong, stupid, unenlightened, and delusional, whereas the collective embracing the scientific method is correct, intelligent, enlightened, and realistic."

"And so every individual human experience, from love to hate, from experiencing to interacting, is labelled an illusion and is denied the status of reality under Sci–Coll."

The doctor nods his head: "Every individual human experience is false, whereas every collective scientific study is true. So the experts—the State and its anointed intelligentsia—always know best. In other words, leave all the decisions to the experts. Trust the experts. Sci–Coll, in the end, eradicates common sense and muddies the concept of the 'individual'. It brainwashes you into doubting yourself, your senses, your mind. But we know that science can be just as fallible as all other human endeavours. The scientific method often ignores many variables—numerous aspects of reality—in order to tease out the main variables or what the researchers consider to be the key aspects of reality. In a drug trial, for example, researchers cannot monitor or uncover every drug reaction in the body, because the body is too complex. So they eliminate many variables, focusing on just one or two main variables to study. Can this process reflect reality? Is it not a necessary simplification of reality, a poor substitute for what is really unfolding in the body? My fine sir, you and I know the answer: once a drug hits the general public and the community starts experiencing numerous undocumented side effects, then you get a clearer picture of reality than the 'reality' presented in the drug's preclinical–clinical research trials. Similarly, all other scientific research involves a loss of information; otherwise, it would be impossible to get anything done. For reality is too complex and chaotic. As a consequence, scientists have to isolate and concentrate on certain parts of their research while ignoring countless other factors. Scientism, though, takes this to another level. It discards all information that is unscientific. So if the scientific method loses certain levels of information, then scientism loses all this information *and* many other levels of unscientific information. Therefore, scientism is a levelling process, just like collectivism is a levelling process: individual details are often glossed over in search of the bigger unifying picture. Scientism–Collectivism searches for the one grand theory to unify everything and everyone. It is the final assault against the individual and individual experience in the pursuit of Enlightenment-driven progress. But I ask you, my fine sir, what is progress? How do you measure it? *Can* you measure progress? And what is the purpose of constant change? What is the final destination? *Can* we ever reach a final destination, a final point of no-more progress? My fine sir, what is the ultimate purpose of Sci–Coll?"

"Didn't you already answer that question, doctor?" I ask. "Isn't the ultimate purpose of Sci–Coll to unify all knowledge and experience—to create one grand theory of the universe?"

"But what is the purpose of this unification?" he asks.

"I guess to achieve truth, happiness, and equality: utopia."

"Garbage. What sort of 'truth' are we living in today? Are we any happier or more equal today? How would you quantify and measure these unmeasurable qualities? How would you even define truth, happiness, or equality? Are any of these aims *ultimate purposes*?"

"Doctor, I really don't know what Sci–Coll's purpose is. To improve society?" I question uncertainly, unsure of where he is going with this.

The doctor squeezes his eyes shut and sighs. He then shakes his head impatiently and says, "Again, what does this word 'improve' mean? It is just as foggy as 'progress'. How can either be measured? Sorry, my fine sir, but you are talking gibberish."

"Well, quite frankly, doctor, you're also spouting mumbo jumbo," I bark back. "You're being abstract and confusing—no different from the political parties you are railing against."

"Please, my fine sir, do not take my probing questions with this poor attitude. I mean you no harm, and you know that. Let us try again. Tell me what you believe the ultimate purpose of Sci–Coll is. Think carefully. Use your knowledge and experience. Put some effort into it. Do not just parrot platitudes."

"Okay, doctor, this will still sound like a cliché, but the answer is *power*: Sci–Coll's ultimate purpose is ultimate power."

"My fine sir, at least you are now trying. The Occidental Union Administrators who embrace Sci–Coll *may* believe that their final goal is to achieve total power and control of society, but I think this answer is wrong. And even though they may be operating consciously on this belief, another unconscious force is, in reality, driving them. One might say that this hidden and subtle force infects all life, including Sci–Coll adherents and the Occidental State. Being a man of science, can you guess what this force may be?"

"I don't know—I honestly don't know," I reply, frustrated and irritated with his questions. "I don't even know where this is going or what you're trying to say."

"Have you ever heard of the *Red Queen*?" the doctor asks, his white eyebrows rising and almost melding with his white hairline.

"Yes, doctor, the Red Queen is a character in a book. But that's all I know."

"You are correct, my fine sir. The Red Queen is a character in Lewis Carroll's *Through the Looking-Glass*. Do you know why I mention it?"

"No idea," I mutter in resignation.

"I mention it because of the *Red Queen's race*. In Carroll's book, the Red Queen says something profound: 'It takes all the running you can do, to keep in the same place.' Do you grasp the greater meaning of this statement—the meaning for life, humanity, evolution, Sci–Coll, and even the Occidental Union?"

"Yes, doctor, I think I do!" I answer, while experiencing a eureka moment. "What is the purpose of life, of evolution? All species (individuals and groups) keep *progressing*—'it takes all the running you can do'—just to keep up with all the other species (individuals and groups), who are also progressing and running furiously to keep up with all the other species (individuals and groups), who are also progressing and running furiously, and so on. Yet, in the end, everyone and everything and every group are 'progressing' at roughly the same pace. So everyone and everything and every group are, in fact, still 'in the same place'. No one moves ahead! 'It takes all the running you can do, to keep in the same place.' Ultimately, there is no such thing as true progress. It is all *relative*. And everything is relative to everything else, while everything has been running as furiously as everything else. Progress is an illusion!"

"*Progress is an illusion*," the smiling doctor repeats. "I develop a knife; you develop a sword. I develop a crossbow; you develop a gun. I develop a tank; you develop a warplane. I develop a ballistic missile; you develop a nuclear weapon. And on and on it goes. The race never ends. There is no such thing as real progress. All progress is relative to other progress—and everyone and everything is progressing relative to everyone and everything else. No end point exists; the race never finishes. And this principle applies to everything in the universe, from individuals to species to collectives to science to evolution. Ever heard of an evolutionary race? Same idea: different species evolving continuously just to keep up with other species, which are also evolving continuously to keep up with other species— and so on. Yet no species is actually progressing. Each species is evolving just 'to keep in the same place'—to maintain its niche. Parasites, pathogens, hosts, prey, predators, competitors, cooperators—all running in the Red Queen's race. There *appears* to be progress, even though there is no progress in reality, in the ultimate picture. Progress is the ultimate illusion. And this desire for constant change—for constant progress—pervades all political parties, and their ideologies, though they fail to consciously realise it. Progress for the sake of progress, but without grasping *why*—without understanding that there is no ultimate destination. Try selling this slogan to the people: 'We do not believe in progress, because there is no such thing as *real* progress. Progress is a powerful illusion.' What person would vote for a party with such a slogan, even though it is the truth?"

"How did I miss this concept, doctor? You are right. For instance, humanity developed antibiotics in the middle of the twentieth century and then arrogantly claimed that humans had won the battle against bacteria. Yet in less than ten years after the first antibiotics were produced, antibiotic-resistant bacteria began to emerge. So, in return, we developed new antibiotics to kill the antibiotic-resistant bacteria—and these bacteria, in return, evolved to resist the new antibiotics. Then, we developed newer antibiotics, and bacteria responded by evolving resistance to these newer drugs. Sixty years later there were bacteria resistant to every known antibiotic. And, today, hundreds of years after the first major victories against bacteria, antibiotics are nearly useless. So we scramble to find a novel weapon, just 'to keep in the same place'. And, likewise, bacteria will always counter our latest advance, just 'to keep in the same place'. It is the Red Queen's race."

"An excellent example," the doctor says. "Medicine is full of such races. But it gets even worse. Say, I have a business selling technological widgets. A competitor then enters the market and improves on my product. I, in turn, improve on his enhancement, and he responds in kind. We continue the Red Queen's race, yet every 'advance' requires more and more energy, and provides less and less returns, just to stay in the same place. So we are expending more and more energy, and running faster and faster, just to stay in the same place. The name given to this universal curse is the *law of diminishing returns*. The race never ends, and we will always be sprinting faster and faster, and consuming more and more energy, just to remain in the same place—to remain in the race. And this applies to many aspects of life and the universe. As our lives become more and more complicated, we depend on more and more and newer and newer technologies, just to stay in the same place. Yet despite these complications, we live the same basic existence as our so-called primitive ancestors. For we do the same things as they did: eat and work and reproduce and die. However, we need to extract and expend more energy—and use more information and technologies—than they did, just to achieve identical goals. So although we enjoy boasting about our 'superiority' and 'progress', we are essentially the same as previous generations. Nothing has changed, except the illusion of progress. Living seems pointless, when viewed from this angle."

"As if life weren't depressing enough," I respond, as fatigue and despondency overwhelm me.

"No, my fine sir, I said life seems pointless when viewed from *this* angle. But this is a purely *physical* perspective. Other perspectives and philosophies exist. My point, though, is that the Occidental Union's ideology of Scientism–Collectivism suffers from the Red Queen's race. No end point exists; no ultimate purpose exists. And we shall always be progressing for the sake of progress, just to stay in the same place. Will Sci–Coll's promised utopia ever arrive? The answer is *no*: Sci–Coll's utopia will always be just out of reach. Sci–Coll ideologues will always be running faster and faster, knowingly or unknowingly, in the Red Queen's race. And Sci–Coll will require more and more energy, and produce less and less benefits for society, just to stay in the same place."

"I am starting to grasp your idea's deeper meaning, doctor. But is there a way to opt out of the Red Queen's race, if I don't want to play? Surely, the race must end eventually? Everything ends eventually."

"Thoughtful questions—but, for all life, I think it is impossible to withdraw *entirely* from the Red Queen's race. The Red Queen rules the universe, from evolution to society. If a person comprehends the rules of her game, however, then this person may choose to diminish her rule in some areas of life. Let me give you an example. Your greatest competitor in life is not some abstract concept of another species; your greatest competitor in life is another human being. And, in society, competition is expressed usually in the social sphere—that is, people compete socially for status. I buy beautiful clothes, and my neighbour buys more beautiful clothes; then, I buy even more beautiful clothes, and the Red Queen's race continues. These competitions can unfold in countless ways, from gaining a higher education to owning technological goods. But, in these kinds of social status races, I can stop running—*if* I choose to stop running. I have the power to decide whether I want to entangle myself in an endless materialistic race for status, or not. This reasoning can also apply to a society, a collective, as a whole. We Copts, for example, choose to concentrate on the spiritual rather than the materialistic, thereby reducing but not eliminating the Red Queen's race in our community. So areas exist in life where, I believe, we can temporarily halt the running or at least slow it down to a crawl. Now, my fine sir, to answer your second question: does the race eventually end? If life exists, then the Red Queen's race will never end. And if we inhabit a closed universe with a fixed starting amount of usable high-quality energy, then I doubt her race will end until all the *usable* energy in the universe is exhausted. For whatever reasons, the Red Queen's race seems to be weaved into the fabric of the universe. So—"

"So entropy reigns supreme," I interrupt. "*The Red Queen rules the universe; entropy is her only curse.*"

"Entropy?" the doctor questions.

"Yes—*entropy*. Disorder. The entropy (or disorder) in a closed system, such as our universe, *increases* with time. Our entire universe is bound by this law: the second law of thermodynamics. It's the law of all laws. *The Law*. It suggests that our universe has a predetermined destiny. My destiny, your destiny, life's destiny, our society's destiny, the destiny of all matter–energy found within this observable universe—it all ends in complete disorder. Or, more accurately, the universe just runs out of steam: it ends with no usable high-quality energy. So it is a sort of death by nothingness. Entropy rules the Red Queen. As a consequence, the Red Queen's race does end, eventually, when all the universe's high-quality energy runs out. Yet when her race does end, the universe will be a 'dead' universe. Therefore, it will be a pyrrhic victory."

"How right you are! Yes, you have given a technical name to the Red Queen's limitations. It has been a long time since anyone has mentioned the term 'entropy'. How interesting that you have read about entropy and our universe's supposed finale. Our universe started in a state of low entropy—one might say a *near-perfect* state. And, with time, according to the second law of thermodynamics, the universe will end in a state of high entropy: death by disorder and the exhaustion of all high-quality energy. It all ends in an *imperfect* state—imperfect for ordered life, at least. *The Red Queen rules the universe; entropy is her only curse.*"

The doctor leans forwards and refills his glass with tea. After taking several mouthfuls, he closes his eyes and begins wheezing. Despite appearing more youthful earlier, an older man with a woolly white beard and a creased rubbery face now sits before me. Even his loose-fitting *galabeya* fails to hide his frail frame.

"Doctor, are you alright?" I ask.

He bursts into a coughing spasm and spits out some phlegm into a handkerchief. As he folds it, I notice the bloodstains. The old, the sick, the weak—tuberculosis avoids discriminating against any of these.

"Yes, yes, I am fine," he answers dishonestly. "I am just an old man who has lived through too much. That is all. And all of a sudden, I feel weary—very weary. Probably from a lack of nourishment. Yes, that is it. Speaking of food, we must sup soon as I am famished. But before we eat, I do have one more thing to tell you—and it is very important. So please listen carefully, my fine sir. Just before I was fired from Worldwide Industries & Finance, I stumbled upon a highly confidential project. This project went all the way to the top of the Occidental State: the Occidental Union Administrators. Do you understand what I am saying?"

"Of course, I do," I reply. "You are about release sensitive information. I understand this, doctor."

"I am just making sure, because it is important you grasp the implications of what I am about to say. Anyway, the Occidental Union contracted Worldwide Industries & Finance to research a new technology—something extraordinary, something this world has never seen before."

He pauses.

"Yes, yes, please continue," I say, growing restless.

"Well," he mumbles, "I don't know how to describe it."

The doctor pauses again.

"Describe what?" I say. "*What?* Please, doctor!"

"Well, I am unsure what it is, because once management discovered I had stumbled upon the project, they fired me before I could delve deeper. But this much I do know: this project, the Occidental State's project, expands on your little discovery."

"My little discovery?" I ask, my curiosity starting to run wild.

"Yes, your little discovery about how the State is drugging the tapwater in order to calm and control the people."

"Doctor, I'm not following you."

"Alright, listen, my fine sir. The Occidental State—and, by implication, this includes the Administrators—is working with Worldwide Industries to create a new technology: a novel technology that will be used to calm and control everyone. *All the people*, all over the world, including the Free Islands. This goes beyond tainting water supplies; this is about worldwide control on an unprecedented scale. It is the final desperate act of a perishing State that is losing its grip on its subjects, a State that is clueless about how to foster a free and healthy society. It is the final stand of Sci–Coll, a Party that deifies science and technology and social homogenisation as the only cure to society's ills. It is the Occidental State's last grab for power and supremacy."

I sit forward, unable to control my excitement. Although I have always dreamt of government conspiracies, the doctor's story exceeds my fantasies. This is *the* conspiracy of conspiracies. This is the big one.

"So how is the State going to control all the people?" I ask. "What is this new technology?"

The doctor shakes his head: "Unfortunately, I have no idea. All I know for certain is that the project is called *United We Fall.* And I think the Administrators will, at first, trial and test the new technology on the one population that the Occidental State despises more than any other: the people of the Free Islands."

~~~~~

The escort is growing impatient. It is late afternoon, and I am still savouring my lunch with the doctor.

"We must go," the escort says. "The Sun will set in a couple of hours, and if we do not leave now, then you will have to walk home in the dark. This will be a problem for you, because the streets outside our community are full of dangers."

"Doctor, I think my escort is right," I say. "I've overstayed my welcome and taken advantage of your hospitality. And I must get home before dark."

"My fine sir," the doctor replies, "please do not say that you have overstayed. You are always welcome in my home. On the other hand, I do understand your anxiety. For the streets after dark can be extremely dangerous, and one should travel during the daylight hours."

As I stand to leave, the doctor also tries to rise from his chair. But he struggles in vain. He is too weak and sick.

"Please, doctor," I say, as he squirms in his chair, "stay seated and finish your meal in peace."

"Reluctantly, I may have to agree with you, my fine sir. These old legs lack the strength to help me stand, so I shall have to wish you a safe journey home from the comfort of my seat. But please do try to visit me again, my fine sir. I insist."

"I promise," I respond. "And if I find out anything about project United We Fall, I shall tell you."

"My fine sir, what do you hope to achieve by pursuing this matter? I foresee problems for you. And even if you do uncover the Occidental Union's plans involving this new technology, what are you going to do about it? What *can* you do about it? You can do nothing."

"Yes, doctor, you are right: I am powerless to do anything. But I need to know. It's my nature. I also need to document the State's actions for future generations—just in case something goes wrong, if we mess up—in the hope that future generations might learn from our mistakes. I think this aim alone justifies my search for the truth."

"A noble pursuit," he says, "a noble pursuit worth the sacrifice. I cannot argue with your reasoning. God bless and protect you on your quest, my fine sir. Perhaps this is His will working through you."

"Thank you for your encouragement, doctor." And just as I am about to say farewell, I remember one final question. "Oh, doctor, I almost forgot to ask you: do you know anything about giant slugs attached to the nape of Occidental Union Administrators? Have you seen or heard of anything like this before?"

"No, not at all," the puzzled-looking doctor replies. "Why do you ask?"

"Because I saw a slug-infested Administrator, in a Temple of the People, while journeying here."

The doctor frowns and then says, "A giant slug? On an Occidental Union Administrator's nape? How bizarre! I have never heard of anything so obscene, and I have definitely never seen such a sight. But I have not even seen an Administrator before, so I know very little about them. Hmm. And, besides, what was an Administrator doing outside of the Occidental Union's capital? They rarely leave their colony. Interesting. Interesting indeed."

The doctor absentmindedly strokes his beard, untangling the numerous knots. My news has obviously disturbed him.

"Have you checked the Internet for anything about slugs and Administrators?" he asks.

"Yes, on my tablet while I was coming here," I answer. "But I found nothing—nothing at all."

"I guess that should come as no surprise. If this information is something the Occidental Union Administrators want to keep secret, then it will be kept secret."

"The other strange thing, doctor, was that I couldn't tell the Administrator's sex from its body or its face. I even failed to gather a hint from its voice, because it was gender neutral. The being was an androgyne."

"Hmm, I do not know what to make of this," the worried-looking doctor replies. "What is the Occidental Union up to? I believe they are planning something sinister: a dangerous new technology to conquer all the people and now this—these androgynous Administrators. No, no, *no*, I hate to think where this is heading—"

"Where do you think this is heading, doctor?" I interrupt, too anxious to control myself.

"What does it look like to you?" he replies.

I ruminate on the events of the day, before saying, "Well, it looks like the Occidental Union Administrators are a new breed—a new caste—of humans. This was my first impression upon glimpsing the Administrator at the Temple of the People. The Administrator *appeared* human from afar—but the more I studied it, the more my instincts told me something was wrong with the Administrator. Its appearance unsettled me. Creepy, not quite human yet humanlike. Then, when you told me about project United We Fall and the novel technology being researched, I thought about an ant colony. You see, doctor, I was observing an ant colony last night, and I was stunned by the physical differences in the various castes. One can be forgiven for mistaking the soldier caste for another species when comparing a soldier with a worker. Yet despite these morphological differences, their collective efficiency was extraordinary. And this got me thinking. A caste system for a social species might be the most efficient way to organise such a species: the greatest benefits for the *collective*, at the least costs for the collective. But forget about the rights of the individual under such a caste system. So, putting one and one together, I would suggest the State is embarking on its most daring social experiment yet: forging a truly collective society by introducing a physical caste system, with the Occidental Union Administrators being the royal—elite—caste. If I were an Administrator, then such a caste system would seem like the next obvious step in human evolution—although this manmade step would, strictly speaking, fail to be evolution by natural selection. But, doctor, I would wager that this is exactly what the Occidental Union Administrators are scheming."

"My fine sir," he says, "this is *precisely* what I think is happening, too. Although the exact nature of the novel technology bewilders me, I believe it will nonetheless launch a new phase in human history. A new phase in Sci–Coll, in Scientism and Collectivism, where the State will finally reclaim its ancient royal status—but on an unprecedented scale of domination, unlike anything history has ever witnessed. This time, the State's power will be unlimited, omnipotent. The State will have conquered finally the problem of the individual and individual freedom. For the Occidental Union still needs the masses. To survive, it requires workers to labour for the Administrators, for the parasitic royal class. And what better way exists to control the workers than to mould a physical caste system? A system where the workers are designed to work obediently for the collective—for the State—no questions asked. We, the people, will be the worker caste; they, the Administrators, will be the royal caste. This is the final phase of collectivism. It is the State's scientific plan to progress society."

"Is the Occidental Union Administration really that deranged?" I ask, trying to absorb the extreme ideas being discussed.

"Yes, it is—just glance at the twisted world around you, the sad society the State has shaped. The Administrators are not guided by a higher authority; the Administrators believe *they* are the highest authority. They worship themselves as human-gods. And do I need to explain to you what unfolds when people obtain power? Read your history. It never ends well. *Never.* Power always—without question, without exception, without hesitation—corrupts."

"It's hopeless, doctor. Isn't it? This time it's going to conclude horribly for everyone. I sense it."

The doctor sighs: "Probably."

"Science and technology were meant to serve us, to make our lives easier—not enslave us," I say. "This time science will fail to solve the problem, because this time science *is* the problem."

Numbed, I stare at the Coptic cross hanging on the wall. The doctor also appears exhausted.

"Anyway, doctor," I mutter, "if you discover anything, then please contact me. Here is my e-mail address, and this is my tablet number."

"And here are my contact details, my fine sir," he says, while handing me a piece of paper. "It has been a pleasure. God bless you, and God help you. If you discover something, then tell the people, especially the people of the Free Islands. Perhaps the various governments of the Free Islands can do something. I doubt it, but you never know. There is still hope."

"As I said before, doctor, I will document everything. Even if we are doomed, at least future generations will have a written record of our mistakes, so they can avoid making the same errors."

I kiss the doctor once on each cheek and then join my escort, who is already climbing down the steps. Exiting the doorway, I glance back at the doctor. Despite his earlier vibrancy, he now appears drained and deathly. I doubt I will see him again.

The escort and I leave the doctor's home.

A cool wind sweeps through the Coptic territories, and threatening thunderclouds hang overhead. The once-colourful lanes now display a muted shade of their earlier brilliance. All the shops have shut for the day. The smells, the sights, the sounds—all these have vanished. We pass no one. Whereas I felt vitality on the journey in, I now sense dullness on the journey out. The desolation I know so intimately has finally reached this community. Emptiness has replaced life. Did I invite the metropolis's despair into the Copts' city?

I hear rumblings in the distance; a lightning bolt branches its way to the Earth. At last the rains will fall and soothe the cracked lands. A blessing from the heavens.

Gazing at the angry black skies, I say, "It looks like it is finally going to—"

"Silence!" the escort snarls back, as he comes to a halt.

I freeze in response, although I hear and see nothing peculiar—just deserted lanes and boarded windows.

"Did you hear that?" he whispers, while staring into the distance.

"Yes," I reply, "it's just the thunder. Thankfully, it will rain soon. The land is so parched."

"No, not that. Listen. There!"

An unmistakable crackle echoes throughout the empty lanes and passageways. It sounds close.

"Yes, *that* I heard," I say, as a second crackle responds to the first.

A sustained exchange then follows, punctuated with sporadic explosions and not-too-distant caterwauling.

"Our community is under attack again! the escort cries out. "Our foes have been relentless recently. God damn those evil bastards!"

"Who is attacking you?" I ask, apprehensive of the approaching turmoil.

"Our enemies, of course!" he says angrily. "We have many. How am I supposed to know which enemy is assaulting us today?"

"Don't tell me the State's armed forces have started attacking you, too?"

"No, that is unlikely. The State would never directly attack us. Such overt barbaric behaviour is not its style."

"So who?" I ask. "Is it the *SS* or someone else?"

But before the escort can respond, a projectile whistles over our heads and crashes into a nearby building. The ensuing explosion catapults me into a wall. Darkness descends around me.

~~~~~

Something is tugging at my arm, and a distant voice is calling my name. I struggle to open my eyes. Everything is blurred, and it takes a few seconds before I can focus on the silhouette towering over me. It is my escort.

"Get up *now*!" he yells, while gesticulating frantically. "We have to flee from here! They are coming this way!"

"What? What, what's happening?" I mumble, as I survey my surroundings.

In front of me sits a three-storey building with one side blown to bits and smoke snaking its way towards the heavens. And even though debris and concrete chunks litter the cobblestone pavement, the lane still manages to retain its quaintness. If anything, the rubble enhances the rustic charm of the maze city.

"How beautiful!" I say.

"Hey! Snap out of it!" the escort screams, while shaking me by the shoulders. "Get up now! They are almost upon us!"

Delirious, I remain sprawled across the cobblestone pavement; in desperation, the escort grabs my waist and jerks me to my feet. Yet despite the grogginess, my memories begin to reform and after a few seconds I recall that we are being attacked.

"I'm beginning to feel better now," I say, standing up slowly yet steadily. "Really, I'm fine and my legs feel strong. Come on. Let's go."

"You sure you are okay?"

"Absolutely," I reply. "Fit as I've ever been. I was just momentarily stunned—that is all. But everything is now back to normal. Let's get the hell out of here!"

"Excellent! I know of a safe place to hide—and it is not too far away. Follow me closely, and do not fall behind."

The escort then bolts down a side passage, away from the approaching gunfire, and I shadow him as close as I possibly can. As we are about to turn the corner, however, I look back and glimpse a hazy figure floating by.

"The State is great!" the figure bellows out. "The State is great! The State is great!"

Other shadowy figures soon trail the first.

"The State is great!" they cry out in unison. "The State is great! The State is great! The State is great! The State is great! The State is great! The State is great! The State is great! The State is great! The State is great! The State is great!"

Seconds later, violent bursts of gunfire fill every lane in the maze city and drown out the coordinated State-is-great chorus.

Booming thunder then shakes the Earth, and the first teasing rain droplets land on my face.

~~~~~

After scurrying through dozens of lanes and narrow passageways, my escort finally stops and points at an inconspicuous crack in the Earth. On closer inspection, I notice a shoulder-width opening nestled between two buildings and camouflaged by the shadows. A giddiness suddenly overcomes me while peering into the Earth's blackness. Perhaps a premonition. But about what?

"Down that hole exists an ancient crypt and chapel," the escort says, panting and trying to recover from the run. "Because I am charged with your safety, I say we must spend the night in the crypt—or at least hide there until the fighting dies down. It may not be the most comfortable place, but you will be sheltered and safe."

"But I really would like to go home tonight. I—"

"No, this is impossible. In case you have failed to notice, a battle is unfolding, buildings are being blown apart, and people are dying. And it sounds like a major incursion, not a light melee. Besides, it is becoming dark, and the rain is getting heavy. You will be drenched before you make it home—*if* you make it home in the dark."

"But—"

"No *but*s. No discussions. No arguments. I am in charge. We stay in the crypt."

And before I can protest, the escort squirms through the fissure and descends into the blackness of the crypt. I peer into the dark, yet I am unable to see anything.

A hollow voice then emerges from the crypt's depths: "Wait where you are while I light a few lamps," the escort orders me. "I shall tell you when it is safe to come down."

While waiting for the escort, the rain begins to fall harder. Despite getting wet, I relish the sensation of the raindrops as they gently massage my face and tickle my shaved head. I have forgotten how mesmerising the simple pleasure of splashing raindrops feels.

An empty metal bucket lies in the middle of the alley, and the pitter-patter of the raindrops as they splash on to the bucket provides the perfect accompaniment to the head-and-face massage. Even the surrounding cacophony cannot spoil the serenity of the moment. I shut my eyes, and my mind drifts to a pristine and primordial place, before man and his civilisation. And my yearning for this virgin paradise—this illusion—grows so strong that it cripples me and leaves me breathless. How I ache to escape this metropolis; how I long to dwell in my unspoilt Elysium. It exists—it must, even if it were for but an instant in my mind—or else all hope would be lost. For this dream keeps me alive. Faith fuels me.

Although I have been indoctrinated into believing that my worldview is rational, that it is based on reason and physicalism, I must confess that faith and hope motivate me to act. I am a dreamer, an idealist. For how else can I describe my longing for Elysium and my subsequent actions to reach it? If I were truly rational, and I confess that I am not that enlightened, then I would see the futility in all actions. I would see the ultimate nihilism and hopelessness of living—and I would stop acting. I would stop moving. I would stop being. Why would I want to live like Sisyphus: pushing a boulder to the top of the hill, just to find that the boulder has rolled back down to the bottom of the hill, and then pushing the boulder back to the top of the hill, just to find it at the bottom again, and then repeating this cursed cycle forever? A rational being who rejects faith and hope would see the pointlessness of these actions and stop acting, preferring instead nothingness (death?) and an end to the senseless activity. For me, inaction would be the truly rational action in the purely physical worldview. Yet no "rational" person stops acting, stops repeating the Sisyphean cycle. So such a person cannot be truly purely rational. Something else besides sheer rationality drives him or her to act.

With the tale of Sisyphus, the Ancient Greeks might have stumbled across the meaning of life, reality, and the universe. Even another universe or a transcendental world, if such a place were even possible, would fail to break this Sisyphean cycle. For if life were to move from one realm to the other, then the endless cycle would also move, along with that life, from one realm to the other. And Sisyphus's curse would still exist. The only real escape—the only true bliss—is death.

Suddenly, a harsh voice shatters my reverie.

"Hey!" the escort yells from the crypt. "You can come down now. It is safe."

A soft glow now emanates from the fissure. I obey the escort's command and squeeze through the fissure. I then crawl down a ten-metre-long shaft and enter a barren grotto. Even at this shallow depth, I can already feel that it is a few degrees cooler than the outside. A metal ladder, screwed to the grotto's far wall, protrudes from a hole in the ground. Looking down the hole, I spot the escort waiting at the bottom.

"Climb down the ladder," he says. "I am in the crypt. You will be safe here."

I climb down the twenty-metre ladder and enter a surprisingly large cave, which is festooned with human bones and skulls—thousands of them. On the left wall, countless skulls are stacked next to and on top of each other; on the right wall, numerous long bones cover every inch of the rocky façade. But the ceiling displays a more artistic touch, with thousands of ribs and short bones pinned together in various geometrical patterns. At the crypt's far end, however, I spot the centrepiece: a massive altar fashioned from ribs, skulls, long bones, and short bones rests against the wall. The macabre scene even appears to be reanimating, for a faint light flittering from the skull oil-burners gives birth to moving shadows and a living creeping terror.

"*What the hell is this*?" I scream at the escort, who is removing his backpack and getting comfortable.

He looks puzzled by my outburst.

"I already told you this is a crypt and a chapel," he replies. "What is the problem?"

"*What is the problem*? Are you joking? There are countless human bones and skulls everywhere!"

"Yes, that is what one usually finds in a crypt," he says calmly.

"Buried in the ground or in a tomb," I reply, "but not hanging from every inch of every wall, like some gruesome parody of the Sistine Chapel."

"Well, this crypt happens to be a chapel constructed from thousands of monks' bones. This is how that ancient order of monks celebrated their brothers' deaths. The monks gloried in the soul's final freedom from its fleshly captivity. For only then would it be able to return to its immaterial creator. And the bone chapel reminded the monks that life in this world is transient—fleeting—and that death is actually the beginning of a new life: a heavenly life. At death, the resurrection occurs and eternal living begins. Thanks be to God!"

"Wow! And they needed the bones of their brethren dangling all around them to remind them of this?"

"Look," the escort says, "please avoid judging that which you know nothing about. This was their culture and their belief system. And who are we to judge the dead and their works?"

"I'm not judging anyone or anything," I reply. "I'm simply talking and making an observation."

"Brother, you are free to say what you like about previous peoples and their beliefs, as long as you show some respect and lose your smugness—your illusion of superiority. After all, these societies survived and thrived and passed on their traditions and culture from generation to generation. Can you even imagine or comprehend what they went through or how they lived? Do you know anything about them or the context of their struggles? Hmm? You, on the other hand, have plenty to prove. How long has your society lasted? How long do you think it is likely to last? Hmm? What have you and your society done that is so wonderful? That is so much greater than the accomplishments of past societies? Sir, do not think yourself so clever or so superior—because neither you nor your society have left any worthwhile or lasting legacy yet."

"My friend," I say, feeling ashamed of my ingratitude and foolishness, "I'm sorry if I have offended you, but I honestly didn't mean anything by the remark. This place unsettles me—that's all. I mean I find it really, really disturbing. Didn't you find this crypt upsetting the first time you saw it? But you are wrong, because I'm not judging those who have obviously passed the tests of their times. I'm commenting about the bones surrounding me. Look around you: thousands and thousands of bones and skulls everywhere. It's terrifying!"

He smiles and palms his chest in a sign of peace: "Okay, okay, brother. I accept your observation. It *is* a bit overwhelming the first time you see it."

I return the Coptic sign of peace and then say, "And, yes, you are right: I have nothing to show for my life. But you can hardly blame me. Can you? Perhaps the miserable society I'm born into has something to do with my failures?"

"Possibly, possibly not," he answers. "Options always exist in life. Only a victim who blames everything and everyone else for all his failures sees no options. Only such a victim, with such a mentality, makes excuses and says, *Do not blame me; blame the environment around me. You cannot blame me, however, for it is not my fault. I am in this hopeless situation, and I have achieved nothing, because of society and bad luck and everyone and everything around me.* But I disagree with this victim mentality and its ceaseless stream of excuses. Look at what we, the Copts, have achieved in the midst of this horrible society, in the midst of the Occidental Evil. We have been wronged—more than you have been wronged—yet we have never played the victim card and surrendered. No. *Never.*"

"You may be right," I say, "but life is brutal outside the walls of your Coptic city. Yet, I guess, life is also brutal within these walls. I really don't know. I have no idea about anything, anymore. I'm so confused and clueless. I'm simply trying to survive, like most people. Again, I'm sorry if I were rude earlier."

"Brother, do not worry about it. Apology accepted. Anyway, our monks do not practise this bone-and-skull tradition. An ancient monk order—similar to the Catholic Capuchin Friars, I think—constructed this crypt–chapel, and we have left it untouched as a sign of respect. I must confess, though, that I do find it secluded and peaceful here. And, on occasions, I shall come down to this crypt to pray, think, and meditate. It is my escape from the world. Believe it or not, this crypt is my private slice of heaven."

I stroll around the crypt, studying its human-made and human-based adornments. Its symbolic artistry and fine workmanship surpasses anything produced by the people of the Occidental Union. Art in the Union consists of tossing a few pieces of junk together and calling it "modern" or "contemporary" or "self-expression". Yet these terms really mean "crude" or "lazy" or "talentless"—or "crude and lazy and talentless".

"Actually," I say to the escort, "the more I look at this place, the more incredible and less disagreeable it becomes. The art is exquisite. It's very human, in more than one way."

He grins. "It is something extraordinary. Is it not? Imagine how they created this chapel. They had to crawl through tiny holes, and then build everything from scratch, by hand. Incredible effort and dedication. And, equally important, the crypt's theme reminds us of humanity's transience and fragility—the ephemeral nature of all life. How humbling."

As the escort finishes his sentence, a nearby explosion rocks the crypt, and the bones begin to rattle with life once again.

"The fighting sounds like it is right above us," he says. "It seems we shall be spending the night in this crypt, although I know that is not what you want to hear."

"Hmm, I think you are right. We lack any other option. But if we are going to be together all night, then at the very least I need to know your name. It's only fair, since you already know mine after scanning my identification chip at the guards' entrance."

He laughs. "A fair point, brother. My name is Hani, and it is an honour to be with you."

"And it is a pleasure to be with you, Hani. By the way, I have been rude. I have forgotten to thank you for your kindness and for taking care of me. I really appreciate your generosity and sacrifice."

"Please, brother, do not mention it," Hani replies. "Thank God, not me, for your protection."

"In any case, Hani, I owe you my deepest gratitude."

He bows his head in acknowledgement. He then eyes his gun.

"Brother," Hani says, "we need to take precautions. This gun is the classic AK-47, the Avtomat Kalashnikova 1947. Yes, the original design is more than two hundred and fifty years old, but it is still one of the most reliable and effective assault rifles ever built. You cannot beat the stuff made during the old system. And because the weapon lacks microchips or other electronics, the Occidental State cannot deactivate it with their military satellites or an electromagnetic pulse."

"Simple yet effective."

"Absolutely," he says. "Brother, do you know how to use an AK-47?"

I shake my head: "No, I have no idea how to use an AK-47."

"Would you like to know how to use it, just in case something happens to me?

"Nothing is going to happen to you, Hani," I reply.

"I said *just in case*."

"Hani, I thank you for your offer, although I shall have to refuse it," I say, trying to be as polite as possible to avoid offending him. "I dislike guns, so I shall side with Dr Tawfik on this one. Besides, if an Occidental Union peace officer were to catch me with this weapon, well, the consequences would be horrible. Carrying firearms is one crime the Occidental Union still takes seriously—very seriously."

He looks puzzled: "As you wish—but it really cannot hurt you to learn how to protect yourself with an assault rifle."

"Hani, it can hurt me. The one thing the Occidental State does not tolerate is a subject armed with a gun; the State excuses only the *SS* from this edict. Otherwise, owning a gun is one of the greatest crimes a person can commit—and for obvious reasons. Imagine how quickly a civil war would erupt, if the people were to arm themselves with guns. The State isn't stupid. It will not allow anything to threaten its power."

"I understand," he says, "and I respect your wise choice."

"Hani, I do have a related question I would like to ask."

"Yes, go ahead," he says.

"If the Church and your community forbid you from fighting and using guns, how come you and your young male friends are going against your community's laws?"

Hani gazes at skull burner for several seconds before responding: "That is a long story, my friend, and quite personal. However, I shall tell you this much: we had enough of being attacked, of being bullied, of being abused. We had enough of intruders torching our churches, looting our property, murdering our people, and kidnapping and raping our women and children. We simply had enough of it! So a large number of young men decided to fight back, and we formed our own militia. Yes, we are disobeying the Church, the elders, and the community—but we believe we must do this to defend ourselves. The Church has its prayers; we have our guns. And for our convictions, we, the rebellious men, have suffered a huge price. For we have been excommunicated from the very Church we yearn to protect and—"

Interrupting the conversation, Hani's radio begins to hiss something largely unintelligible, with "help" the only clear word being repeated. But despite fiddling with a few buttons, the radio's reception fails to improve.

"I must go above ground to receive a clearer signal," Hani says, while climbing the ladder. "I shall be back in a few minutes."

As Hani climbs the ladder and disappears, I seize the opportunity to call Bulla and ask her to take care of Anup during my absence. I unwrap the tablet computer from around my forearm, but, like Hani's radio, the signal bar is missing. No underground reception. To exit the crypt, however, would require too much effort. And, besides, the crypt's macabre yet captivating art is teasing me into inspecting it more closely. So I forget about calling Bulla and home in on the bone altar instead.

Despite its gruesome grandeur, something else about the altar captures my attention: a small bone-constructed door lies partially concealed behind it. The door is blocking a natural opening in the cave wall. My curiosity swelling, I try pushing the altar out of the door's way. But the massive structure barely budges. This is a job for at least two men.

A drenched Hani then returns to the crypt.

"Hmm," I say, as he tries shaking off the excess rainwater, "it appears to be pouring down hard."

"Yes—but that is the least of our problems," he replies.

"What's the matter?"

"Our community is under attack, a huge assault by several neighbouring districts."

"Who are they?" I ask.

"The *SS* and other assorted human garbage. They have always envied and resented us—partly thanks to the State, which is constantly whipping them up into a murderous rage against us. It is always blaming us for all society's ills, for we are an easy and obvious scapegoat. But I fear I may have to depart soon and join my brothers, because this is no ordinary attack. We may be witnessing *the* final stand. Although we have tried to survive for as long as possible, we all knew this day would come. Their numbers are too great, and their hate is too consuming."

"But why do they hate you so much?" I ask. "Is it just because of the State and its propaganda?"

"They have always hated us, from time immemorial. But our recent tiny successes, our flourishing community, have fuelled their loathing more than ever. Dr Tawfik says they suffer from the *Fourier complex*—that is, they want to level our community to the ground so that we may live in misery, just like them. They do not care that our destruction will not improve their living standards. They just want to see us obliterated, because they envy and resent our success, our strong family bonds, and our happy thriving community. Our failure will please them, even though our failure will neither enhance their lives nor improve their standard of living—a classic case of schadenfreude. But here is my question: what if there were another neighbourhood that had even less wealth and a lower standard of living than our attackers? And what if that poorer neighbourhood were

135

also to suffer from the Fourier complex and thus decide to punish our attackers the same way they are punishing us? In life, inequality of all sorts will always exist. And some people will always be blessed with spiritual and material fruits, whether they be talents or success or loving relationships, that other people lack and desire. But if the Fourier complex were to inflict every person, then what would stop such inflicted persons from meting out the same 'solution' to our attackers, as they are meting out to us? Such a cycle of envy, resentment, and levelling will never end, until all has been levelled—until everything has been annihilated."

"So you are saying this hatred is mainly over envy and resentment?"

"Yes, never underestimate the devastating power of the big three: pride, greed, *and* envy," Hani responds. "Although we are warned about the evils of too much greed, the Occidental State worships envy and wields it as a political weapon. The State uses the politics of envy to keep the people divided and bickering and to distract them from the real disasters and the State's own misdeeds. Today, society even praises envy, calling it a good quality rather than something bad. But envy can be just as destructive as greed."

Hani then rummages in his backpack and pulls out a pocket Bible: "Because envy can completely consume a person and cause so much damage, God lists it as a sin in the Ten Commandments of the Old Testament: 'Thou shalt not covet thy neighbour's house, thou shalt not covet thy neighbour's wife, nor his manservant, nor his maidservant, nor his ox, nor his ass, nor any thing that *is* thy neighbour's.'"

"I never knew the sin of envy was one of the Ten Commandments," I say. "But, come to think of it, I know only three of the Ten Commandments: do not murder, do not steal, do not lie. Oh, and now I know four! Do not be envious. Sorry to disappoint you, Hani, but I'm not religious."

"Well, neither am I, not anymore, considering that I have been excommunicated!" he says with a chuckle—though I doubt he finds the situation that funny, for his banishment from the community and its ancient traditions must have shattered his spirit.

Another explosion then rattles the crypt, and a staccato of gunshots erupts nearby. Then yelling. Then screams. Then the terror.

"Hani," I say, "I think they are fighting right above us!"

"Yes, you may be correct," he replies. "I hate to do this to you, but I must leave you soon to help my brothers. Our attackers have never penetrated this far into our city. So it seems this will be our final battle—and my people will need all the help they can get. My community needs me. But before I depart, I shall have to give you some final instructions."

"Yes," I say apprehensively.

"You cannot stay in the crypt on your own tonight. Our city will very likely fall—perhaps in the next few hours—and you must not be here when they take us captive. You have no idea what they will do to us—what they will do to

137

you if they capture you. They enjoy torturing their victims. So you must leave now. You must go home tonight."

"I figured as much, Hani. Anyway, I was going to suggest that I leave, after hearing all the gunfire."

"So now for your two options—each bad."

"All right, Hani," I say. "Give them to me."

"The first option: we try to get you out of the neighbourhood by going above ground and weaving our way through the smaller alleys. But the enemy has already captured many of our lanes and buildings. They are stationed everywhere in our city, and their numbers are huge—and growing. They also carry better weapons than us, and they are better trained."

"That sounds extremely dangerous. What about option two?"

"Okay, option two," Hani says, while pointing at the bone altar. "Earlier, as I was climbing down the ladder, I saw you trying to push the altar in order to expose the door hidden behind it. Funnily enough, option two involves that small hidden door. Come and help me push this altar out of the door's way."

I join Hani, and we shove the altar, again and again. With each shove, we shift it an inch—and after a minute, the entire door is exposed. Hani then grabs a key from a skull on the wall, unlocks the door, and pulls it open. Past the door lies blackness—nothing but blackness.

"Okay, this is option two," Hani says, indicating the mysterious blackness. "Beyond this tiny doorway exists a huge cave system, which eventually connects with the metropolis's catacombs."

But before he can continue speaking, I shake my head in protest and say, "Hani, you want me to crawl through these caves and then find my way out through the metropolis's catacombs? Are you crazy? Have you heard the stories about the catacomb dwellers?"

"Those stories are exaggerated. I have passed through the catacombs many times, and nothing has ever happened to me. No, the catacombs are not the dangerous part of this journey: you will struggle in the caves. In many parts, you will be wriggling through tight spaces, whereas in others you will be climbing across ledges. And most of the cave system is damp, cold, and miserable. Unfortunately, it gets worse. It will take you about fifteen hours to squirm through the caves and arrive at the catacombs. But once you hit the catacombs, it will take you only fifteen minutes to walk to the exit point—and reach daylight."

I snicker at the ridiculousness of the second option. "Hani, you've sold me on option one and the gunfight. I'll risk going above ground with you rather than crawling around underground alone."

"I am sorry for presenting them as two options," he says, while shaking his head. "Actually, only a single option exists: option two—the caves and catacombs. I was hoping you would choose this option by yourself, after grasping the impossibility of option one."

"*Are you serious*?" I shout. "No! I refuse to enter the caves! I am going to risk your neighbourhood's lanes with you."

"Brother, I am afraid you fail to grasp the seriousness of the situation above ground. We have lost. It is over. Every entrance is blocked—captured. The enemy has encircled our entire community. No escape exists, and no help is coming. We are finished."

"Finished?" I repeat.

"Finished."

"It's that serious?"

"It is that serious," Hani answers.

"So what are you going to do up there, in the city? Die with your friends?"

"I will fight till the death," he says. "In a way, I now feel this is my fault—the fault of my militia. I think Dr Tawfik was right: we broke God's commandments and abandoned our faith. We placed our faith in guns and manmade technology instead of God and his natural laws. We cursed this community."

"Hani, why don't you join me? We can travel the caves and catacombs together, and then you can stay with me. There are plenty of empty apartments in my building, and you can live there for free. The State doesn't seem to care anymore about who stays where. So what do you think?"

Hani mulls over my proposition for a few seconds before saying, "Thank you very much for the offer, but I cannot go with you. This is my home, and I must stay with my brothers and sisters—no matter what fate awaits me." He then gawks at the ceiling, as if someone or something were lurking within the bones. "I think I must find a priest as soon as possible and confess my sins," he mutters to himself. "Yes, yes, I must confess my sins and go back to God and His laws before I die. Yes, yes, yes, I must do this quickly. This is urgent." He then looks at me and says, "Come on! We must hurry!"

Hani shoulders me aside and gropes for something in the darkness beyond the bone door.

"We keep two backpacks full of caving supplies ready at all times," he says, as he locates and drags out two large backpacks.

Hani dumps their contents on the rocky ground: four bottles of water, twenty military rations, two caving coveralls, two head torches, four spare batteries, two hunting knives, two matchboxes, two lighters, two maps, and two machetes. He grabs a map, a coverall, and a head torch, and then stuffs everything else into one backpack.

"Slip this caving coverall over your clothes," Hani instructs me, "and then strap this head torch around your head." I comply with his orders, while he continues talking. "Brother, you will also be taking this backpack full of supplies. You will need it on your journey. Now, listen very carefully, for what I am about to say is incredibly important. Your life will depend on it."

"I'm listening carefully, Hani," I reply calmly, despite my growing anxiety. For I shall be travelling alone, underground, in a dangerous and alien environment.

"Okay," he says, "each head torch can remain on for roughly three hundred hours, before you will need to replace the batteries. So you can switch on your head torch now, and leave it on during the entire duration of your underground journey, without worrying about the batteries running out of energy. Okay?"

"Okay," I reply, as I switch on the head torch.

"Good. But I warn you, brother: do not turn the light off, even for one second. Because without any light the caves will be a thicker deeper black than anything you have every experienced before. Blacker than the blackest black soot. I cannot stress this enough: keep your head torch on at all times."

"Understood, Hani," I respond, my stomach feeling sickly tight. "The head torch light shall remain on—all the time."

"Excellent. Now, the map will lead you through the cave system and the catacombs," Hani says, while unfolding the map and pointing out a dot. "Look, we are here, at this point—and your path to freedom is drawn in yellow. See, you will exit here, at this point," he says, indicating a second dot on the map's extreme right. "You will exit the catacombs exactly on the coast, on the eastern side of the metropolis—not far from where you live. Once you are above ground, you can easily find your own way home. But the most important thing while in the caves and catacombs is to make sure you *always follow the yellow path drawn on the map*. Okay?"

"Okay," I reply. "Always stick to the yellow path drawn on the map. Got it."

"Next, as an added layer of safety, you will know you are on the correct path because we have chiselled tiny crosses throughout the cave system." Hani then grabs my shoulders before continuing: "Brother, listen very carefully. The crosses are chiselled, at knee level, on the left and the right walls. So when you are crawling through the caves, you will see the crosses at eye level. But remember that the correct path has one cross chiselled on the left side and one cross chiselled on the right side—that is, crosses on both sides. Okay? *On both sides*."

"Yes, Hani, I shall remember this," I say. "Don't worry."

"Brother, remember this information, because we have also chiselled decoy crosses on decoy routes. On the decoy routes, you will find crosses chiselled on just one side—only on the left side, or only on the right side. But decoy routes never have crosses chiselled on the right side *and* the left side—never on both sides. If you find that you have taken a passage with crosses chiselled on only one side of the wall, then you have taken the wrong route. You are on a decoy route and must turn back. Am I perfectly clear?"

"Yes, crystal clear," I answer. "Crosses on both sides, at knee level. Done."

"Excellent! Then, my brother, you will be safe. It is a tough journey, but you will make it. You are strong. As I said, the journey through the caves will take roughly fifteen hours, with the occasional break; however, the journey through the catacombs will take only fifteen minutes. So this is what I suggest: crawl through the caves for a few hours until you are exhausted. And then take a four- or five-hour nap. You will be safe sleeping in the caves, because very few people are aware they exist, and humans rarely enter them. And no living creatures inhabit the caves—except for one particularly nasty type of maggot, similar to The Nightmare. While you sleep, this maggot will wriggle into your ears and bore into your brain. It is a slow and horrible death, so be sure to plug your ears when you nap."

"What the—!" I snap, utterly terrified. "Hani, you've got to be joking! I'm not squirming through any cave system that has brain-eating maggots. Forget that rubbish! I'm going to risk dying with you, in the lanes of your city."

Hani bursts into laughter, tears streaming down his cheeks.

"Brother," he says, "I am joking! There are no maggots. You should have seen the look on your face. It was priceless!"

"You mean there are no cave-dwelling brain-eating maggots?" I ask, relaxing a little.

"Of course, not. There is no such thing! I just want to lighten the mood. God knows, we need a laugh with all this doom and gloom."

I chuckle. "Nice one, Hani. Actually, you have brightened things up a little. So there *really* is nothing alive and dangerous in the caves?"

"Nothing at all, brother. The caves are tough and tiring—yet safe. There are a few ledges, with long falls, but you will be careful when climbing across these. And you will be safe. I am sure. But, jokes aside, now it is almost sunset, and if the caves will take you roughly twenty hours, including a five-hour nap, and the catacombs about fifteen minutes, then you should make it above ground midafternoon tomorrow—if you leave now. This will allow you plenty of time to walk home during the daylight."

"This plan seems quite reasonable, Hani—much better than my first impression. I shall do it!"

"God bless you, brother," Hani says, while patting my back. "I have a warning, though. The stories about the people living in the catacombs are semi-true. So once you crawl out of the final cave passage and enter the catacombs, you should arm yourself with the two machetes."

"Oh, come on, Hani! You said it was safe."

"I said *the caves were safe*. And I am telling you now that the catacombs are somewhat safe. I have wandered alone through them several times, without any major incidents. But people do live in them. Rainwater drains into several underground canals that pass through the catacombs, and there is also an endless supply of fresh meat: rats and mice. As a consequence, vagabonds do reside in the catacombs, since there exists a steady supply of food and water. So you have to be careful—just as you have to be careful when you bump into any vagabond in the metropolis's streets."

"Hani," I say, "I'm upset with this development."

"Brother, honestly, you have nothing to fear. The machetes are for your safety, and they will act as a deterrent. Yet I highly doubt you will have to use them. Trust me. It will be fine."

I inhale deeply and ponder Hani's words.

"Okay," I say, "it doesn't sound too dangerous—and I don't have any other options. Do I?"

"None."

"So I guess I'll just have to be careful, as if I were walking the city streets at night."

"Exactly," Hani replies. "And, with that, I think we have covered everything. Do you have any questions, brother?"

"No, nothing else comes to mind," I answer, while examining my backpack and other equipment for any last-minute concerns. "Oh, Hani, your contact details!"

After we exchange e-mail addresses and tablet numbers, Hani says, "So this is it, brother. It has been a pleasure knowing you, even if it were for just a short time."

"The pleasure is mine, Hani," I reply. "I cannot thank you enough for everything you have done for me. And—"

"Please, do not mention it. I pray you will make it home safely. That is my only wish. If you were to achieve this, then believe me, brother, my heart would rejoice. Be safe, my friend."

"And I really hope you, and all your community, will be safe, too," I reply. "Hani, I don't know what else to say or—"

"Brother," he interrupts, "goodbye and may God protect you. I shall offer you some final advice to help you on your journey. For you will be physically, mentally, and spiritually tested in the caves. Yet do not despair. Do not surrender to your fears. Do not let your imagination play tricks on you. The silence, darkness, and cold harsh monotonous environment will drain you of your spirit. So your will must be strong, if you want to survive the caves. Do you grasp what I am trying to say, brother? Your greatest enemy in the caves will be you. The darkness feeds on your fear and despair. Your mind—your will—shall either save you or destroy you. But the choice will be yours. Always. You will decide your own destiny."

I contemplate Hani's words. For a young rebel, his wisdom displays the maturity of an Ancient Greek philosopher.

"Hani, brother, thank you for your guidance," I say, as my anxiety fades away and a pure sadness replaces it. My soul aches. I know I shall never see Hani's kind face again. These people, the Copts, are doomed. We all are. All life is cursed. An Ancient Greek tragedy.

"I shall close and lock the door, after you enter the cave," Hani says, changing the subject. For we share each other's pain; our eyes fail to hide the anguish. "And if possible, I shall try to find someone to help me push the altar back into its original place. That way, it will block the door. However, I doubt I will find anyone. So try to hurry through the caves as fast as you can for the first hour or so, to make good distance between you and this crypt—just in case the attackers enter the crypt and decide to discover what is in the caves. But I doubt they will even find this crypt. Go now, brother."

"Perhaps we shall meet again some sunny day," I say, without any real hope.

"Perhaps."

We hug each other, one final time.

I then adjust my backpack and crawl through the narrow doorway. The door slams shut behind me, and I hear the lock click. I am alone in a tight subterranean passage.

~~~~~

3

The air is dank, still, and earthy, and a silence grips the cave system—a suffocating silence, the absence of something, of everything. For nothing exists, here, deep within the Earth. Nothing stirs. Nothing cries. Nothing lives. Yet it takes time to adjust to the nothingness, just as it takes time to adapt to any change. And if my head torch were switched off, then the nothingness would be complete: neither sight nor sound to disturb the senses. Yet, even here, something *does* exist. The ground alternates between rough–abrasive and muddy–squishy, and these sensations, registering in my mind, remind me that something exists. That I exist. And, then, of course, there is that lingering dirt-Earth smell. That, too, is something.

~~~~~

For the first hour or so, I follow Hani's advice and hurry through the cave system; then, having distanced myself from any potential pursuer, I slow down yet refuse to rest.

Hour after hour, I squeeze and squirm through the Earth's belly. One rocky passage soon blends into the other: tortuous and monotonous and mesmerising. Yet despite the dullness, I am living in the moment. My previous life is becoming a blurred vision, and memories of the above world are dimming and shrinking the farther I crawl into the Earth. The dullness, the silence, the quasi-nothingness—all are blacking out my thoughts and feelings. My "I"ness is being wiped out slowly. Everything I thought I knew, everything I thought mattered in life, is fading into the cave's darkness. Society's struggles seem trivial, down here, in the smothering silence. Existence seems trivial. Even I seem trivial. Nothing matters but the cave and *this* instant. The dirt's grittiness. The rock's cold coarseness. The air's mellow earthiness. And for the first time in my life, I fear nothing and no one, not even the State. I picture the State receding into the distance of my mind's horizon. The State is collapsing into a speck—a pathetic and insignificant grain of nothingness.

And I have crushed it.

~~~~~

I recall Hani's instructions and double check my route by tracing out the map's yellow path and by searching for chiselled crosses on both sides of each passage. After crawling through countless passages, many barely wide enough to host me, fatigue begins to cripple my progress. I have been caving now for several hours, and every thrust forward is becoming a struggle, as my arms and legs begin to drag awkwardly. A dark haze clouds my mind. The atmosphere in the cave system darkens and thickens. All my motivation disappears into the darkness—the darkness that is always behind me, stalking me, and the darkness that is always ahead of me, lurking at my light's boundaries and waiting to ambush me.

And, then, I hear a shuffling movement behind me. I turn and look, but my torch's light illuminates only a few metres ahead and ends at the previous junction. Yet whatever made the noise is skulking just past the junction. Dare I return to the junction and search for my stalker?

A muted childlike giggle creeps its way towards me.

What might be slinking in the cave system with me? Hani swore nothing inhabited the caves. And I am more than ten hours away from the catacombs, so it must be something living in the cave system. But what? Unless someone has followed me from the crypt–chapel in the Coptic city. But what sort of person would wriggle through kilometres of caves for hours just to giggle at me in an unsettling childlike voice?

"Hey, arsehole!" I yell in the direction of the previous junction. "I'm armed with machetes—and if I find you, I'll butcher you! That's not a threat; it's a promise. You piece of bloody shit!"

I freeze. No response, not even a rustle.

Then, another chilling giggle. It is so soft, though. And although I initially thought it was human, I am now doubting my senses. What might it possibly be? A troglobite of some sort?

I arm myself with a machete and remain motionless, waiting to hear the creature move or giggle again. If I can pinpoint where the sound is coming from, then I shall pounce on my stalker and kill it before it can attack me. But I cannot let it live and trail me and ambush me.

Seconds and minutes pass in disturbing silence. The anticipation is unbearable. I now want to confront my stalker, whatever it is, and end this stand-off. Budding rage is replacing my dying fear.

More silence, not even hushed breathing.

Having had enough, I decide to retrace my movements past the previous junction and hack into my stalker before it even realises what is happening. But as I turn the corner and lunge at my mysterious foe, I clash with—nothing. The tunnel is empty. So I retrace my steps even farther back and hasten through another tunnel, until I reach the next junction. And, again, nothing.

Were there any shuffling movements? Any giggles? Or is the cave system muddying my mind?

If something were stalking me, then I would have heard it scurry away from me as I chased it down the tunnels. But only silence greeted me as I stalked my stalker—and only silence continues to greet me now.

Nothing lurks in these caves except for me and my imagination. I am alone.

Extreme mental and physical exhaustion suddenly overwhelms me. I must rest.

~~~~~

I sit down and fumble a military ration and a water bottle from my backpack. Although the cold rocky ground is jutting into my bruised flesh, the rest instantly begins to relax me. The tension of marching through the metropolis, running for my life in the Coptic city, and crawling through kilometres of caves has sapped me of all my energy. And despite the cave's recent mind tricks, I feel oddly content— alone yet at peace with myself and my surroundings. I have toiled and earned this simple yet satisfying reward. So I gulp down the sweet cooling water and tear ravenously at the ration's freeze-dried rice and vegetable mix, which bursts with unexpected flavour.

After swallowing all the food and washing it down with several final swigs of water, a comfortable emptiness begins to numb my mind. I have, for now, conquered this cave system. And I fear nothing. No despair, either. Just a warm fuzzy tiredness washing over me. Muscles melting. It must be almost midnight. Too exhausted to check the time on my tablet computer. I shut my eyes. Darkness immediately engulfs me. Heavenly nothingness.

~~~~~

I cannot stop shivering. The cold and dampness and lack of movement have drained my body of all its heat. My fingers and toes are numb. My skin is clammy. Even my mind is reacting slowly, partly frozen along with everything else.

How long have I been asleep? According to my tablet computer, I have slept for six hours—too long for these frigid conditions. Now, my body is shutting down: cell by cell, organ by organ, system by system. And I shall die, unless I can raise my temperature quickly.

But my will—that unconscious fire fuelling my existence—refuses to ignite me into action. For the cold and inaction have doused it, too. I want to surrender, to remain still, to curl up into a ball and sleep. A part of me grasps the deadly consequence of such a decision, whereas another cares little. Yet the latter is dominating. What do I have to live for? I detest this life. This is the perfect place to die. Deep within the Earth. Alone.

I shut my eyes. My consciousness begins to flicker. I am here and not here. My "I"ness is dimming, a dying ember in a once-brilliant blaze. And I do not care. The outside world seems so remote, in space and time. Drifting away. Surprisingly serene. Struggle free.

But something is anchoring me to this world, to this body. My time has yet to come. And that unknown-unknown something is rekindling my flame, my will to live. That unknown-unknown is vanquishing the all-consuming despair. No more flickering consciousness, a solid "I" is reforming—and I command my body to action.

So I start hurrying through the cave system as fast as I can move my heavy limbs. And with each motion my body's temperature increases and my mind clears. A sharpness of vision, a clarity of thinking, a verve to live— together, these supplant the despair and sluggishness of moments just passed. Yet despite the vigorous exercise, it takes more than an hour for my temperature to become normal and for my body to stop shivering. I have finally beaten the hypothermia.

~~~~~

It is becoming a brutal slog. Every passage resembles every other passage: lifeless, colourless, meaningless. My knees hurt. My muscles ache. My body is bruised. I despise this cave system. It is hell, and I long to escape it. Another hour passes, yet it feels slower than the previous. How many more hours to go? A couple? A few? Longer?

I am now counting the seconds rather than the hours. Every few moments I check my tablet, hoping that by some miracle the time has ticked by faster than I expected it to. Instead, it slows with each glance. I am obsessed with the time, for this is all I have left. No other distraction exists down here. And I am growing frustrated and agitated.

Again, my will to act is being tested. Why continue acting or moving at all? I feel like Sisyphus, except my circular punishment is this never-ending cave system. With each passage conquered, I find the exact same passage confronting me—and, then, on conquering this passage, another identical passage lies ahead. For all I know I might be crawling around in circles. This may be Hani's idea of a joke; after all, he must have overheard my conversation about the illusion of progress with Dr Tawfik. And my progress in this cave system definitely appears to be an illusion.

But, then, I stumble across something peculiar, which briefly severs my circular hell. An inconspicuous side passage leads to four separate room-sized chambers.

In the first chamber, thousands of bones and skulls from different animal species are scattered everywhere. A plaque secured to the chamber's entrance reads, "Temporality. Plurality. Reality."

In the second chamber, dozens of human skeletons are buried up to their necks, with each skull facing the same direction and positioned equidistantly from its neighbour. A plaque says, "Humanity: mass psychosis. Collectively gawking at an illusion in the future or the past while missing the reality of the moment."

In the third chamber, two human skeletons lie in the centre. They are curled up and desperately clinging to each other. A plaque at their feet reads, "The awakening. The terror. The despair. The loneliness."

And, in the fourth chamber, two human skeletons rest in opposite corners. The first skeleton has its skull smashed in and is missing a lower leg; deep marks are carved into the femur, just above the missing lower leg. The second skeleton, complete and intact, has a rusted hunting knife and lower-leg bones resting next to it. A plaque has been fixed to the third cave's entrance:

According to the natural law, we are imperfect beings—beings that have needs and wants. As a consequence, we must act—move—to satisfy our needs and wants. All life, all imperfect beings, share this burden.

Only a perfect being lacks needs or desires. A perfect being has no need to act or move, because it has already achieved a perfect state. And any movement away from this perfect state would only end in imperfection. If this were to happen, then the being would cease to be perfect. Needs and desires would then arise to motivate the being and help it regain its previously perfect state. So a perfect being lacks needs, desires, and movement. A perfect being is motionless.

Although the concept of a perfect and an imperfect being emerges from Ancient Greek philosophy (later Christian philosophy builds upon the Greek), a similar idea also exists in Buddhism. In this tradition, desires lead to suffering. So to reduce suffering, one must decrease his desires. One must pursue perfection—a heavenly state lacking desire and suffering. This transcendent state, where even the self dissolves from a lack of desire, is known as nirvana.

Yet everlasting perfection will always elude humanity, because, to quote Charles Darwin, "Man still bears … the indelible stamp of his lowly origins." We are, as always, imperfectly evolved beings cursed with needs and desires.

Imperfection means action to achieve perfection; perfection means inaction to maintain perfection. In death, one finally attains perfection.

After I finish reading the plaques, I rush back through the side passage and continue my original journey. Even though this detour has broken the grinding monotony, it has also conjured up haunting visions. Perturbed, I move through the remainder of the cave system at a blistering pace. I have to act, because I am an imperfect being who needs to satisfy a desire—the desire to end this underground nightmare.

~~~~~

After roughly twenty hours, I finally reach the end of the cave system. For the next passage connects with the catacombs—and, from there, it is just a fifteen-minute walk to the above-ground world and freedom. And Hani's calculations were perfect: my tablet indicates that it is midafternoon, so I shall have plenty of time to walk home in the daylight.

I climb out of the dirt-encrusted caving coveralls and toss them away. But I hesitate to arm myself with the two machetes, as Hani suggested. Instead, I ready the machetes by attaching them to the backpack's sides, within easy grasp if required. I then squeeze through the last ragged tunnel and step into the catacombs.

~~~~~

A storm drain splits the chamber into two, and the sound of trickling rainwater fills the catacombs. The soothing drip-drip and cool still air begin to relax my frayed nerves—but, then, I remember that I am strolling through an underground cemetery crammed with walled-in skeletons, scuttling roaches, and inquisitive rodents. A distant bang also shatters any illusions of serenity and warns me that larger animals than roaches and rodents reside in these tunnels. At least I can walk upright—a huge relief from the stooped torture of the caves.

I follow the route marked on my map and hurry through the various tunnels, chambers, and ossuaries. The majority of the deeper tunnels and rooms are empty, and this aids in my quick progress. But as I approach the surface exit point, I stumble across an increasing number of the catacombs' inhabitants. In a particularly large chamber, I notice a

157

campfire burning in the centre and sinister shadows darting around the room. A voice wails, "Alloooooo!" But I neither stop nor respond. I then race past another chamber, where I overhear pants and grunts emerging from the blackness.

One ossuary, however, halts my dash through the catacombs. Yelping, howling, caterwauling—these and other woeful cries are originating from this ossuary. And as I peer inside, the light from my head torch reveals dozens of cats and dogs chained to the walls. Several of the wretched creatures are missing limbs; the majority are bleeding, bruised, and battered. A stench—part faeces, part dried urine, part gangrenous rot—saturates the air. Despite being inured to foul smells, this one's pungency overwhelms me and I collapse under its physical presence. What is this perversity? An abattoir? A meat storage room? A torture chamber? Out of all the species on the planet, only humans breed other animals—innocent sentient beings—*specifically* to enslave them, torture them, use them, abuse them, mutilate them, experiment on them, butcher them, and eat them. I have been blind to this hidden underground horror, just like the majority of people. All of us wilfully blind. All of us equally guilty. If morality were real and absolute, then we—humans—would be the most immoral species ever to walk the Earth. And, "If possessing a higher degree of intelligence does not entitle one human to use another for his or her own ends, how can it entitle humans to exploit non-humans?" wrote Peter Singer in the twentieth century.

As I am trying to recover from the obscene scene confronting me, something shoots out of the darkness and knocks me flat on my back. Stunned, I instinctively grasp a machete while getting up. The amorphous mass pounces on me again, but as it does I swing the machete with all my might. The sharp blade slices deeply into my ambusher's flesh—the momentum stopped only by crunching bone. My ambusher screams, an awful shriek that penetrates every inch of the catacombs. Although I should flee from this place before all the sewer dwellers respond to their comrade's cry for help, my rage consumes me and I hack into my attacker until blood and chunks of flesh are splattered everywhere. A mangled mass of meat rests at my feet. Faraway calls begin to ring throughout the catacombs' branches. I cannot save the chained animals; I can save only myself. So I bolt for my life.

A couple of hundred metres later, a blast of sunshine vanquishes the darkness and exposes a ladder leading up to an open manhole and my freedom. But skulking in the darkness, separating me from my prize, glares a deranged bum with soiled rags wrapped around his body. I squeeze my machete's handle.

"Oi!" the bum yells. "Whadya doin' here, mate?"

"Nothing," I reply. "I just want to pass through peacefully and climb up the manhole and leave."

"Nah, mate, this is me home," the bum says, before clearing his congested sinuses and spitting the gooey gunk in my direction. "Ya think ya can just walk through me home, ya wanka?"

"Look, sir, I didn't know this was your home. I would be happy to—"

But just as I am about to offer him some food and consumer goods for safe passage, the bum pulls out a dagger from the folds of his rags and lunges at me. With one swift motion, I slash at his throat with my machete. The blade carves effortlessly through his neck meat. I then jump backwards and watch as blood spurts in short bursts from his severed carotid arteries. After a few seconds, he drops to the ground, while clenching his throat and gasping for air like a landed fish. But my machete has also cleaved his trachea, and bloody bubbles foam angrily around the slit in his neck. Soon after, his struggle ends. A dark liquid begins to pool under his motionless body. The liquid then creeps towards the manhole ladder and turns bright red as it leaves the darkness and enters the sunlight.

Shuffling noises, distant yet drawn towards the commotion, surface from the catacombs' depths, and a wicked smell drifts through the tunnels. The horde is coming. It is time to go. I leap over the bum's body and climb up the ladder as fast as my weary arms and legs can move.

The darkness, my constant companion, scatters as I emerge from the manhole and into the light.

I weep, I sing, I rejoice! For the Sun bathes me with its life-giving rays. The gentle warmth immediately begins to crisp my clammy skin and energise my depleted spirit. How glorious and brilliant you are, oh radiant Sun! I now grasp your allure, your power, your divinity. I understand why previous people treasured and worshipped you as the ultimate God. For you warm and nourish and nurture all your creations, all your earthly children. Without you, I would be dead—all life would vanish. You are magnificent.

And yesterday's blackness retreats—for now.

~~~~~

The Sun's intoxicating warmth soon fades away, however, and yesterday's darkness returns thereafter. For thick smoke is billowing from the metropolis's western horizon, from the direction of the Coptic city.

I unwrap my tablet and call Hani and Dr Tawfik. But neither person answers, so I leave them messages. Fearing the worst, I click on *The Indymedia Daily* website, a politically independent non-State news outlet, and search for this city's latest news. The first article confirms my fears: "Fires and Firefights Level Coptic Territories". According to the news item, "Although a handful of survivors fled the Coptic city, the majority died … Heavily armed State's Spawn murdered countless Copts … The *SS* marauders also ignited numerous fires, which killed hundreds of thousands of Copts … It was a shocking massacre—much worse than the recent inferno that razed an inner-city slum to the ground."

But on other news outlets' websites, such as *The Occidental Times* and *The Occidental Herald* (both State owned), no mention exists of the *SS* or their mass murder. *The Occidental Times*, for instance, mentions something about a "massive fire and a tragic accident", yet blames the Copts for "failing to abide by the State's town-planning rules and regulations". And *The Occidental Herald* writes, "Since the

161

Copts spent their entire lives resisting secular reason-based progress and State-led centralised planning—designed to make the people's lives safer, fairer, and happier—then the Copts have no one to blame for their misfortune but themselves and their insular irrational thinking. Let this be a lesson to everyone: the State and its experts know best. This is why we have a centralised system, where the Occidental Union Administrators collaborate with leading experts, scientists, and academics to plan a better world and a progressive rational society."

So the State has finally defeated its ancient foe. The Copts—the last bastion of Christianity in the Occidental Union—are dead.

But what now? Without that "old whore Christianity" or that "old bitch capitalism", who will the State scapegoat for all the ills of society? Who will the people blame for the inherent flaws in human nature? For the State needs an enemy to survive, and all people thrive on conflict. Lacking a common foe, perhaps the State will wither away and the people will perish.

Right now, however, I am too drained to feel either loss or grief for the Copts' eradication. Just an uncomfortable nothingness taints my mind and afflicts my soul. Although it is the height of self-centredness, I need to get home and see my Anup. I miss his adoring stare and soft coat. Yet what else can I do?

~~~~~

Less than a couple of kilometres away from home, I happen on the largest Temple of the People located in this part of the metropolis. Despite this Temple hosting a solidarity event on most days, today's event must be huge, judging from the hubbub. The Temple and surrounding streets are buzzing with activity.

The Ancient Romans used to say, "Keep the people fed and entertained, and you can take away all their freedoms." Yet nothing much has changed thousands of years later, for these State-run and Worldwide Workers Union–coordinated solidarity events exist for this purpose. It is mind-numbing entertainment of the people, by the people, for the people.

My curiosity growing, I approach the Temple with caution. Today's solidarity event may involve the Copts and enlighten me further about their fate.

Several-thousand people, all wearing the Occidental Union's black attire, are crammed into the Temple, and shouts and screams ripple throughout the homogenised mass. Something big is brewing. And the rabble is becoming frenzied, which suggests the tapwater must be clean today.

At the Temple's far end, a group of Occidental Union officials and several representatives from the Worldwide Workers Union are taking their seats on either side of a stage; meanwhile, a young blonde in a white figure-hugging dress is pacing up and down the same stage. And even though she does not need the help, the afternoon sunlight does highlight her high cheekbones and enhance her exquisitely sculpted features.

Next to the stunning blonde hangs the sacrificial catch of the week: a white-bearded scrawny old man dangles upside down from a rope tied around his ankles and secured to the stage's ceiling. He is completely naked, except for some metal wire wrapped around his torso and arms. Between the crowd and the immobilised man, a line of shield-carrying peace officers forms a human barrier.

Without warning, the stunning blonde points at the naked old man and shouts into the microphone: "And this is why we have this piece of human garbage—this filthy scum—here today!"

In reply the crowd claps, roars, and wolf whistles, many barely able to control their rage and hatred. A few well-aimed beer cans and bottles strike the man's scrawny body, but he refrains from flinching. He just hangs there limply.

The attractive hostess then continues with the show.

"*This priest,*" she squeals, "must pay for the sins of his Fathers, for the sins of their past, for all the problems they have given us today."

The throng erupts in excitement. A drum beat floats over the Temple. If it were possible to eliminate the rage and human sacrifice, then the spectacle would boast a Mardi Gras flavour.

"And this priest will pay—*today!*" the woman screams, as she punches the priest in the gut. He grimaces in pain yet remains silent.

Approving of the violent entertainment, the people start hooting and stomping the floor. The Temple of the People vibrates with the fury of the people.

The rabble then chants, "Ho hum, ho hum, kill the Christian scum! Hum ho, hum ho, the priest's head must go! Ho hum, ho hum, kill the Christian scum! Hum ho, hum ho, the priest's head must go!"

And with each incantation, the mob's demeanour becomes more vicious.

After the chant dies down, the woman then clutches the priest by his white beard and says, "This bigot, this misogynist, this hate-filled man—if we can even call him a man, judging by his tiny dick—is the reason we are living in hell today. His Church raped innocent children and women under its care, and his Church butchered and massacred and exploited every innocent native people they conquered! These genocidal Christian men killed billions of non-Christians and stole all their lands and wealth and property. These Christian pigs, these oppressors, these fascists, raped the environment and killed all the native species—drove them to extinction. And all this they did in the name of their greedy white-male God! In the name of Christianity, in the name of their white-male religion, and in the name of white-male capitalism, these rich Christian pigs tried to obliterate every other race, every other culture, every other religion, every other living creature! These rich greedy Christian fascist Nazi-scum pigs tried to exploit and subjugate everyone and everything! Death to all Christian rapists! Death to all Christian fascists! Death to all Christian mass murderers! Death to all Christian Nazi scum! Death to all rich greedy Christian capitalist exploiters!"

Dozens of individuals in the crowd then start bellowing, "Death to all rich Christian capitalist pigs! Death to all greedy Christian Nazi scum! Off with their heads—the whole bloody lot of them!"

After the threats subside, another singsong slogan arises from the horde's midst: "Hum ho, hum ho, to Christian bigotry we say no! Ho hum, ho hum, we demand no more priests—none! Hum ho, hum ho, all Christians must go! Ho hum, ho hum, gut the capitalist scum!"

Tears begin to stream down the priest's forehead and zigzag their way between spindly tufts of white hair before dripping on to the stage floor. A glistening pool soon collects beneath his head. And despite the sunlight warming his body, he is trembling. Even I am terrified for the priest.

"*Once spirit was God, then it became man, and now it is even becoming mob*," the priest cries out to the crowd. "Friedrich Nietzsche said this hundreds of years ago. Do any of you understand the meaning of his words? What about you, oh wise officials of the Occidental Union? Do any of you understand the meaning of his words?"

The crowd boos and shouts down the priest, preventing any officials from responding. A barrage of beer cans and bottles then batter his body, badly bruising it. But the priest has more to say, and he waits for a break in the abuse before continuing.

"Tell me, what have I done wrong?" the priest asks, staring at the officials on stage. "Tell me *one thing* I have done wrong. Just one! Huh? What have I done wrong? Nothing! I have done *nothing* wrong! This is perverse! God have mercy upon all your souls, for you are all sick. *Sick*! This society is sick. All the people are sick. Everything here is sick. God have mercy. *Kirieleison. Kirieleison. Kirieleison.*"

The religiously infused invective infuriates the irreligious people, who respond by lobbing more beer cans and bottles at the priest. Several projectiles slam into his head, bruising and piercing his flesh. Blood runs down the priest's forehead and then mingles with his pooled tears on the stage floor.

Once the mob finishes its assault, an Occidental Union official stands up and says, "Priest, the Honourable Occidental Union Administrators have already administered your case, and they have judged you *guilty*. Guilty!"

The crowd claps and cheers on hearing the guilty verdict.

"Priest," the official continues, "the Honourable Occidental Union Administrators have also administered your sentence, and today you will serve your public punishment. Time for justice, old man—so do not act all innocent with us. Exploiters like you disgust our honest, peaceful, and egalitarian community."

I snigger at the farce, the sickening display of State totalitarianism merged with mob tyranny and human depravity. Do these people believe any of this? Or do they realise that this is a choreographed perversity and that they are wilful agents in a crime against an innocent man? Or perhaps the line between lie and truth has been erased a long time ago. No lie, no truth. Just the will of the State, the will of the people.

"Yes, priest, don't act all innocent with us," the stunning blonde interjects. "You know exactly what you've done wrong. But let me tell the good people gathered here today what you've done wrong, just in case anyone doesn't know."

The blonde strolls over to a bag resting next to a union representative. She then reaches into it and says, "Besides the countless sins of your so-called holy Brethren and Fathers, which I've already described, I'll tell you what *else* you've done wrong. You, priest, have violated the most important law of all. You have been hoarding the old system's ultimate symbol of filth and exploitation: gold and silver bullion."

As she says "bullion", the blonde removes a gold bar from the bag and holds the brilliant bullion like a trophy above her head. The priest shakes his head in disbelief.

"Yes, good people of the Occidental Union," the blonde says, "this rich greedy scum was caught stockpiling gold and silver in the form of coins and bullion. And he was even caught trading with them! This degenerate priest is guilty of embracing the evil old system. He is guilty of being greedy. He is guilty of exploiting the land and the environment and stealing its mineral wealth for his own selfish desires. But most importantly, he is guilty of exploiting us, the people!"

These charges against the priest ignite the volatile and unstable rabble, and several spectators, inflamed with self-righteous rage, try to scale the stage. But the line of peace officers holds its ground and protects the stage and priest from the stage jumpers.

"Good citizens, please calm down!" the blonde cries out apprehensively. "Do not worry: one of you will be picked at random to punish this piece of shit, this enemy of the people. It's time for social justice!" She then picks up a tablet computer, glances at its screen, and says, "Okay, good people, a programme has randomly picked a person by scanning your implanted microchips. And, yes, we have a winner! The following person is to administer the priest's punishment: Mr Jacobin. Mr Jack Jacobin. Is there a Mr Jack Jacobin in the crowd? Please, Mr Jack Jacobin, you are to come to the stage."

Instantly, a young man, not even twenty years of age, starts ramming his way through the crowd.

"I'm Jack!" he says, while shoving aside several waifs. "That's me! Yes, *finally*, it's me turn!"

"People! People!" the blonde announces, as she grabs an electric stock prod from the same bag that housed the gold. "Please, good people, let Mr Jacobin through."

After a minute of violent shoving and pushing, Jacobin reaches his prize and springs on to the stage. He smiles sadistically at the priest. The priest, in return, squeezes his eyes shut and silently mouths what is probably a prayer.

Eager for the torture to begin, many in the crowd start cheering and jeering. A chorus then fills the Temple: "Tweedle dee, tweedle dum, butcher the priestly scum! Tweedle dum, tweedle dee, hang the priest from a tree!"

The blonde waits for the din to die down, before handing Jacobin the stock prod and saying, "Jack, this is a modified electric stock prod. Each time you jam it into the priest, he will receive a high-voltage shock. Actually, it's a juiced-up prod, so it has extra bite. And the longer you jam it into the priest, the more damage it does. You know what I mean: more burning and searing and sizzling of the flesh. If you want my advice, I'd target the most sensitive parts of the priest's anatomy and then deeply thrust that prod into him for *your* maximum pleasure—not his." She giggles and, winking at Jacobin, says, "Go ahead, sexy—the priest is all yours. Give it to him with your big stick."

Jack Jacobin, drooling from all the excitement, advances on the helpless priest.

"Please stop, good sir!" the priest pleads, while gazing at Jacobin's demonic eyes. "I have done nothing—harmed no one. I help people, not hurt them. I even cry when I see a stray dog in pain. I beg you, good sir, do not take part in this vile crime. Please, this is a huge mistake. I have never kept or owned any gold or silver. I know the law. I know the law, and I do not break it. That is not my gold. This is all a lie—a set-up!"

And with these denials, the bloodthirsty horde erupts in wrath. The black mass seethes towards the priest. Nothing will placate the people now.

As the first rioters reach the stage, the peace officers fire their nonlethal acoustic devices (disc-shaped sonic blasters that can concentrate disabling sound waves at specific targets). Even from this distance, I can feel the sound waves piercing my skull, and I keel over in pain and nausea. But after a minute the screeching noise stops, and I glance at the stage to see rioters swarming over the peace officers and bludgeoning them to death with beer bottles and other makeshift weapons. No officers escape. All the State officials and union representatives are also being battered to death. No State contract can save them now. And lacking any State security, the immobilised priest has certainly been condemned to join them in death.

The priest shrieks and flaps pathetically as his first attacker, Jack Jacobin, jabs him—again and again, harder and harder—with the stock prod. Seconds later, however, the horde swallows up the priest, and he vanishes within wave after wave of roiling turmoil. A thin scream of dread his final act.

The horde then focuses its terror on the stunning young blonde. Her stupid grin of self-assurance disappears; pure horror now contorts all her features. I recognise that awful look—that instant when any warm and fuzzy feelings about the goodness of the universe fade away. It is the realisation that it is over. That mother nature is, at heart, apathetic and capricious—not loving and predictable. That one is neither unique nor special.

Thriving on her fear, dozens of ferals start yapping excitedly like hyenas. Feeding time is here. And they begin snapping at each other, as they encircle their prey. For each desires the prime piece of meat for his own pleasure.

A moment later the pack attacks and shreds the blonde's white figure-hugging dress to pieces. Foraging fingers then claw at her soft milky flesh and tug at her long lustrous hair. And, in an act of cruel irony, a few ferals even flaunt tufts of her hair—still rooted in chunks of bloody flesh—above their heads as trophies. Others bite and chew whatever womanly body parts they are able to mouth. And though the woman screams repeatedly for mercy, she receives none—just like she showed the priest none. Another act of cruel irony. But unlike the priest's struggles, which ended quickly, the woman's are just beginning.

The mob knows no mercy, no reason, no dialogue. When man no longer believes in any narrative, when the collective clearly grasps the grand delusion that it—itself—

helped construct, then the mob is born in a final act of group self-destruction. For the mob is the raw will of the disillusioned collective, before it turns on itself and devours its own.

Howling and yowling, here and there. Mayhem and madness engulf the Temple and adjacent streets. Packs of feral young males splinter and scatter in every direction, sowing senseless violence wherever they roam. Already crumbling buildings are pelted with projectiles and then torched, hastening their inevitable collapse. Sporadic explosions shake the Earth. Gunshots pepper the metropolis. Fires flare up all over the neighbourhood, and the atmosphere thickens with smoke. The Sun disappears behind the rising darkness. Desperate screams penetrate the air as ferals hunt down unfamiliar men and pack rape the women and children sheltering in nearby apartment complexes. Yet the ferals' evil baying and cackling eventually overpower the muffled cries for help, until only the predators' calls dominate the metropolis.

Building after building, street after street, neighbourhood after neighbourhood, is submitting to the will of the mob—to mob annihilation.

The Occidental Union is dying. And this time man will find no salvation in myth or religion, reason or enlightenment, progress or humanism, scientism or technology, socialism or collectivism, liberalism or conservatism, democracy or monarchy, despotism or totalitarianism, fundamentalism or absolutism.

Seeking fresh victims, a pack of feral youths starts sniffing in my direction. Somehow they can smell I am not one of them, like an immune system detecting a foreign body. So I grab both machetes and prepare for violence. I shall fight like an animal stripped of all its dignity. And before they can butcher me, I shall slaughter as many of them as I can. We shall die together.

A naive feral, intoxicated with the thrill of anarchy and mass destruction, breaks away from the pack and zeroes in on me. Caterwauling and swinging a metal pole, he charges at me, but I sidestep him and strike him across the back of the knee. The machete slices through nerves, tendons, ligaments, and blood vessels with clinical precision, and the feral instantly collapses in agony.

Value pluralism dictates that we must embrace different values at different times. No one value is always and absolutely correct at all times. And when one is being attacked, then it is right—morally correct or conventionally acceptable—to defend oneself using violence. Although pacifism might be honourable most of the time, savagery also has its rightful place. Without the State, without its security apparatus, without its rule of law, only savagery exists.

And now is the time for savagery.

While the feral is down, I hack into his neck until I slash through the vertebrae and his head rolls away from his body.

"Come on, ya pricks!" I roar like a deranged lunatic at the advancing pack members. "I've been waiting for this moment all my life. I can't wait to dice all a'ya into pieces!"

The ferocity of my bloody attack, coupled with the crazed bloodlust in my eyes, serves its purpose. For I see the terror emerging in the pack members' faces. Like all hunters, these ferals prefer the weak, the maimed, the old, the young, the scared, the defenceless. But there is one thing all hunters fear: the prey that chooses fight over flight. And these pack members now fear me. After sizing me up, they decide to abandon the hunt and seek easier prey elsewhere. So they flood instead into an apartment complex down the road—and the ensuing shrieks confirm that they have indeed tracked down easier prey.

Despite my long and tiring journey, the danger of mob violence has invigorated me. Nothing like an existential threat to rouse someone from a muted existence. Life does hold meaning—it does have purpose—when faced with the peril of no life, of dying. And the meaning of life becomes clear during terrors such as this: for all actions are taken to survive and thrive.

~~~~~

4

She is dead. On entering the apartment, I find Bulla twisted into a grotesque pose on a chair. Her glazed eyes stare vacantly at the ceiling, and her still-warm porcelain-like flesh feels rigid, almost ossified. Yet I cannot detect any signs of violence. She seems to have died from a disease or a natural cause. But what kind of disease freezes a person into a statue? Nothing fits such a description. Even an environmental toxin would fail to leave a body in this condition.

I cover Bulla's body with a tarpaulin scavenged from an abandoned apartment down the hall and then drag the corpse outside. Dazed and drained, I mutter a few random words and chuck several handfuls of dirt over the body. A pathetic finale to an ignoble existence.

Although I should be upset over Bulla's death, I feel nothing. I have experienced so much death and destruction in the last twenty-four hours that little else but an unsettling emptiness dwells in me. My numbed mind is shutting out much of the environment.

Everything is crumbling around me: society, the metropolis, the Occidental Union, all basic services, the social and physical infrastructure. And now even my own home—my sanctuary—is being assaulted. Nowhere is safe.

I *was* Progenitor A—one Progenitor among many and nothing more than a State-administered human contract. But, *now*, everything has changed. In an instant, all the previous manmade contaminants have begun to vanish from the world. The State is fading away and with it my identity. Who am I?

~~~~~

Anup is sleeping next to me. Last night, at about the same time, I was lying alone on the cold rocky ground of a cave; tonight, I am curled up in my soft bed next to another living being. I run my fingers through my dog's thick coat and delight in its softness, which I find surprising after the relentless hardness of the caves. He radiates warmth, and his rhythmic breathing comforts me: in through the nostrils, airways, and lungs, and then out through the lungs, airways, and nostrils. Always the same routine. So simple, so essential, so natural. Almost hypnotic. But there is something else, something familiar about his breathing. An ancient message passed from organism to organism over hundreds of millions of years is encoded in this primordial act.

I study Anup's perfectly formed features as he sleeps, happily oblivious to humanity's deteriorating world around him. What would it feel like to be Anup? How does he experience reality? What sort of sensations rule his existence? What is unfolding in that mind of his?

I think and experience consciousness mainly using words, sometimes conjuring up images and other fuzzy mental representations, but rarely does my mind venture far from this narrow comfort zone. However, for a pure animal uncorrupted by words and language, how does the world appear to Anup? What is streaming in his mind, in his consciousness? Is he thinking through smells, sights, and sounds? Does he dream of a different past, present, or future? Can he dream of such things? Does he love and hate? Who is Anup?

How I long to experience reality through another mind, another animal's mind. But I cannot. For I am bound, in solitary confinement for the duration of my bodily sentence, to never truly know another mind. Although another living being—another mind—is situated right next to me, I might as well be all alone in another universe. An unconquerable vastness separates Anup from me; an impenetrable barrier isolates me from every other living being, from every other mind. I, like every animal, am doomed to a lonely existence.

~~~~~

My tablet computer vibrates just as I am about to doze off. It is a message from a personalised web-spider, a software agent that hunts down online articles for me. The message says, "I've found something you may find interesting. Click on the link. But before you do that, don't forget to turn on the fan—it's a hot day today." The "fan" is code for *Naughty Ape*, a programme that erases all digital footprints and allows a person to surf anonymously while bypassing State filters, monitors, and Cleaner software agents. So I activate Naughty Ape and then click on the link:

The Indymedia Daily, *"The Occidental Union releases 'technological marvel' in desperate final act"*——*The Occidental Union has become a dangerous place to live. Life is miserable. Work has dried up. Goods and services—the essentials of life—have vanished. Safety and security are faded dreams. Civility is lacking. Families, communities, and civil institutions have been eliminated. The natural environment has been degraded. The Great Heat is relentless. The State's food and clothing handouts are disappearing. And even the State's welfare and essential services have withered away. But if life is currently dreadful, what will happen when the State completely fails? When the Occidental Union collapses?*

So how did we arrive here? A poem written more than one hundred years ago by an unknown author may shed some light on our current predicament:

The universe is an unsolvable equation

The darkness defiled the lands of the Earth,
From east to west, it signalled a stillbirth.
They called it the epoch of misery, scarcity, and pain,
Which had to surface after the centuries of easy gain.

For what goes up must come down, our ancestors once said,
But who cares about ancient wisdom, which is now dead.
So the hubris of the people and experts inflated,
And their demands and expectations could not be sated.

Blinded by arrogance, they all missed the signs,
Displayed here, there, everywhere, and at all times.
And when it was too late and nothing could the hoi polloi do,
They cried innocent victim—whom can I blame, whom can I sue?

Nature can be brutal and merciless—and so can God be,
These truths the people forgot, drunk with cheap sentimentality.
For when the resources grew scarce, all the low-hanging fruit taken,
The dark side of nature emerged, all the societies shaken.
But people were already soft, decadent, uninspiring,
Spending most of their lives studying, just before retiring.

Microbes ravaged the people, while growing resistant to all drugs,
Ancient plagues now incurable, just like the virulent new bugs.
Obesity and chronic ailments scourged the young and old alike,
Processed foods and virtual living triggering the big spike.
But there is nothing to fear, said the new science priesthood,
Fresh technologies will save us and raise man from beasthood.

Although up was now down, hot was now cold, and black was now
white,
This puzzled all the people: what is now wrong, what is now right?
All experiences are an illusion; the mind and senses are a deception,
The people must reconstruct reality according to the experts' conception.

179

But there is nothing to fear, said the new academic priesthood,
Scientism will save us and raise humankind from beasthood.

Plenty of time passed yet nothing was fixed,
Leaving the experts divided and mixed.
And the arguments raged: progress has failed,
Who's listening, the panicked people railed.

Democratic nations then forged sideshows in the name of freedom,
safety, and human rights,
And costly wars were waged against drugs, dictators, terrorism, and
countless other fights.
Yet the truth, hidden behind these words, was simpler and more
mundane,
All struggles are about control and coercion—nothing arcane.

In the meantime, the standard of living sharply declined,
As the prices of food, energy, and essentials climbed.
But there is nothing to fear, said the new economic priesthood,
More debt and spending will save us and raise humankind from
beasthood.

So central planners and bankers began their manipulations,
To camouflage the true burgeoning debt of failing free nations.
Printing more money was the Keynesian answer to all the crises,
Though the central-planning experts ignored the warnings of von
Mises.

Yet the people's standard of living continued to plummet,
Except for a few insiders whose lifestyles reached the summit.

But there is nothing to fear, said the new bureaucratic priesthood,
A bigger government will save us and raise mankind from beasthood.

So it began with the State sowing hatred, envy, and fear,
Though joy, safety, and equality—these the State pledged were near.
And through simple slogans and promises of a grand solution,
The State spewed out lies, tainting and moulding minds with its
pollution.

But the first step needed to cure the people's trouble,
Was to grant the State more power, at least by double.
And so through democracy and the voting process,
The State began to mushroom and consume more, not less.

Legislation after legislation was introduced,
And all the citizens were mesmerised, awed, and seduced,
By the temptation of a land of milk and honey,
If only the people would give the State more money.

So our freedoms died inconspicuously, one by one,
And taxes tacked on everything, even the air and Sun.
State-sponsored science and research supported all its actions,
Which helped silence dissenting ideologies and factions.

Yet the sworn utopia failed to arrive,
And the State said it would continue to strive,
But more money and power did it need,
For it to complete the difficult deed.

Meanwhile, the State infiltrated the schools and the academia,
Even free speech died at the hands of the State-infected media.
Central planning, central banking, and central reserves,
No power left to people, who became the new serfs.
Never throughout history had such an assault taken place,
As the one State expanded everywhere: matter, time, space.

And more and more handouts did the State purposely give,
Thus spawning State-suckled masses needing it to live.
The State fed, clothed, and sheltered its chosen ones,
And groomed them for violence and armed them with guns.
Yet these brutal mobs also gave the State its required votes,
And helped it enforce tyranny and slit its enemies' throats.

Still, utopia never came,
So the State had to lay blame,
Pointing the finger at capitalist scum,
Accusing them of every evil, every slum.

Next came the stealing of private property, precious metals, and
production goods,
Though the State called it nationalisation for the benefit of
neighbourhoods.
The businesses busted, the entrepreneurs fled,
The economy stalled, the community bled.

Yet one worldwide company and one worldwide trade union did
remain,
Helping the State secure power while sharing the insider's gain.

But no other competition would the State tolerate,
So it destroyed them all through legislation, lies, and hate.

The demonising of rival collective ideologies then began,
And religions, in particular, felt the full force of the State's brutal ban.
Although the State's ultimate aim was to place the individual in
chains,
What better way to achieve this than spout the righteousness of
collective gains?

So the family unit was next to go,
Turning each one against the other in woe.
Now, the State became parent, husband, and wife,
Pervading every part of a person's life.

The job of completely subjugating and dominating the individual was
almost done,
Freedom, property, family, and equality in the eyes of the law—a
person now had none.
Yet, still, these triumphs failed to satiate the hungry State,
It needed each person's mind and soul to be truly great.
And after the State became subjugator and achieved all this,
It dismantled the democracy that helped it achieve State bliss.

Without light, its darkness shrouded every land,
As nation by nation could no longer stand.
And this stifling State, it did so spread,
Leaving everything in its path dead.

The State's perfect and righteous ideology was then publically declared,
In the name of Scientism and Collectivism, no one—nothing—was
spared.
The individual must prostrate himself before State science and the
collective,
This is how the State justified every atrocity and every new directive.

The State's official name, the Occidental Union, was the perfect fit,
As the Occidental Union devoured all the Occident before it,
Subsuming and homogenising all other peoples and cultures,
The few remaining scraps swallowed whole by the State-entitled
vultures.

Omniscient, omnipotent, omnipresent—it feared naught,
Yet in nature's oldest trap the disdainful State was caught.
For mankind's arrogance will eventually bow,
To nature's eternal and unbreakable vow:
The Red Queen rules the universe;
Entropy is her only curse.

And everything will fail,
For this is nature's tale.

Jump forward more than one hundred years, and this brings us to the
dysfunctional present—where crime and insecurity, conflict and
atavism, have replaced peace and security, cooperation and stability.
Liberty, free trade, the rule of law, the protection of individual rights,
and the respect of person and property and the fruits of one's labour are
distant memories, perhaps even ridiculed ideals.

But the State, facing annihilation, has declared war. One State official, a Sci–Coll Party member who spoke on the condition of anonymity, said, "Things haven't gone to plan, and in hindsight we've made one mistake after another. We now have no option, however. The Occidental Union is collapsing. And if you think I am joking, then try visiting District Five, formerly known as the United States. I dare you. It will be your final journey."

The Party member then described the "ultimate solution" to all of society's troubles: "Seriously, we've run out of options. Future generations will look back at us and say only one thing: we saved society, because we used and released this new technological marvel—the ultimate solution. Why won't the future generations say anything else? Because if we don't use this new technological marvel, the ultimate solution that Worldwide Industries & Finance Co. developed at the State's request, then there will be no future generations. Society will crumble, and we will slaughter each other. So there is no public debate. This is a necessity. It is the ultimate solution to all of society's troubles; it is the ultimate solution to the problem of individuality. And we—the State, the experts—are going to do what's necessary to save society, to save the people, to save our beloved Occidental Union. In the name of Scientism, Collectivism, and the Occidental Union—one State, all men."

So what's this incredible "ultimate solution" that will save society? It is a "new technological marvel" called …

But the rest of the article refuses to load. The screen remains frozen just before the article reveals the name of the "new technological marvel". So I turn the tablet off and on and then reload the article, yet this time the article freezes as it loads. And, finally, the link dies altogether. The article, and everything associated with it, vanishes. Someone or something, most likely a Cleaner software agent, has deleted it.

Although the name of the new technological marvel remains a mystery, I try instead to unearth more information by plugging the article's title and other key words into an online search engine. But all my searches fail to produce anything useful.

Irritated with technology's fickleness, I grab a pillow and slam it against the wall. Anup wakes up and whimpers his distress.

"It's okay, boy," I say, as I massage his ears to calm him down. "You haven't done anything wrong. I'm angry with something else. Go back to sleep, Nups. Sleep and dream of curious smells and tasty treats."

And, within a few seconds, Anup shuts his eyes and resumes his sleep.

I then recall the conversation I had with Dr Tawfik. He talked about a highly confidential project, United We Fall, which the State had contracted Worldwide Industries & Finance to work on. A project that scared him. A project to restore the State's power. A new technology to control all the world's people. A new technology that would be trialled first on the despised people of the Free Islands. Is United We Fall the same project as the "new technological marvel", which is described as the "ultimate solution" in *The Indymedia Daily*? And what about Bulla's death? Does it have anything to do with this new technology or the ultimate solution?

More than ever, I need to uncover the truth. What is this new technological marvel?

~~~~~

Nightmares haunt my sleep, and I wake up in the middle of the night paralysed. My legs and arms refuse to respond to my commands. My body feels like a dead weight. I cannot even turn my head. My eyes are open, though, and I am gazing ahead. Something shadowy and menacing is lurking at the foot of my bed. Although I can glimpse the figure in my peripheral vision, I cannot move my eyes and focus on it. For my eyes are locked, immobilised, just like the rest of my body. I fight. I struggle. I plead with my body. But I am powerless. My body ignores me. It feels alien. And "I"— that self-conscious and experiencing being—seem so insignificant, like a passing side effect soon to redissolve into the black fabric of space and time whence my "I"ness emerged.

Yet the figure is persisting right there. Motionless, floating, watching. An amorphous blackness. Darker than the night. More threatening than anything I have ever experienced. What is it? And why is Anup sleeping? Why is he not attacking it?

It wants me. I can sense this now. It abhors me. It wishes to consume me. It is pure evil.

I try to shout out to Anup—*Help me, Anup! Please, Anup, save me! Kill it!*—but the words are forming in my mind, not on my tongue and lips.

My heart is now racing and pumping harder than I can bear. If the intruding entity does not devour me, then I shall probably suffer a heart attack. Yet the shadow does not advance. It remains floating threateningly just outside my central vision.

With renewed determination, I concentrate all my willpower on moving my head. It turns slightly; then, bit by bit, I regain control of all my body. I sit up and snap on the light and ready myself for a fight. Yet nothing is levitating in the corner. Apart from Anup, the room is empty.

But how can this be? I was awake; I am sure of this. I was awake, *and* I saw a dark hostile figure hovering at the foot of the bed. I even felt it. Something inhuman. Not animal, either. But *something*, nonetheless.

What was it? Was it real? Or am I losing my mind?

The night has assumed a new feel: fear fills the atmosphere. Menacing figures now skulk in every corner of the apartment. It reminds me of my childhood, when monsters hid in dark places waiting for the right moment to pounce on me.

Sleep eludes me, so I patrol the apartment for imagined or unimagined threats. After searching every inch of the place and finding nothing, I decide to call the ghost hunt off. Yet that shadowy terror still torments my mind.

~~~~~

INTERLUDE

Handbook for Occidental Union Administrators
Philosophical Foundations for a Sci–Coll Worldview

Article 46: Man-Animal

You begin to die from the moment you are born. Yet this fact only becomes crippling, once you gain awareness of its implications later in life. When you understand the meaning of "I", at the point of self-awareness, then you begin to dread that instant when the "I" shall cease to exist.

Deny it, delay it, or deride it, you *will* eventually die. For you are animal. You share a common ancestry and a similar lifecycle with all other animals. You eat. You excrete. You breed. You die. You rot. The same as all other animals. But you, *man-animal*, adorn yourself with layers of illusions and delusions to try to escape from this inescapable burden. Perhaps you endure a greater curse than all other animals, because you appear to be the only animal that can grapple with its death and nonexistence. Other animals enjoy the luxury of not knowing, of living in the blissful ignorance of the here and now. For man, however, you live in constant terror, in the eternal shadow of death. And this unending horror has twisted your mind.

Perhaps one might compare this psychological assault with the Stockholm syndrome, where hostages grow to like their captors and sympathise with them. Such battered victims have even died defending their abusers. So maybe humans have developed a similar relationship with death. Death, and its perpetual presence, has battered you into willingly defending it. Although you cannot vanquish death, you can change your attitude towards your captor. And, as a result, you create mentally soothing myths to deal with death. No other book has influenced man more than the book of death.

Occidental researchers have tried to view human history through the evolution of this death syndrome. Analysing countless studies, they have identified one question that has always gripped humans and humanity, whether in the past or the present: how do we reconcile our existence with our annihilation?

Maybe an eternal, timeless, immaterial, omnipotent, and benevolent god might do the trick. So you create god in your own image—but instead of saying humanity created god in its image, you announce that god created man in his image. You then claim that god planted in man an immortal and immaterial soul—a mysterious and undetectable substance melded with yet separate from man's material body. But what about all the other animals? Does each animal also have an eternal soul? An eternal existence? No, for god has blessed only man with an eternal soul and an eternal life. And this move is necessary, because you need to distance yourself from animal. That is the whole point of the exercise. For you are now no longer animal. Unlike all these miserable mortal creatures, you have unshackled yourself from the decaying material world and triumphed over death. You are man, god's chosen one. Special. Eternal. Immortal.

How you despise the animal lurking in you. You hate it for what you think it means: death, decay, despair. And you would do anything to remove this indelible stamp from your being. *Animal be gone! God be! Death be vanquished!* you say.

But along comes the enlightenment and the birth of the scientific method. And one man, in particular, shatters your faith in god and an immortal soul: Charles Darwin. Myth slayer. Revelation exterminator. Now, you cannot deny your animal heritage, nor can you reject your animal nature. You are animal, yes, but it is much worse than that. For you also share a common descent with all other animals. You are right in the mortal mess of things. The stench of death surrounds you.

And you have returned whence you started—back to man-animal.

Still, few people can absorb this indigestible truth, so witness the birth of the liberal humanist. You now claim a fresh myth and a new god to sustain the ego. The myth is progress; the god, humanity itself. Though man has evolved from animal, he differs from every other species. For man possesses something that no other animal shares: reason. And reason can save humanity. Reason applied correctly and consistently to all human endeavours can lead to progress. Progress can tame nature and mould her into something benign. Progress can forge utopia. Perhaps progress can even triumph over animal and death. In some techno-surreal futuristic world, man can once again reclaim his immortal throne, stamp his authority over the cowering cosmos, and proclaim himself god of everything.

Yes, you say smugly to yourself, no other animal resembles man. Man is unique. Man is special. Man perches on top of the evolutionary tree. For unlike every other animal, the reason-gifted man can shape his own future. The new man, or superman, can progress where no animal has gone before. Mortal man-animal can be immortal *man-god*, once again.

And wallowing in hubris, you declare yourself the pinnacle of evolution. You go further still: you announce that the new man is post-evolutionary man. Evolution no longer restrains you, since you have progressed beyond nature and evolution. You have redesigned your biology and genetic make-up. You have built megacities and removed nature from the natural equation. You have deconstructed the cosmos and reconstructed it in the image of man-god.

But gaze at all the life around you and take note: you are *not* the pinnacle of evolution. All present-day life—this includes you—has evolved from the one common ancestor, which means all life has been evolving for an equal length of time. In other words, every single creature alive today is just as evolved as its neighbour. Complete evolutionary equality. So the trillions of bacteria residing in and on you are just as evolved as you. The flies buzzing around your head are just as evolved as you. And the pond scum inhabiting your local waterway is just as evolved as you. Evolution has no peak; all animals are created equal.

Instead of producing the first humanist, Darwin gave birth to the animist—and animism was the primordial religion meshing man with animal and nature. What an ironic conundrum for the human trying to free himself from the animal dwelling within and neutralise all its beastly implications.

Animal you are, once again.

And isolating yourself from your animal heritage and your fellow animals will only end in disaster. For you need other species to survive. Without microbes, plants, and animals, you lose your food, health, wealth, and consumer goods. That is, you perish. But without you, all other animals can survive—indeed, thrive.

You depend on more than just other species for survival, though. Today, embracing progress, you have chosen the path of never-ending scientific and technological change. You need novel medicines. You need more consumer good. You need enhanced shelters. You need constantly advancing materials. You need increasingly powerful computers. You need smarter phones. You need bigger factories. You need more efficient industrial farming, improved mass slaughter techniques. You need ever evolving militaries. You need greater energy. You need new technology to fix the destruction of old technology. You need *newer* technologies to fix the destruction of the new technologies. And your needs keep growing faster and faster every single day. You have entered into the Red Queen's race. And if you stop running—stop producing stuff and cease expanding your industries—then you will face annihilation. Billions of humans will instantly die. For scientific, and technological, progress now determines your collective fate.

But what progress? Are you not doing the same things your primitive ancestors were doing for tens of thousands of years? Are you not doing the same things that other animals have been doing for billions of years? You eat, excrete, breed, die, and rot—though you need a million more resources, gadgets, narratives, and ideological systems to complete these same simple tasks. This lifecycle will always remain fixed, even if you think yourself more advanced or civilised or progressive than those who passed before you. And whether you are religious or irreligious, reasonable or unreasonable, animist or humanist, you will still struggle to survive and thrive like every other animal. Your worldview changes nothing.

Narratives based on "salvation" or "progress" will always remain useful fictions to numb your pained mind, make your life "meaningful", and separate you from your animal essence. Eliminate these illusions, though, and you are confronted with this raw truth: despite being enslaved in a finite body, you are an infinite mind yearning to make sense of a perplexing yet terrifying reality. A reality that also happens to be pointless, purposeless, meaningless. However you try to frame it, this universe ruled by randomness cares nothing for you or your delusions of grandiosity. You, like all the other animals, are alone and insignificant.

The most you can hope for is to die quickly and mercifully. But even here, the senseless cruelty weaved into the fabric of this apathetic cosmos means you will probably die a slow and nasty death—the last insult to your absurd life. A special and unique individual? Nothing of the sort. You are doomed animal.

So go ahead and fill your days with whatever helps you to forget your ludicrous life and your destiny with death. Have sex. Buy colourful clothes. Think pleasant thoughts. Surround yourself with pretty things. Gorge on good food. Travel the world. Do religion. Have faith in god, a heavenly saviour. Claim an immortal soul. Do liberal humanism. Believe in progress, an earthly saviour. Seek utopia. Enslave and torture and kill other animals. Keep on clicking your mouse and tapping your tablet. Watch silly shows and feel-good movies. Read self-help books. Wonder about how special you are. Self-actualise. Delude yourself. In short, flood your lifecycle—from birth to death—with whatever makes you feel non-animal, immortal, and superior to nature. And reproduce and reproduce and reproduce, until you swamp the Earth with humans and drive other species to extinction. Then, you can choke yourself to annihilation.

But, in your rarer instants of anguish, when reality has stripped you of all your pomposity, then remember this: you are still animal. Man-animal.

Recommendations for Occidental Union Administrators

As Occidental Union Administrators, we need to accept that the previous information applies to the majority of people—even today. The knowledge and denial of death has shaped our collective human development, and the knowledge and denial of death continues to shape the individual's development. Our greatest mistake would be to ignore this death syndrome. The Occidental population, no matter how hard we try, will never come to grips with death and a random meaningless universe. The masses will always seek escape from pointlessness, annihilation, and their animal nature. For few people can grasp or accept the concept of existential nihilism. Man-animal fears and despises his absurd mortal existence.

Administrators, on the other hand, should embrace existential nihilism. Though life lacks meaning and death is guaranteed, we are free to be. Nihilism is liberating. A random universe means no purpose and no absolute morality: no good or bad, no right or wrong, no should or ought to.

If we examine history, we discover how "morality" has changed over the centuries and differed from culture to culture. Take homosexuality. In different places and at different times, various cultures have considered homosexuality either "immoral" or "moral", according to the majority consensus. And we find the same cultural shift in countless "moral" categories, from sexual norms to slavery and human rights. "Morality" is pluralistic. It never progresses, because it has no end point to progress to. "Morality" changes with time and from culture to culture.

So we can reduce "morality" to *normative conventions* that are endorsed by the majority—and these normative conventions differ with time and from place to place.

Although "morality" does not exist, accepted conventions do exist. And they emerge as soon as two individual animals (man-animal or other animal) cross paths. Conventions help lubricate social interactions by maintaining stability and enhancing predictability.

Without conventions, society would collapse. For instance, we need *informal* conventions guiding language and communication, and *formal* enforced conventions regulating law and order, trade and property. Such informal and formal conventions form the foundation of society.

As Administrators who plan and micromanage every aspect of the individual and society, we must perfect the science of creating and enforcing conventions. We must ensure that conventions—and their subsequent elicited *actions*—produce the least suffering for the greatest number of beings. For this is the only way to forge a stable society.

Every Administrator must also digest this truth: action—constant yet pointless change—governs the universe. God, purpose, progress—these are all just illusions conjured up by the ignorant and the desperate. But once we confuse action and constant change with purpose and progress, then we fall into the trap of denying reality and our animal nature. We move from man-animal to man-god, and thus unleash all the damage associated with this subtle change of mindset.

Despite the universe lacking *ultimate* meaning and purpose, islands of *proximate* meaning and purpose have

197

arisen from this ocean of futility. We see a similar paradox emerging from the second law of thermodynamics. Although our closed universe is moving inevitably towards greater entropy and disorder, pockets of increasing order have bucked the trend and emerged from the landscape of increasing disorder. Now, why local meaning should arise from a meaningless universe, and why local order should emerge from universally increasing disorder, continues to baffle us. But for our purposes here, we are only interested in the consequences of these phenomena. Meaning and purpose do exist at the local level of life, even though the greater universe lacks any ultimate meaning or purpose. So we live a meaningful and purposeful life, despite inhabiting a meaningless and pointless universe. A paradox, indeed.

As a result, we can only embrace nihilism at a universal or bigger-picture level. Yet, at the local level of life, we need a practical philosophy to plan, administer, and micromanage individuals and society. Sci–Coll, Scientism–Collectivism, is our local philosophy of politics and society. For the pursuit of scientific knowledge and the mastery of nature define the Occidental Union. These aims provide us with our proximate purpose, and to achieve them we have to collectivise and subjugate society to our will.

We have now defined the Occidental Union's proximate purpose and shown that the universe, having evolved from randomness and physical necessity, is ultimately meaningless. From both these points, we arrive at the following conclusion: Occidental Union Administrators should dismantle all barriers that prevent the pursuit of scientific knowledge; that is, every avenue of scientific research must be explored. We should even pursue research that carries a risk of human extinction—or total Earth life annihilation. For if life is a random occurrence, and if morality is just a matter of convention, then no argument can refute our position or block a programme of unrestricted scientific research. We can present this logic in the following way. First, conventions are what we, the Administrators, declare—and we declare that all life can be sacrificed and that no convention should inhibit scientific research. And, second, life on Earth has arisen from randomness and universal physical laws, which suggests that the process may not be unique or difficult to replicate. So if we were accidently to obliterate life on Earth, then life would probably re-emerge randomly elsewhere in the universe. We might even expect life to re-evolve here on Earth, at a later time.

Therefore, no good arguments exist for restricting any form of scientific research. No risk is too great—not even death or the annihilation of all Earth life.

~~~~~

5

The red fog blankets everything, and I am unable to see a couple of metres ahead. The surrounding trees and shrubs look like blurred-red shadows. Even Anup, who is next to me, is a hazy scarlet.

A sickly-sweet metallic odour also lingers in the predawn air. It is as thick as the red mist, and the combination of the two are overwhelming. I feel possessed, as if some unseen entity were wrapping itself around me and penetrating every part of my body.

I lift my hand and stare at a shapeless red blob. I then wave my arm through the red fog, and it parts in response. After a second, it recollects and appears to swallow my arm. The fog seems to be alive, for it is collecting around my arm and enveloping it. I inspect the fog closer and notice tiny particles clinging to my arm and climbing up it.

Is such a thing possible? Of course not. The bloody fog is just playing tricks on me. Nothing more. It is a red fog, and no red particles are scrambling up my arm.

But what is this early-morning fog? Why is it so thick? And why red? Is it possible for fog to bleed like this?

I have never experienced anything like this before. A surreal dawn. A glowing eerie red mist. It unsettles me.

The red fog also perturbs Anup. And even though he is unleashed and free to roam the coastal park, he remains glued to my side. He begins to whimper and rubs his head against my thigh—his way of saying *something is wrong*.

"I know, Nupy," I say, while patting and reassuring him.

Anup's whimpering changes to growling. He freezes and pricks his ears. Something apart from the red fog is disturbing him. Yet I can neither see nor hear anything.

An unnatural silence haunts the park. At this early hour, the birds should be singing and squawking as they start their daily routines. But not today. Nothing stirs. Nothing squeaks. Everything, including the air, is deathly still. Something is wrong.

A distant rustle.

"Anup, shhh!" I whisper, as I place my hand around his muzzle.

I listen for even the faintest noise—but I hear nothing. And although Anup is gazing ahead, indicating that something is hiding in the barely visible shrubs, I see nothing. I sense something is wrong, though, and I clench my machete, its familiar handle comforting me. I feel secure with Anup at my side and my machete at the ready.

A twig snaps. Closer than the previous rustle.

I glance at the direction of the sound and strain to see the culprit—yet nothing emerges from the thick red fog. Just more thick red fog. And then the silence returns, the still air and opaque red mist augmenting its absoluteness.

Anup shakes free from my clasp and begins to growl again. It is guttural and angry. My feeling of security disappears and is replaced with dread. Something is stalking us—something big enough to snap a twig. And this something fears neither man nor dog.

A surge of adrenaline rushes through my body. My mouth dries up, and I start to tremble in response to the fight-or-flight hormone flooding my cardiovascular system. Anup, reacting to my fear, also begins to quiver.

Another rustle—but this time the noise emerges from behind us. I can feel my heart thumping in my chest. My hands are sweating, making it difficult to grasp the machete.

A second later, a weird human–animal sound surfaces from the same vicinity of the rustle. Yet nothing appears. Just the heavy scarlet mist.

I drop my backpack and seize the second machete, as the threatening sounds inch closer and surround us.

Anup looks puzzled. He turns nervously to face every new noise, snapping this way and that way but always remaining glued to my side. His growls become barks; his barks, yaps. His brave-faced façade is slipping.

The threatening noises draw nearer—fearlessly, relentlessly homing in on us.

The red fog is even heavier now, and I can barely see one metre ahead. Despite this, I glimpse something weaving its way through the trees. The thing zooms in on us but then fades away as swiftly as it materialises. Another red shape materialises, darts towards us, and disappears. And then another and another, from every direction. It is an ambush—too many of them.

My heart beats faster and harder as their game continues for what feels like several minutes. They are testing Anup and me—sniffing out our weaknesses and trying to wear us down. They are hunting us, and they will attack if they can ferret out an opportunity, an opening. But if we run, we die. For nature's ancient law dictates this. Anup and I must confront our attackers. Here, now, we make our stand. And it is as good a place and time as any. So I hold my ground and swing my machetes—with all my might—at every fleeting scarlet spectre.

With every thwarted attack I grow more confident, and my fear quickly turns into rage. It is my right to fight; it is the natural right of every living creature to defend its body, and property, against an aggressor. My strengthened will also triggers something primaeval within Anup. He instinctively grasps our predicament. He understands the ancient natural law, too. He knows his rights. For we have evolved from the same seed, the same Word, the same bit of information: *it from bit*. All life is one, and one rule binds all life. Anup's fear then turns into rage, and his growls rumble, once more, with the authority of a top predator.

Sensing our increasing strength, several red spectres dart simultaneously towards us in a final and desperate attempt to overcome us. Although they coordinate their strike, they have misjudged the psychological timing. A mental switch has snapped, and Anup and I wield the power. Both my machetes slice through different attackers, and Anup sinks his canines into one after the other. A collective shriek penetrates the air. A hasty retreat follows. And the silhouettes recede into the dense fog.

The red tide has turned. Anup and I have won this battle.

Although silence reclaims the park, it lasts only for a short time. A few minutes later, the birds begin their singing and life resumes its routine. The Sun's first golden rays pierce the heavy red fog, and within moments it scatters and then vanishes. Despite the early hour, I can already feel the Sun's warmth. It is going to be another hot spring day. I take a deep breath and savour the surprisingly fresh air. Even the sickly-sweet metallic odour has vanished along with the mist.

Oddly, I feel good. The ambush is a faded memory.

~~~~~

Anup and I leave the coastal park and travel west into the heart of the metropolis. We are heading for the Scientific Facility, a massive structure owned by Worldwide Industries & Finance. There, I might uncover some truths about the new technological marvel, before departing from this metropolis forever. Although the journey to the Facility will take roughly two hours by foot, I can already see the destination glinting in the distance.

"Nups, say farewell to this park and our home, because this will be the last time we see them. We're leaving this city for good. We're going to find greener pastures, a new land to call home. This place is now too dangerous, and it is only going to get more brutal and depraved as the final remnants of the State collapse."

Anup stares at me quizzically. He lets out a chipmunk-like sound.

"I just hope we can make it out of the city alive," I mumble to myself, recalling yesterday's riots.

Countless smoke plumes dominate the city's landscape; many buildings must still be ablaze from the mob violence. But despite this, I fail to detect a single sign of human life. A suffocating silence surrounds the metropolis, and the local streets lack human activity. The place is a ghost town.

As soon as we hit the first major square, though, I notice it: the weirdness. Hundreds of people are immobilised. Many are standing motionless. A few are crouched or sitting down. Others are sprawled awkwardly across the ground. Yet all remain perfect statues. It reminds me of Bulla's condition.

Nearing the first frozen collective, I grab my machete and prepare myself for the Occidental's usual violence. But Anup, just as curious as me, rushes towards the nearest group before me.

"Anup! No!" I command, in a hushed tone, not wanting to draw any attention. "Come here, *now*!"

After a few seconds of deliberation, Anup accepts my command and then joins me while whimpering his unease with the unsettling scene. I stroke his coat, and this calms both of us. Despite the din, however, not a single person reacts to our presence. Just silence and stillness.

Anup and I approach cautiously the inanimate group. Still no movement, not even a twitch, from a single person. So I poke the nearest upright person with my machete's tip. No reaction. The woman's eyes are dull; her breaths, rapid and shallow. Barely alive, she appears to be paralysed. I touch her arm. The red-tinged skin is clammy, and her muscles are hardened—knotted—just like Bulla's. I know that tetanus, a bacterial disease caused by *Clostridium tetani*, causes muscle rigidity. But spasms accompany the involuntary muscle contractions caused by tetanus. These people's muscle contractions are different, however. The woman's muscles are solidified, without any spasms. And her flesh feels like concrete—as if she were dipped in resin and then left to set. I have never seen or heard of anything like this.

An adolescent stands next to the woman. I prod him with my machete. No response, similar to the woman. I nudge him a little harder, and this time he begins to wobble like an unsteady bottle. After a couple of seconds, he topples to the ground while maintaining the same ossified shape. He stays where he has fallen. But the crash has disturbed something, and an angry buzz fills the air. And then I detect it—the unmistakable stench of putrefying flesh. The Nightmare has struck this adolescent. I investigate several other human statues and notice that many are either infected with The Nightmare or dead. It appears that paralysis is the first step in this disease process, with death the inevitable outcome.

Terrified, I leash Anup and hurry away from this graveyard, before its deadly mystery infects me. But if the unknown agent is airborne and contagious—and all the clues do hint at this—then it may be too late. I might already be infected.

~~~~~

While marching west, towards the Scientific Facility, I puzzle over what I have just witnessed. Were those paralysed people aware of my presence? Though their eyes were locked, this might have been because they were unable to move them. It does not mean the people were unconscious, for they might have been paralysed yet conscious. Consider *tetrodotoxin*, a neurotoxin produced by bacteria living in certain fish species such as pufferfish. If this potent toxin were to be ingested, inhaled, or injected, it would paralyse the subject while leaving the person aware of the surroundings. The condition resembles a living death, a zombielike existence. So perhaps the paralysed people in the town square are experiencing something similar.

Yet why would the Occidental Union aerosolise a deadly toxin? For what purpose? Although the Administration is parasitic and lives off the people without giving them anything in return, a parasite needs a weakened yet *healthy* host to drain slowly and continuously. A dead host provides no ongoing free benefits. So the Administration, from its point of view, should be striving to forge a docile and compliant host population. The Administration must also avoid killing its workers—because if they die, it dies. Consequently, the perfect mind-moulding tool should weaken the will and make the people more submissive and manageable. But the current plague sweeping the land and killing the people is failing to achieve these ideal parasitic goals.

In any event, no known disease or environmental toxin could have caused that strange muscle rigidity.

Whether it is a failed experiment to control the people or something else, the entire scourge stinks of project United We Fall and the Occidental Union's new technological marvel.

~~~~~

In contrast to yesterday's chaos, the streets are hushed—not even a birdsong breaks the surreal serenity. Every so often, though, I hear a scream or a moan echo throughout the ghostly metropolis, and even less often I bump into a person wandering aimlessly. A few paralysed or dead humans are scattered across the city but nothing like the macabre scene in the square.

Decaying buildings line every street, each structure blending with the other. A homogenous strip of dirty-grey concrete and shattered windows. But nothing stirs inside the countless apartment blocks. No vagrants, no residents, no State officials.

Sad, spent, squalid—this is the metropolis. The public transport system, which consisted of a metro and light rail, shut down many months ago. We awoke one day and all services had stopped, without even a warning. But just until a couple of days ago, State emergency and essential services—paramedics, peace officers, sanitation officers—

were responding sporadically to calls. Today, however, they are all absent. Like the apartment blocks, nothing moves on the streets.

Private transport, including motorised and nonmotorised vehicles, was banned and eliminated before I was born. In the name of safety, and to reduce emissions, the Occidental Union announced the final phase of human transportation: a completely public and environmentally friendly mass transit system. Yet the underlying motives were obvious: power and paternalism. For unlike the citizen-serving governments of the Free Islands, the Occidental State fails the good governance test. The Occidental State has no interest in the flourishing of its social and natural environments or in advancing peace and stability; rather, the State cares only about enhancing the power and wealth of a politically entitled few. And even though it camouflages its true selfish agenda in the benevolent language of "environmentalism" or the "social good", anyone who knows anything about history or politics should be able to see through the State's sleazy veneer.

Still, the State failed to eradicate or manipulate all traces of our history and culture, and I have read articles and seen documentaries about bicycles and private motor vehicles— wonders of the old system. Yet aside from my visit to the Free Islands, that is as close as I have come to such historical curiosities. So I rely on my feet to get around town. The State, despite its totalitarian ideology, has ironically taught me to be self-reliant.

The sages of the past valued self-reliance as a virtue, and I now grasp the meaning of their words: "Society everywhere is in conspiracy against the manhood of every one of its members ... The virtue in most request is conformity. Self-reliance is its aversion." Although Ralph Waldo Emerson wrote this in the nineteenth century, his wisdom still applies today. For Sci–Coll espouses one main virtue: conformity. And conformity results in reliance on others, on the collective. But I have never accepted Sci–Coll's so-called virtue as a true virtue. I guess self-reliance flows in my blood, because I enjoy accomplishing a goal on my own. I thrive on thinking through dilemmas as an individual. And no amount of indoctrination has been able to change my nature, my biology. They tried, from birth, to mould me into collectivist thinking, into adopting the verdict of a group of State-picked "social experts" as my own. They tried to homogenise my mind—and spirit—as they had done with the rest of the masses. But they failed.

I am an individual—a thinking man who rejects groupthink and demagoguery and authoritarian rulings, if they are irrational or offensive or simply wrong.

A primatologist once said that humans can behave in one of three ways: the chimpanzee way, the bonobo way, or the orang-utan way.

Chimpanzees live a hierarchical, patriarchal, and violent group existence. The troop is ruled by an alpha male who brutalises all those below him into submission. After the alpha, the beta male is in charge—and so it goes down the chain of command. This hierarchy applies to the females, too. An alpha female rules over those under her and so forth. Yet females also use sex as a bartering tool to win over the allegiance of multiple males. This strategy can help protect her life by pitting male against male.

However, this violent group existence becomes even more violent when different chimpanzee troops clash. Such encounters end in shocking cruelty and gruesome deaths. Allegiance to one's tribe exists in many species; humans are not the only animals who will kill, or even die, for the tribe.

Bonobos, in contrast to chimpanzees, live a hierarchical yet *matriarchal* group existence. Although violence does exist, it is much rarer than in chimpanzee communities and usually occurs when several leading females gang up on a rebellious male and bash him into obedience. Besides being ruled by a matriarch and living peacefully, the main difference between chimpanzees and bonobos lies in their sex life. Although female chimpanzees use one-on-one sex to curry favour with different *individual* males, bonobos engage in bisexual group sex to *collectively* cement relationships. These clashing behaviours give rise to the following motto: chimpanzees make war, not love, whereas bonobos make love, not war.

Then, there are the orang-utans. Although chimpanzees and bonobos survive in groups, orang-utans live a semi-solitary existence. They are social and peaceful, with fights erupting rarely. If friction does occur, it usually unfolds between two flanged males competing over a sexually receptive female. Yet even in such situations, males often decide on the "winner" through a dominance display instead of brawling.

So what do these three ways have to do with me? I live the orang-utan way. I am the social yet semi-solitary ape stuck in a society that sometimes resembles the chimpanzee way and other times the bonobo way. Individualism is planted in my biology, and self-reliance sprouts naturally.

~~~~~

"We'll rest here for ten minutes, boy."

Anup tilts his head as he grapples with the meaning of my words. He whines a melody of distress: *I cannot understand what you are trying to tell me*, I imagine him saying.

"It's okay, boy," I reply while scratching his rump, just above his tail.

This is the itchiest part of his body, and he sways ecstatically while emitting his little chirping noises.

"You are a funny little boy. Aren't you, Nupy? Yes, you are."

Anup unleashes a playful growl and jumps on me, knocking me to the ground. We rumble for a minute before calling it a draw. He then sits, lifts his right paw, and stares me in the eyes. Despite his seated position, his tail still manages to flick from side to side.

"Oh, you're hungry, Nups," I say, as I fumble a military ration from the backpack. "Look—I've got something special for you."

I open all the food compartments of the ration and place the tray on the ground. Anup sniffs it and then begins wolfing down the food. Long tongue strokes empty each compartment, and in less than two minutes the entire tray is clean.

"That tasty was it, Nupy? What a good boy. Here, have some water."

I remove a bottle from the backpack and pour some water into the tray's empty compartments. After lapping up all the water Anup lies down, exhausted yet content. He gives me a side glance and decides that I shall not disappear and that it is safe to get some shut-eye, for a minute or two. The warm sunshine simply sweetens the deal.

I also enjoy the break from all the morning's adventures. This is a tranquil place to rest, for we have stumbled across an old fountain nestled in the centre of a battered and vacant square. At the centre of the fountain's classical sculpture lies Pliny the Ancient, who adored basking in the Sun. A fifteen-metre-wide pond surrounds the fountain, and thousands of mosquitofish dart around the water under the cover of floating lily leaves. Every so often, an insect lands on the water's surface—and if it is lucky, it avoids becoming lunch for one of the voracious little fish patrolling underneath. Life is thriving in this little ecosystem, in the middle of this dying metropolis.

Life always finds a way to survive. Always. Why is that? How is that? Although no central Administrator has planned this pond paradise, life has nonetheless managed to mushroom and make the most of the mess.

What is this thing we call *life*? And why is it struggling to live, to spread, and to occupy any abandoned niche? What is the point, the purpose, of all this effort?

Despite my upbringing and previous certainty, I am beginning to doubt that life is meaningless pointless randomness.

The State and Sci–Coll and all the academics and intelligentsia have been drumming the same message into the people's heads, at every available opportunity: life has no aim, no purpose, no design. Meaning is just an elaborate illusion—a mind trick. If you believe there is more to life, then you are experiencing an *epiphenomenon*—a mental and illusory side effect that emerges from matter. For your mind has evolved to see meaning where there is no meaning. A child, for example, thinks a cave was designed for shelter, whereas an adult knows that a cave emerged as a natural side effect of erosion and land movement. And even though animals and people might use a cave for shelter, this is just a secondary use, or side effect, of a random and natural process. The cave, in reality, exists for no reason whatsoever. It formed randomly. Likewise, the universe—at its foundation—has no design, no intention, no purpose. Everything emerges as a side effect of randomness, of natural processes. Chance rules. There is just mindless matter: molecules in motion. This is the ultimate truth. Agents, like you and me, mean nothing—for we are mere epiphenomena, side effects of randomness and natural processes.

"We are just meat," says professor Katy Stevens, the greatest neuroscientist in the Occidental Union. "Values, reason, meaning, rationality, intentions, morality—all these are illusions, worthless side effects of random material processes. We are walking talking meat. Nothing more. Just meat."

So reality is absurd; sentience, a ridiculous side effect of meaningless matter.

But observing this pond full of life, my mind begins to question and reject Sci–Coll's lifelong indoctrination. Meaning does flood this pond; meaning *is* this pond. And matter appears to be the *vehicle*—perhaps even a side effect—of the information and higher meaning emerging from this pond. From an agent's point of view—that is, my point of view or the fish's—information and meaning form the foundation of life and reality, whereas matter and energy are just vehicles for sending and receiving information and for creating a rich and meaningful universe.

It from bit. A *bit* of information creates *it*—constructs matter. So *it* emerges from *bit*: matter emerges from information. And beings use this information to sculpt meaning. But if meaning were meaningless, then why would it mould matter in a meaningful manner? Meaning saturates the universe. Meaning shapes reality. Meaning is life. Without life, meaning does not exist; without meaning, life does not exist. Both complete the circle.

Sci–Coll's carefully crafted façade is cracking. Sci–Coll's micromanaged materialist society is crumbling. Sci–Coll's totalitarian mind-control prison is collapsing.

The degrading programme is being erased. The nightmare is ending. Sci–Coll is losing its grip on my mind, body, and soul.

"You are nothing," I can hear an Occidental Educator telling me. "You are a means to an end. You are not the end. You are neither special nor unique. You are a cog in the machine. Your concept of free will and 'I' is an illusion created by your mind—and your mind is an illusion projected by your brain. And your brain is meat. Your brain is matter. So you are just meat. You are just matter. Nothing more."

But I am starting to see the world clearly now. Although everything is collapsing around me, and I might have been exposed to a lethal pathogen or toxin, a sudden rush of joy engulfs me as I absorb the meaning of life. The feisty fish. The calming water. The lush green leaves. The sumptuous sculpture. The cool blue sky. The gentle and warm sunshine. My loyal, loving, and protective friend. The beauty. The richness. The symphony of life and meaning.

And, then, an insight strikes me: why this spontaneous order from the inevitable disorder? Why a pocket of increasing order—why *anti-entropy*—in a universe ruled by increasing disorder (increasing entropy)? If the unbreakable second law of thermodynamics says that entropy or disorder must increase with time in a closed system such as our universe, then why should life—which is an increasing-order or decreasing-entropy or anti-entropy process—arise and flow against the iron law of increasing disorder? This can be compared to a tiny stream suddenly springing up in the middle of a raging river and then flowing *against* the river's direction. So what gave rise to this countercurrent stream? This revolutionary programme we call life? This programme that conflicts with the second law of thermodynamics and the fabric of the cosmos? And who or what created this deviant programme—and for what purpose? Chance, *alone*, cannot account for life or increasing order or anti-entropy in a universe bound by increasing entropy over time. Chance fails to explain why pockets of increasing information should exist in a universe that annihilates information. For chance would *naturally* and *necessarily* lead to disorder or increasing entropy or loss of information over time: that is the ultimate point of the second law of thermodynamics. By chance, or randomness, the entire universe must increase in entropy with time— must become more disordered and contain less usable energy over time. The universe must lose information and become meaningless in the long run.

No. In a universe governed by increasing entropy, the sudden appearance of antithetical decreasing entropy—life from randomness, order from disorder—must be accounted for using an explanation other than randomness alone. To quote chance as the source of anti-entropy would be absurd—a self-defeating explanation. And this is impossible. Sci–Coll's explanation is not an *explanation*. It may be a partial *description* of the unfolding physical processes, but that is it.

Sci–Coll, however, is not interested in unlocking the truth. It has another agenda: to reduce all the universe and everything in it to a simple material process—a single mathematical equation that captures yet diminishes the complexity of life, reality, and the cosmos. To achieve this aim, Sci–Coll tweaks the data and conclusions to avoid mentioning any evidence for beings, agency, intelligence, design, goals, purpose, reason, rationality, or meaning. For all these so-called epiphenomena—or illusions or side effects of matter—are the enemy of Sci–Coll and its ultimate pursuit of nihilism.

But to express in words why a car exists, say, requires two answers. First, we need to *describe how* the physical processes allow the car to exist. The scientific method, based on physical laws and particle motion, rules this domain. Second, we must also *explain why* the car exists. Without agents—intelligent beings with needs and desires—a car would fail to exist. For the processes and machinery behind car manufacture did not evolve from randomness and physical laws alone: they evolved from the actions of beings. Beings uncovered the underlying physical laws and mathematical equations. Beings mined the mineral resources. Beings built the factories and manufactured the car parts. Beings created the factory assembly lines. Beings forged the societies with economies of scale. Beings desired and bought cars and ignited the need for their manufacture to begin with. Yet without beings—without thinking and acting agents, without needs and desires, without meaning and purpose—no cars would exist. So a car exists because of physics *and* agency. The universe contains physics *and* agency.

Whether Sci–Coll realises it or not, its obsession with reducing everything to the *purposeless* motion of matter is, paradoxically, a *purpose* in itself. For Sci–Coll, despite pursuing the concept of nothingness and trying to force reality to conform to its nihilistic ideology, is pursing something. Sci–Coll's superficial meaninglessness betrays a deeper meaning.

Although I lack the answers to the mystery of life and reality, I now know that Sci–Coll is just as clueless as me— perhaps even more so. At least I abstain from displaying the Administration's arrogance and smug self-certainty, when faced with doubt and unknowability. Voltaire said, "Doubt is not a pleasant condition, but certainty is absurd." Yet every generation throughout history has believed—had faith—that they know, or can discover, the answers. Every generation has trumpeted the certainty of their knowledge. Every generation has fancied that it, unlike previous generations, now wields the tools to master nature and unearth all her deepest secrets. And every generation has failed. Our generation is no different. It will also fail, despite its certainty in Scientism.

I have accepted that humans, being a tiny subset of the universe, will never grasp the ultimate truth: the whole set of the universe. We have our limits, and they bind us to forever knowing just a fraction of reality.

Here, in this isolated pond of nothingness, life and meaning have emerged against impossible odds—and they bring a message of hope.

~~~~~

After an hour's walk, my destination looms ahead. The Scientific Facility is striking: a giant metallic pyramid, with each side exactly two thousand one hundred and eighty-five feet in length. The entire surface seems seamless. And even though the morning Sun is still weak, the pyramid shimmers with activity, for it is converting the sunlight into electricity.

Reports suggest that the Scientific Facility extends many kilometres underground. Some say that what we are seeing is just the tip of a superstructure stretching under the entire metropolis. Yet even if these reports were false, the above-ground pyramid, by itself, would still be an engineering wonder.

I gape at the behemoth before me and marvel at our predecessors' prowess to build such a structure. For the Scientific Facility is more than one hundred and thirty years old—the lasting product of the old system. We could never construct anything like this today. Just to maintain the pyramid challenges us, and I notice, on closer inspection, the countless cracked solar panels enveloping it. The Facility's functioning days are numbered, along with everything else in this metropolis.

As Anup and I near the pyramid, my tablet computer begins to vibrate. I tap on the new message, a link from *The Free Islands Telegraph*. The report, written by Adam Smithy, is titled "The Red Fog of Death":

To my fellow citizens of the Free Islands,

This will probably be my final report, because I have been exposed to the Red Fog of Death. That is the name our scientists have given to the dense red fog that is visible only during predawn and dawn. For once the Sun's rays strike this strange blood-coloured mist, it quickly vanishes. Unfortunately, our scientists have discovered little else about this deadly phenomenon. We, at The Free Islands Telegraph, have gleaned the following titbits from various scientific sources—may God save us all.

First, the Red Fog of Death is not a fog at all. Using electron microscopes, scientists have found that the Red Fog consists of exotic nanoparticles or nanodust—nanometre-sized particles that can be seen only with the most powerful microscopes. For comparison, the smallest known virus is about twenty nanometres, which is roughly twenty times as large as the average nanoparticle observed in the Red Fog of Death. So these nanoparticles are ridiculously tiny.

Second, and incredibly, the nanoparticles appear to be animate! They respond to their environment. They seem to communicate with each other and coordinate their actions. They have even been observed connecting with each other to form larger units. And they can replicate in any environment, even those lacking oxygen. Beyond this, the scientists know little. What do these nanoparticles want? Are they really alive? What do they consume? How do they communicate? What is their chemical composition? Where did they come from? Can they be stopped? Can they be killed? What is their purpose, if they have any?

Third, the nanoparticles are paralysing every animal they encounter. Scientists, however, remain clueless about the physical process. And although different animal species have different response times, every species eventually succumbs to the paralysis. With time, the paralysis then becomes a death sentence. Every animal ultimately stiffens like a rock and dies. Even plants, fungi, and microorganisms (such as bacteria) are not immune to the Red Fog of Death. In all these groups, the nanoparticles appear to dissolve the cell membranes or cell walls of the infected host cells—thereby killing the cells. In other words, the Red Fog of Death is attacking and killing all life—every *plant, animal, and microorganism on the planet. Everything, including humans.*

All life on the planet is being exterminated.

My brothers and sisters, we have reports coming in from various locations around the Free Islands that entire communities—and ecosystems—are dying. In the last few hours, we have even received similar reports from cities located in the Occidental Union.

The Red Fog of Death is annihilating everything—and it is happening all over Earth.

If you see the Red Fog of Death at dawn, then I am afraid your fate has already been determined. According to different sources, after exposure you will have between six hours and two days before you are paralysed. Death follows soon after the paralysis. Yet what about those people who do not see the Red Fog of Death at dawn? How can they tell if the nanoparticles are in their environment? Well, other symptoms do exist. Nausea, giddiness, hallucinations—all these have been reported. A few victims have also described a feeling of wellbeing, even under stressful circumstances. But these symptoms are anecdotal findings. Paralysis and certain death are the facts, however.

And I am sad to say that I saw the Red Fog of Death this morning. That was almost seven hours ago. So it seems I am now living on borrowed time.

Do I feel differnt? wll, yes an no. i guess i shuld be mor upsett butt im not. aftwr all i m dyin. so. oh mu god! i i csnnot contril my .., o ni.!.d.f.f.kd.

~~~~~

Although I have always understood that I am a mortal being, for the first time in my life I am living a mortal existence. I am dying, and I am unable to change it. My life does not belong to me; it is only on loan. And the universe would like to reclaim its loaned property, soon. I collapse on the harsh concrete, and gawk at the monstrous pyramid facing me. It will stand here tomorrow, whereas I shall probably be dead. Extinct. All traces of me wiped out. As if I never existed. How can that be? It is incomprehensible, preposterous. One instant "I", the next instant—

How many times has death stalked me? How many times has the darkness threatened to consume me? How many times has the nothingness imperilled my mortality? Yet only now, with death's guarantee stamped on my soul, do I grasp the true meaning of this nonnegotiable contract: my time—my "I"ness—is almost concluded. I have a few more hours, perhaps a day or two at most, to engage with this world, with this body, with this mind. After that, in a flash, everything I have ever seen, heard, smelled, tasted, touched, known, hated, loved, experienced, and assimilated will be erased. I—my consciousness, my self-awareness— will evaporate. My reality will vanish; all reality will disappear. Everything will return to nothingness, a concept that even now I fail to grasp. I realise the nothingness has almost caught up to me, but I cannot imagine nothingness. For I am something. And something cannot be nothing, no matter how much that something tries to be nothing or tries to imagine nothingness. Nothingness is true meaninglessness, yet I am meaning. Perhaps visualising the temporary nothingness of sleep is the closest I can get to nothingness. What does sleep and its lack of consciousness feel like? But even this simulation is still something, for I am trying to experience sleep and its nothingness. I am trying to think about how it feels to be nonsentient and nonexistent. This is absurd, though, because "I" am still in the picture. *Something*—a sentient "I"—can never be *nothing*. The two ingredients resist merging into one.

The "meaning" and "message of hope" that I just found while pondering over the fishpond have faded away as quickly as they appeared. Absurdity and futility have supplanted them: the absurdity and futility of life, of sentience, of reality. I have been dying since the day I was born; there, in that one statement, I have captured the inanity of reality.

And what was it all for? *What?* To experience exceedingly rare moments of unsatisfying or temporary contentment—dare I utter the word "happiness"?—during a short and brutish struggle for existence?

But all life is facing my individual fate. We shall die together. The collective will become one—one individual—and perish in its final act of unity.

~~~~~

Anup is licking my neck and cheeks and trying his best to break my trance. Although I long to hug this warm inviting bundle of love, my mind is stunned and my body immobilised. But this is not the paralysis of the Red of Fog of Death. This is the paralysis of hopelessness, of emptiness, of defeat. I lack the will to move. What is the point?

And then Anup does what his instincts command and what I am hardwired to respond to: he starts chirruping like a fledgling and wriggling his body with joy. To entice me further, he flicks his tail and nudges my face with his moist muzzle.

I cannot resist his play any longer. I look into his expressive eyes and realise, then and there, that his devotion to me will end only with his last breath. His life is mine. He lives to please me. He adores me. I owe him so much.

I hug my dog, and for a moment I forget about the future. I lose myself in this instant of purity. The mid-morning spring sunlight feels good—a gentle breeze balancing its warmth. I am alive and happy. I adore these simple things. These good moments, they flood life. But rarely have I taken the time to sit back and absorb them. *This is life! now, here*—not yesterday, not tomorrow, not that memory, not that fantasy. And life is good— overwhelmingly good. How did I miss it? Why was I so self-absorbed? And now that I yearn to live more, to experience this goodness, how can I stretch out this instant forever? It is impossible. For everything passes. My emotions overwhelm me, and I begin to cry. And then I smile. And then I laugh. And then I sob some more. After several minutes my body begins to convulse, and I am soon drained of energy. The sadness and happiness end. I wipe the tears and mucus away.

Composed, I stand to face my destiny. The Scientific Facility beckons. I still need answers, and I shall find them in that monstrous pyramid.

And perhaps not all hope is lost. Perhaps a cure exists. Perhaps I shall find salvation in that pyramid. *Perhaps.*

Even now, faced with certain death, my mind refuses to accept reality. My mind has already gone into repair mode and is drip-feeding me *hope*. For how else can the infinite mind, trapped in a finite body, grapple with the concept of mortality?

Yet the question remains: *is it false hope?*

~~~~~

Although I used to work for Worldwide Industries & Finance, I have never entered its Scientific Facility. It is strictly off limits to everyone, except the highest-ranking employees of the company and the Occidental Union Administrators, who have access to every building in the land. I have, nonetheless, seen the pyramid many times from the outside, and the gates and doors have always been secured shut. Today, however, they are open, and no peace officers are protecting the entrance. The entire area lacks any sign of life or activity.

Anup and I approach the main eastern gate. Despite his reassuring presence, I decide to leave Anup outside the building. He may upset the peace, and I want answers, not problems. So I secure him to a pole and then step inside the pyramid.

Silence greets me. The place is empty: no security, no cameras, no reception desk, nothing. From the cloakroom-sized vestibule, I enter a long narrow corridor. A soft white light emanates from the floor, ceiling, and sidewalls—and everything seems to be constructed from this same lustrous metal. A gentle hum and a flowery fragrance also accompany the illumination. The ambience soothes me.

Numerous side corridors branch off the main one. Each side corridor ends in a cul-de-sac, though. I enter the first side corridor and touch its farthest wall. My fingers slide off the metal's velvety, almost frictionless, surface, and an instant later the white light emanating from the wall dims. A number then flashes on the centre of the wall: "012". After a few seconds the number fades away, and the light's intensity returns to normal. I repeat the same procedure with all the side corridors. Although different numbers materialise on each wall, nothing else happens. Every passage stays blocked.

Only one wall remains untried: the far end of the main corridor. So I approach the wall, which looks identical to the others, and I slide my finger across it. The number "000" takes shape. A few seconds later it disappears, and the entire wall slides open to reveal a cavernous chamber, roughly a hundred metres in length and width and height. It is stuffed with scientific equipment, and every surface is emitting the same soothing light as the corridor.

Dozens of scientists dressed in white laboratory coats are buzzing around the place. A few notice my presence but ignore me. They appear to be focusing all their energies on thousands of quartzlike objects, each approximately the size of a matchbox. On my left, however, three scientists are slumping lifelessly against work benches. And to my right, a few metres from the entrance, two others are staring at the ceiling. Both are motionless. Meanwhile, at the opposite end of the chamber, another scientist is screaming at no one in particular.

A beetlelike man in a yellow-stained coat scuttles towards me. He is barely the size of a twelve-year-old child.

"Do you not know that this place is forbidden to the likes of you?" he snaps, while pointing one of the quartzlike objects at me. "How dare you! *How dare you*! How dare you enter this spectacular erection of a building!"

I stare silently at the scientist.

He looks me up and down, left and right, before continuing with his inquisition: "Did you understand what I just said, you imbecile? Or are you as stupid as the rest of the serfs and *SS*?"

"Oh, I heard you," I reply nonchalantly. "I just don't give a damn."

"How dare you! *How dare you*!" he yells, as froth piles up over the corners of his mouth. He then begins jumping up and down, like a beetle trying to take flight. "*How dare you*! How dare you reply to me in such a manner, you slimy little maggot."

Smirking at the scientist, I say, "Tiny man, surely you know that it's all over, don't you? Surely you know that you have no authority here or anywhere else? Surely you know that the Occidental Union is finished? Surely you know that the State is gone? Yes, Sci–Coll is defunct, and the law no longer exists. So it's back to the state of nature, as Thomas Hobbes would say. And I'll do whatever the hell I want to do. And I'll go wherever the hell I want to go. And there is nothing you, or anyone else, can do about it. Understood?"

The silver-haired scientist glares at me. "B-b-b," he stammers, "but what about—"

"There is no *but* or *what*," I interrupt. "There is only this fact: the State has been toppled—and, with it, all authority has vanished. Including yours. Now, get over it, because we don't have much time left. Do you understand me?"

The scientist instantly deflates. After a few seconds he sighs. The truth, which he already knows, is sinking in.

"Yes, yes, you are right—I suppose," he says, while relaxing his muscles and slumping his shoulders. "I guess it *is* all over. I am just so used to, well, so used to, to, to—"

"To the old routine, to what is now the old system," I say, helping him find the correct words.

"Yes, that would be correct, I presume. I am used to our system, which is now the old system, I guess. The old routine—it is concluded, finished. Oh, dear. Oh, my! The Occidental Union is dead! I cannot fathom such a disaster. It, it, it is incomprehensible, unacceptable, outrageous! How dare it! How dare it."

The scientist then keels over and shakes his head while making grinding beetlelike noises. This continues for more than a minute.

After recollecting himself, he says, "I simply cannot believe it. I simply cannot imagine that in a couple of days there will be nothing left. Nothing! Can you imagine such a preposterous outcome? Why, it is downright barbaric. Barbaric!"

I nod my head but refrain from responding. I grant him his moment of grief and disbelief. But even with all his bellowing, not a single scientist glances in our direction.

The system really has collapsed. Without the State and its contracts, little binds these strangers together.

"So what is your story?" the scientist eventually asks me. "Why are you here?"

"I'm looking for answers. I *need* answers, and I think this is where I'll find them."

"Answers?" he says, while raising his bushy monobrow. "Answers pertaining to what specifically? Perhaps I may be of assistance to you."

"Yes, perhaps you might be—or if not you, the person in charge of this facility."

The scientist sniggers.

"*My* name is Dr JJ Russoo," he announces, crooking his head up, "and I am the Chief Scientific Officer in charge of Section Forty-Seven. I am responsible for preparing all quartz data storage units for ejection into space. Thus, if I lack the required expertise, then I am afraid to say that no one else here will have the answers."

"Then, I guess, I have found the right man," I say, astonished at my good fortune, which is a rarity. "But what is it that you are in charge of exactly? I've never heard of such a thing as a 'quartz data storage unit'."

"Of course, you would not have heard of such a high-tech and confidential project," Dr JJ Russoo replies, while crooking his head up even higher and looking down on me. "This is an emergency, and we are in crisis control. We are in the process of saving all this planet's history—all its natural and manmade history—on to quartz data storage units. And, as we speak, hundreds of Worldwide Scientific Facilities around the globe are engaging in this project. We are also imprinting genomes, the DNA sequences of tens of thousands of species, on these quartz storage units."

"But why?"

"Because these quartz storage units are almost indestructible, and they will last for hundreds of millions of years—even under the harshest conditions of interstellar-space travel. After saving the Earth's vital information, we shall then rocket all the quartz units into space—thousands of quartz units fired into every direction of space. Imagine such an accomplishment! Utterly magnificent! We are gods!"

I glower at the pathetic little beetle-man, while trying to hide my disgust at his deluded arrogance. People like him destroy the world and then claim they are saving it.

"Please forgive me, Russoo," I say, "but I'm still confused. For you haven't answered my question. Again, why would you want to do such a thing? Why would you save all this information on to quartz units and then launch them into space? What is the purpose of this exercise?"

"Well, is it not obvious?" he responds.

"No," I answer.

"We want to make sure that the Earth's life lives beyond this planet, even if it were to exist just in the form of pure information. You see, comrade, these quartz units will travel to every corner of this galaxy—and they will carry with them the information needed to recreate Earth life. This includes the genetic information required to reconstruct man. Think of this project as an insurance policy. If an advanced alien civilisation were to exist now or in the future, then they might chance upon our quartz data units in space and learn about the Earth. And who knows—maybe if they were technologically advanced enough, then they might be able to reconstruct us. Therefore, this project represents humanity's final testament. It is Earth life's final will."

"So, Russoo," I say, assimilating all the information, "you have been preparing for humanity's final testament and Earth life's final will? So Worldwide Industries and the Occidental Union Administrators have known about the Red Fog of Death—the nanoparticles—all along? So this destruction is all your doing? This tragedy is the State's doing? In other words, you people are responsible for unleashing the Red Fog of Death and condemning all life to death?"

"The Red Fog of Death?" Dr JJ Russoo inquires, squirming nervously. "Ah, yes, you mean the *picodust*. That is what it is officially called: picodust. I tell you what, comrade, I shall be forthright with you due to our impending doom. After all, the system has collapsed and there will be no adverse consequences for disclosure of previously classified material. Correct? We, this group of scientists you see here, are trying to complete the quartz storage project: the final and highest-level directive ever issued by the Occidental Union Administrators. We are doing this in order to preserve this planet's all-important information. For it is now about salvaging information. *Information* is the key to the future—to life beyond this world. Information means salvation; information means *re-creation*. So, I guess, I have already answered your first question."

232

"And what is that?" I ask, perplexed.

"Your first question: *is there a cure?* No, there is no cure. The picodust cannot be stopped. It is everywhere and will consume and kill everything. The picodust will exterminate all life—visible and invisible. I am sorry to be the messenger of such dreadful news."

"So it *is* true: we are all going to die, and nothing is going to save us," I say, emotionally deadened. For I have already heard this news. It is old. The scientist has just murdered any remaining hope—that is all. "I really don't know how to respond. What do you say to such news?"

Dr JJ Russoo bows his head and stares at the floor. Several minutes of silence pass between us, yet life, nonetheless, continues to unfold around us. Scientists dart all over the chamber, trying to complete their final assignment—humanity's final quest. Heated arguments erupt between workers. Cries of anguish overcome others. But despite the frenzied activity, an underlying futility taints the atmosphere. Every action and interaction lacks meaning, sincerity. Life has been hollowed out. The façade has fallen.

Yet curiosity ultimately arouses me. "So, Russoo," I say, "is the picodust the technological marvel that I've been reading about? Is it project United We Fall?"

Dr JJ Russoo looks surprised.

"Now, comrade, how would someone like you know about United We Fall?" he asks. "That project was highly classified. Only Occidental Union Administrators and the highest-ranking Worldwide Industries personnel, such as myself, would have had access to that record. Please enlighten me about how you are aware of such classified information."

"Russoo, it doesn't matter how I know about it, because we don't have much time left. I want you to tell me everything you know about the picodust or the nanoparticles or the Red Fog of Death—or whatever it is you call it. Tell me everything about project United We Fall."

"What difference does any of this make?" he asks, annoyed at my evasive reply. "If you know the truth or not, either way you—we—are doomed."

"For me, it makes all the difference!" I snarl back. "At least I shall die knowing *why*. *Why*. Yes, it's all about *why*."

I then slap Dr JJ Russoo on the face, and the blow's force knocks him over. He gets up. Shocked yet docile, he cowers before me. Not a single worker even peeks in our direction.

"You gonna answer my questions, or not?" I ask. "Because I'm losing my patience."

"Yes, yes, of course I shall," he replies. "No need for violence, please! If it means that much to you, then I shall comply."

"Good. No more violence. I promise," I say calmly. "And I'm sorry for slapping you. I don't know why I did it. It just happened. I guess I'm just sort of pissed off with everything you people have done. Anyway, just answer my questions, and everything will be fine."

Dr JJ Russoo straightens his lab coat and then anxiously flicks his hair to the side. I smile and nod my head, and this assuages some of his fears.

"Okay, okay," he says, glancing cautiously in my direction yet refraining from making any eye contact. "Project United We Fall was top secret—the highest-classified project in the Occidental Union's history. But you already know this. You may, however, wish to ask the following question: what prompted the project to commence? And the answer would be the need for control—control of the minds and, therefore, the bodies of the workers. For if one controls the mind, then one also controls the body. You see, good comrade, workers are motor units, and the Occidental State needs their labour to get things done. It is really that simple. The Administrators do not actually do anything. They do not produce anything, and they cannot survive by their own labour. As a consequence of this survival challenge, the State must compel and coerce its workers to work so that it, and all its dependents, can live. Project United We Fall—that is, the picodust, or what you would call the nanoparticles or the Red Fog of Death—was meant to solve this problem."

"The ultimate solution to all of society's troubles," I say, recalling the words printed in last night's news article. "It is the ultimate solution to the problem of free will. For if the State were failing to manipulate workers into toiling and producing goods and services, then what would be the solution? One solution would be for the State to use force to dragoon the people into working and doing what it desires. But this would pose many logistical problems for the State—and, frankly, it would not be that efficient. Protests. Revolutions. Civil war. Loss of life. And this disruptive cycle would continue ad infinitum. Another solution, though, would be technological. If a technology were to exist that could control the minds and, therefore, the bodies of the people, then the State would have forged the ultimate solution to the problem of its survival. The Occidental Union Administrators—holed up in the Occidental Union Capital—would parasitise the people and, as a result, get all the 'willing' manpower needed to run all the State's plans. The Administrators would have finally solved that most ancient of problems—*the* problem that has haunted all previous rulers: how to control the masses and force them into doing thy master's bidding."

"Right you are, comrade," the scientist says, trying to flatter me. "Yes, excellent deductions and superb logical thinking. But United We Fall was not just about control. It was also about making the people feel safe and content. The picodust was meant to make the people feel good about working. It was supposed to make them pleased about taking orders from the Administrators. So, one might say, the picodust was going to transform the masses into *willing* and *ecstatic* workers. Consequently, it was hoped that it would be a solution on two levels. First, the rulers would be able to micromanage and administer every aspect of society and consumption and production. And, second, the masses would find their ultimate life purpose and pleasure in obeying their rulers' orders. In return, the Administrators would keep the masses fed, housed, safe, healthy, and materially equal. The workers would not have to worry about anything. Therefore, it was supposed to be a win-win solution for everyone."

"You call that a win-win solution for everyone?" I ask. "I call that the vilest and most immoral form of slavery ever devised. An oligarchy of Occidental Union Administrators ruling the entire world with absolute and guaranteed authority. And *you* cooperated with this evil plan."

Dr JJ Russoo shakes his head, as worry disfigures his face. "No, comrade," he says, "I did only as I was ordered to do—please do not hit me again!"

"I said I won't hit you again, and this means I won't hit you again."

"Thank you, comrade—thank you so very much. I appreciate your kindness and fairness. Anyway, as I was saying, I was not even that high up in the chain of command. In fact, my main job was to ensure that all the quartz storage units were kept up to date, just in case an adverse event—such as this current disaster—were to transpire. But may I add that from a scientific point of view project United We Fall had another important potential benefit—something that, I think you may agree with, was well worth the risk."

"And what might that be, Russoo?" I ask.

"Ultimate knowledge. Unravelling the mystery of life and the cosmos. Why is there something rather than nothing? Why does anything at all exist? What is life and reality? Why are we here, and how did we get here? And is there a purpose to it all? These are the hard questions that we have been unable to answer using reductionism and the scientific method. And even though we humans have tried for millennia to solve these problems, we have encountered barrier after barrier. As a result, we became desperate—so we thought the picodust might help provide the answers."

"The answers?" I ask. "But I thought Sci–Coll had declared that there were no answers to these types of questions? For didn't the Administration and Worldwide Industries scientists say that 'why' questions are stupid questions, the wrong questions to ask? Haven't we been taught that everything, including life, is just molecules in motion? That we are just meat? That consciousness is just an illusion—an epiphenomenon or a side effect of matter? That the universe is just a random accident, lacking purpose or design or intention? That life is meaningless and absurd?"

"Well," he replies, while clearing his throat, "*I* do not agree with these conclusions. And I think you will find that many Worldwide Industries scientists were beginning to question this line of thinking, too—dare I say this line of *nihilistic* thinking? For example, we know that randomness and chance fail to explain the incredible fine tuning of our universe for life. In fact, chance cannot even explain why our universe exists the way it does, with its precise physical properties, laws, and constants. We were, thus, confronted with three alternatives in order to explain why our universe exists with its precise properties and why it is tailored for intelligent life. The first answer: our universe is part of a *multiverse*—a huge 'mother' universe that keeps on spitting out billions of different 'baby' universes, such as our own universe. As a result of this huge number of independent and unique universes, a few universes hospitable to life were bound to appear by chance and with time. And we, residing in *this* universe, exist as a consequence of being in one of these 'baby' universes that displays the correct ingredients to give birth to life. So we are able to wonder about why we inhabit this 'goldilocks' universe, because we just happen to live in one of the life-friendly universes. However, the problem with the multiverse hypothesis is that we cannot detect the mother universe or any other baby universes. For we live in an independent universe that is *completely disconnected* from the mother universe and every one of its baby universes. Hence, there is no way to know whether a multiverse, or any other universe, exists. It is pure speculation. And we are, unfortunately, physically bound and limited to this universe. As a consequence, we cannot explore anything 'outside' this universe, if such a thing even existed. But apart from the complete lack of physical evidence for such a hypothesis, the multiverse fails to solve our original problem. For the obvious question then arises: what give birth to the original mother universe? Where did it come from? And why does it exist? So, by speculating wildly about a multiverse, we have just pushed the problem back one step. We would still need to explain what gave rise to the multiverse, to the mother universe. Yet the multiverse idea also breaks Ockham's razor, because it multiplies the number of assumptions needed to explain the original problem. We are thereby increasing the complexity of the answer to the original problem instead of simplifying it. Comrade, are you following so far?"

"Yes," I reply, "I think so. I've pondered over these very questions many, many times. So I'm interested in what you're saying."

Dr JJ Russoo peers suspiciously at me. "How is it that you are able to follow all these complicated philosophical and scientific arguments?" he asks.

"Russoo, we don't have time for this. I need information about the picodust and project United We Fall. And time is running out. I need to know."

He nods his head. "If it is one thing I respect," he says, "it is knowledge. The pursuit of knowledge—the truth—is the highest virtue in the world. Therefore, I shall continue and grant you your wish. So where was I? Oh, yes, the second answer. Now, if the multiverse hypothesis were to fail, then this would leave us with two other choices: either an unknown-unknown explanation—that is, the universe is a *brute fact*, a physical necessity, and that is the end of the story—or the traditional deist or theist explanation."

"The traditional explanation? You mean *God*."

"Yes, God—that wildest of speculations. But I have many reservations about this answer. For saying 'God did it' explains nothing at all. It is intellectually lazy and practically useless. So why even bother with such a fuzzy concept that neither explains nor solves anything? Absolutely useless, primitive, ridiculous—that is the God concept in a nutshell."

"Okay," I say, "if you despise the concept of God, then what are you left with? An unknown-unknown explanation for life, the cosmos, and reality. Not even an inkling of an idea. No real explanation. Just a brute fact. Is that it? Is that the third option?"

"Well, yes. And you are correct: this is an unsatisfactory conclusion. Perhaps, though, we have missed something subtle yet crucial in our cosmic investigations. Perhaps we need a different point of view, a different kind of intelligence to guide us in the right direction. So besides taming the masses, it was also hoped that the picodust would enhance our collective intelligence—which would help us crack the problem of why anything at all exists. Thus, many Occidental Union Administrators and Worldwide scientists honestly thought that the picodust would solve all society's problems *and* provide us with the answers to the mysteries of life and the universe. The majority believed that the picodust was worth the gamble for ultimate power—and ultimate knowledge."

"The pursuit of ultimate knowledge," I say, "it's a trap, a delusion. We can't achieve ultimate knowledge, because we are just a miniscule part of the universe. How can a part grasp the whole? How can a subset comprehend the complete set? Where is our humility? Why can't we accept our tiny role in the greater scheme? Why can't we learn to live in balance with all life? Russoo, we were warned, thousands of years ago, that we would fall if our pride blinded us to the reality of things: we can never possess ultimate knowledge; we can never be gods."

Dr JJ Russoo, failing to grasp my allusion, gawks at me. He is clueless about our culture, history, and ancestors' wisdom.

"Anyway, Russoo," I say, changing tack, "tell me about this picodust, this strange material that the Administrators and scientists placed all their faith in. What is this thing? And what went wrong?"

Frowning, he replies, "Well, I do not really know what the picodust is. I mean, I doubt anyone does. No one knows where it even came from. There are rumours, but they are just rumours."

"Rumours? What sort of rumours?"

"A couple of higher-ranking scientists at Worldwide Industries have hinted at the picodust being not terrestrial. They claim that the Saturn Rover Space Mission brought back core samples from Saturn's icy moon Enceladus, and that these samples contained the picodust. Apart from this anecdote, though, I know little else about the picodust's origins."

"So that's it?" I say. "We don't even know for a fact where the picodust came from?"

"That is it, I am afraid. The secret of the picodust's origins will remain a mystery. I do know more about its composition and behaviour, however. The picodust, as you probably already know, is an exotic nanomaterial. But here is where it gets interesting: each individual nanoparticle—by itself and isolated from other picodust particles—cannot possibly be alive. For it lacks the necessary and sufficient machinery to 'live' on its own. Consequently, an individual particle does nothing."

"So this suggests that the picodust is not life as we know it. It indicates that it is inanimate matter."

"Not quite," Dr JJ Russoo answers. "Although each *individual* particle appears lifeless and is incapable of life on its own, things change when individual particles gather in a *collective* and reach a certain concentration, a tipping point. At this point, the picodust appears to be alive."

"Extraordinary," I say, feeling invigorated by the scientific information. For I am, at heart, still a scientist and will always be one. "But how do you know this? If what you're saying is true, then the picodust might be a new form of life altogether—something we haven't even imagined."

"Exactly right," he replies. "The implications are staggering, because it has always been assumed that life can be described only at the level of the individual organism— and that is it. However, it was never even considered possible that an individual of a species, on its own, might be inanimate, yet on amassing might suddenly transform into life. We know, for instance, that a bacterium behaves differently when it is in a collective. But an isolated bacterium is still alive. The picodust, on the other hand, is nothing like bacteria. An isolated picodust particle is lifeless and lacks the basic machinery for life—but when more than a trillion particles form a group, the entire collective comes to life and acts as a *single* living organism. I think the closest word we have for describing such a collective of living picodust particles would be *superorganism*."

"Perhaps *alien superorganism* would be even closer," I say. "Isn't it ironic, though? The greatest scientific discovery in history ends human history."

Dr JJ Russoo snorts gleefully at my statement, which was not meant to be amusing. After calming down, he says, "You see, the initial experiments involving the picodust were conducted by scientists in a secure and controlled environment. They first tested the picodust physically and chemically, and after that they started introducing it to different species. And that is when things became really interesting—"

Dr JJ Russoo then pauses and glances at three scientists who have just stopped moving. More and more scientists around us are submitting to picodust-induced paralysis and death.

"I am sorry, comrade," he says, "but we must terminate our discussion very soon. I have to ensure all the quartz storage units are loaded and ejaculated into space as soon as possible. My scientists, alas, are dying faster than I predicted, and I am afraid that my turn will soon follow. And if that happens, then I shall have failed my assignment."

"But why should you care if you fail?" I ask. "The Occidental Union has collapsed, and no one is going to punish you. So why even bother with this task? If I were you, I'd end my days on Earth doing something I wanted to do."

"*This is something I want to do.* You do not comprehend how important this project is. For, as I have already told you, this is humanity's last chance to send a message to the past, present, and future—to any one or any thing that might be alive in the cosmos. This is our final will and testament. And if we fail to send this message—this information about Earth life—then we, along with every other species, shall truly perish. No record of life's existence on Earth will exist. But if we succeed in sending this information, then, in a way, we and all Earth life shall live on. For this condensed information might be used by an advanced alien civilisation to recreate Earth life. Now, comrade, do you grasp the gravity of the situation? Matter is the messenger, but information is the message. We must propagate the message."

"I understand," I say, "and I agree with you: information and messages are crucial. For life emerges from meaning, and meaning emerges from information. So we are more than just meat. Anyway, Russoo, I shan't distract you from your task much longer. But if you would finish what you were saying about the picodust, then I'd be grateful. As you feel compelled to finish your project, I also feel compelled to learn the truth."

"It would be a pleasure to share as much information with you as I can in the next few minutes. But that is as much time as I can spare."

"Thank you," I say, while bowing my head in gratitude.

"So where were we?" Dr JJ Russoo asks. "Ah, yes, the picodust and the scientific experiments. Okay, so the Administrators and scientists first experimented with simple life forms. They exposed bacteria and fungi to the picodust, and then they introduced it to insects, fish, and even reptiles. Although the results were varied and fascinating, I lack the time to describe the details. But I shall talk about what the Administrators and scientists did next."

"Yes, yes," I say, "go on, please."

"Well, they decided to try something unusual. They wanted to see how the picodust would interact with an ape—an intelligent and sentient being. So they introduced chimpanzees into a sealed room full of picodust. These initial tests using chimpanzees revealed something stunning: the picodust subdued them—*and* changed their brain anatomy and general physiology. The chimpanzees became obedient servants, and their intelligence increased. They understood and accepted simple orders. In other words, they became servile workers. There was a catch, however. The chimpanzees, even with their enhanced intelligence, failed to understand or to perform more complicated or delicate tasks. So—"

"So," I interject, "the Administrators and scientists decided to test the picodust on humans."

Dr JJ Russoo nods in agreement and then says, "Yes, comrade, that was the obvious next step. Although the scientists tested the picodust on human subjects, they conducted all the research deep underground, in the most secure laboratories on Earth. For an alien entity—a new life form as powerful as this—must be clinically tested thoroughly, before releasing it into the wild. Any mistake might be lethal for all Earth life. It is similar to releasing any alien species into a native ecosystem. Unless we are absolutely certain the ecosystem can handle the intruder, we should never introduce it. Do you, for instance, know what happened when Hawaiian cane toads were introduced into the former land of Australia in the twentieth century?"

"Ah, no," I respond, "I don't know what happened."

"Well, scientists released cane toads to control cane beetles, which were destroying sugar cane crops in Queensland, Australia. But the alien toads ignored the cane beetles and decimated instead the populations of almost every other native species. And, making matters worse, the cane toads had no natural predators in the virgin ecosystem.

So it was an ecological disaster. Hence, our initial trepidation with the picodust."

"So what happened to the picodust tests on the humans?"

"Interestingly," Dr JJ Russoo replies, "the initial results were unbelievable! The human subjects were willing to obey any order—and they were happy. In addition, they developed enhanced intelligence. It was too good to be true—as if the picodust were merging with the humans and creating a new hybrid species. A cooperative and super intelligent species. And, to top it off, there were no obvious adverse reactions. No side effects. None. So, buoyed up by this research, the Administrators and Worldwide scientists decided to perform a multitude of additional randomised double-blind placebo-controlled clinical trials. Each study was a success, an amazing success. Perfect results, no side effects."

"So I guess the Occidental Union Administrators then decided to unleash the picodust on a live population: the people of the Free Islands."

"Yes," Dr JJ Russoo says, "once again, you are correct. As you are probably aware, Sci–Coll and the Administrators loathe the Free Islands and its people and their free-thinking ideology. So if anything were to go wrong with the experiment, the Occidental Union could quarantine the Free Islands and—"

"And nuke the Free Islands, its people, and the picodust problem—everything solved in one shot," I interrupt. "The Administrators would finally have the perfect utilitarian excuse to conduct such a genocide: it was done for the *greater good*. Because if the people of the Free Islands had caught a 'mysterious' disease that threatened the rest of humanity, then the obvious greater-good argument would be to 'contain' the infected population. And what better way to ensure containment than to blow everyone and everything to smithereens. The former United States also used a similar greater-good argument when it dropped two atomic bombs on Japan in the twentieth century. Dropping the atomic bombs, the US Government argued, would save more lives in the long term by forcing a quick end to World War II. So more than one hundred thousand innocent Japanese civilians died, in the short term, during the two atomic bombings—and they died for the greater good. Their sacrifice 'saved' many other people from dying. But excuse me if I don't agree with this utilitarian argument or its hypothetical claims. Real people lost their lives for the sake of hypothetical people—that's ridiculous."

"You are spot on, though," Dr JJ Russoo says. "The entire plan involving the picodust and the Free Islands would have been the perfect solution, either way, for the Occidental Union Administrators. If the picodust experiment were to progress smoothly, then the Occidental Union would subdue and enslave the entire worldwide human population. And if the experiment were to unfold poorly, then the Occidental Union would use the disaster as the perfect pretext to obliterate the Free Islands. However, the Administrators ignored a crucial historical lesson, as you have already mentioned, comrade: that of hubris. Nature can neither be contained nor controlled. And all experiments involve an interaction between the experimenter and the experimented. *All* experiments. This is the golden rule of scientific research. Although researchers can try their best to avoid contaminating, influencing, or interacting with what is being studied, they can never fully succeed. All experiments involve an experimenter interacting with and influencing an experimentee—and vice versa. No experiment can be fully contained, controlled, or isolated."

"Okay, Russoo," I ask, "so what went wrong?"

"At first, the experiment neither went right nor wrong," Dr JJ Russoo responds. "In fact, the experiment looked like a complete failure, because no changes occurred in the subjects. The people of the Free Islands were going about their daily routines oblivious to the fact that the Occidental State and Worldwide Industries had released an unknown alien artefact all over their islands. All the Island people were behaving as they normally would. No positive changes. No negative changes. No changes whatsoever. Consequently, the Administrators and scientists thought the entire experiment was a dud. They even carried out environmental studies yet could find no trace of the picodust. As a result, the scientists assumed the picodust had somehow been destroyed."

"Huh? Destroyed naturally? But how could that be?"

"Indeed, how could that be. That was the question plaguing the scientists' minds. But here is the thing: the picodust was very much in the environment. It was, in fact, hiding. Can you believe it? Actually hiding! Avoiding detection!"

"But why would it do that?" I ask, intrigued by the scientist's story.

"In order to spread undetected all over the planet. Imagine that! It was reproducing, camouflaging itself, and planning a worldwide dissemination strategy. Only when it reached a specific density of particles worldwide did this tipping point then trigger a new phase in the picodust's life cycle. And that new phase involved a coordinated worldwide attack. Can you grasp the meaning of this?"

"Of course, I can," I answer. "It means the picodust is alive; more than that, the picodust is an intelligent agent."

"Exactly. That was the only inference we could make. The picodust was mounting a worldwide invasion. Nevertheless, the details remained sketchy: where did the picodust come from? Did it originate from Saturn's icy moon Enceladus or somewhere else? And who or what created the picodust? Or had it evolved naturally? And what *exactly* was it—its composition, its metabolism, its lifecycle, its strengths, its weaknesses, its needs, its desires, its *ultimate* purpose, if any? Everything remained unknown. But by its actions, it was possible to deduce this one fact: all the alien nanoparticles were coordinating their actions and communicating with each other for a greater purpose."

I lock my eyes on to the scientist's and say, "So what is the picodust's greater purpose? What does it want?"

He shakes his head and replies, "I do not know the answer to any of your questions. No one does."

"But the picodust is killing everything! All life!"

"Yes, that is unfortunately true. But it fails to change the following fact: we do not know *why* the picodust is wiping out Earth life. We do not understand the picodust's ultimate purpose, or if it even has a purpose. Perhaps all this paralysis and death is just a side effect. Perhaps the picodust has no intention of killing all life, but in the process of living and reproducing it might be excreting a waste product that just happens—by chance—to be toxic to Earth life. For instance, the first photosynthesisers to evolve on Earth (some three billion years ago) produced oxygen as a waste product, yet, unlike today, oxygen was lethal to much of early Earth life. Something similar might now be unfolding with the picodust. There are, however, too many possible scenarios to explore. And though we can speculate all we want, it will change nothing. Our time is running out, and we are powerless to halt the picodust. In a few hours, perhaps a day or two at most, we shall all be dead. All life on this planet will be exterminated."

The scientist's words hit hard and leave me emotionless and thoughtless and speechless.

Sensing my growing despair, Dr JJ Russoo dips his hand into his coat pocket and pulls something out.

"Here," he says, as he hands me two tiny blue tablets. "Take *the Tablet*. It is a gift from me to you."

"Thank you," I reply, while pocketing the two tablets. "But what are they? What do these tablets do?"

"It is *the* Tablet. You have not heard of the Tablet before?"

"No," I reply.

"Okay. Do you know what *the Pill* is?"

"Yes, the Pill was an old medication, which taken in the twentieth and twenty-first centuries to prevent pregnancy."

251

"Similarly," he says, "*the Tablet* is a modern medication taken to end life and prevent misery. If you swallow the Tablet, you will die peacefully. You will experience no pain. Therefore, I suggest you swallow the Tablet at the earliest hint of tingling, numbness, or paralysis. These are usually the initial symptoms of the picodust infection. Or, for peace of mind, you can swallow the Tablet well before the first symptoms—in order to avoid being completely paralysed and unable to place it in your mouth. I have also given you a second Tablet, just in case you lose the first."

"So you are recommending that I suicide?" I ask, as my anxiety mounts. This is it. This is really happening. This infection is not some passing drama. We shall all perish. I am going to die.

"I do not want you to do anything, comrade," Dr JJ Russoo says. "I like you. I now feel we are kindred spirits. I even understand why you slapped me. Anyway, I want to give you the option of a serene death—a blissful final exit."

"Aha. Well—"

"Oh, and by the way," he continues, "the Tablet is extremely rare and hard to obtain. I have only a few left. And *I* am definitely going to take one, when the time comes. I strongly urge you to do the same. The Tablet will prevent any possible suffering."

"Thanks, I guess. Wow—I don't know what else to say."

Whereas I was—only one moment ago—thoughtless and emotionless, countless thoughts and feelings are now rushing through my mind and merging with one another. Reality is spinning out of control. The chamber seems distant and surreal; the floor, soft and unreal. Every object appears translucent, as if matter were an illusion. And my "I"ness, my centre of being and reality, is fading away. What is happening? Is this all a nightmare?

"Oh," Dr JJ Russoo says, as I muster all my mental powers to focus my attention on his voice and face, "there is one more thing, before I get back to work. Comrade, would you like me to take a sample of your DNA, and save the sequence on to a quartz storage unit? Your information will live on for hundreds of millions of years in space. And, who knows, if an intelligent alien species were to stumble across your quartz unit in space, then they might recreate you from the stored information. Therefore, in a way, you might live on, after your earthly demise."

I dwell on his proposal, as my concentration gradually returns.

After a few moments, I say, "Even though I think you're wasting your time and no other life, let alone intelligent life, exists in our part of the galaxy, I don't see why I should refuse to give you my DNA. After all, I've got nothing to lose. Am I right?"

Dr JJ Russoo smiles and plucks a hair from my head.

"All done," he says. "One hair is all I need."

"Thank you, Russoo, for all your help."

And, without any farewells, I leave the chamber and exit the pyramid.

~~~~~

Although time is running out, I must reach one final destination before the picodust cripples me. I have a closing task I would like to complete. So Anup and I march on towards the coast, towards the east.

We trudge through a crumbling city and a perishing planet. A disturbing stillness infects the land and air. The invading army is mustering its forces, preparing for the Ultimate Annihilation, while Earth life is passively awaiting its destined occupation. How can we defend ourselves against an invisible alien army, if we know nothing about them? Are we truly this helpless, when nature decides that our time is over?

Despite this foreboding, something deep within me impels me to keep moving. And each step vivifies me and reminds me that I am alive. I am the living.

A distraction soon halts our progress, however. Hundreds of dead or dying people are dotted around a Temple of the People. Many assume contorted standing positions, as if they were wax exhibits in a museum. Meanwhile, a malodour—part salty, part metallic, part rancid—is wafting out from the Temple. And moans and wails, also originating from the Temple, are floating along with the odour.

Anup and I proceed cautiously towards the Temple's side entrance. I peer into the building and witness a sea of flesh: milky flesh and dark flesh, young flesh and old flesh, all writhing together in a final act of sexual solidarity. Thousands of people. And even though many are already dead or paralysed, this fails to prevent the living from copulating with all—corpse or not.

In the centre of the Temple, a young man is anally penetrating an older gentleman while bashing the recipient's head in with a metal pole. And a few metres away, a group of men are swamping a young women, every now and then flashes of her flesh betraying her position. Near the Temple's main entrance, a petite brunette is pinned down by a boil-blighted bedbug-bitten big brutish man. He grunts and thrusts into her—again and again and again—and with every offensive she presses her hips against his and groans in rapture. Surrounding the copulating couple, many other men are impatiently awaiting their turn. A few metres away, manacled to a column, an innocent-faced girl submits to her many masters as they subject her to their masochistic experiments. And on the other side of the same column, a chained blonde corpse is attracting just as much attention as the living girl.

Yet similar scenes, employing different actors, are being replayed throughout the Temple of the People.

Cheering and screaming, pleasure and pain, horror and desperation.

And The Nightmare, aroused by all the fresh wounds and bodily fluids, has also gathered in enormous numbers. Millions of infuriated flies darting here and there, ovipositors penetrating the soft flesh and depositing eggs into the helpless human victims. An orgiastic feast of the flesh.

Despite all the hubbub, a naked man in his early twenties spots me and Anup. "Aye, tha, ya dirty cocksucka!" he yells from inside the Temple, while pointing a finger at us.

Several other Temple dwellers snap their heads in our direction, as their enraged bloodshot eyes lock on to Anup and me. Although they are human, their faces lack any sign of warmth or intelligence or humanity. They lack that which makes *Homo sapiens* human: a soul.

Warlike howls and yelps begin to drum throughout the Temple. Bored of the violent sex, a few Temple dwellers have found a novel amusement: us.

"Oi!" shrieks another nude man, as he disengages from his shackled victim. "Whe da ya fink ya goin'? Ya piece o' shit! Get ova 'ere, an' brin' that friggin mutt o' yours. We wanna taieste bof o' ya!"

The commotion attracts the attention of many other Temple dwellers, and one by one they stop raping each other to leer at Anup and me. Then, from various sections of the Temple, several figures begin to zero in on us.

I unleash Anup and give him the command for "it's okay to fight and bite". I then grasp both machetes and begin to retreat, while eyeing the Temple dwellers pursuing us.

"Anup!" I cry out, as I navigate through the maze of human statues surrounding the Temple. "You come with me, and don't you dare leave my side!" He reluctantly obeys my order, despite his excitement and desire to charge at our stalkers.

Moments later, two unarmed men splinter from the pack and race towards us. Anup, ignoring my previous order, pounces on the first assailant. He screams as Anup tears at his neck. Blood spurts in bursts from the wound, and after a few seconds the man collapses. Yet Anup refuses to let go, even though the man's struggles are petering out.

On seeing his comrade injured, the second assailant lunges at Anup—but I slam my machete into the attacker's head, just before he reaches Anup. I feel the man's skull crack under the blow's might, and an instant later he drops to the ground. He lies motionless, blood gushing out of his deeply parted flesh. Seconds later the blood stops draining, and I glimpse the glistening cream-coloured furrows of his exposed brain.

Anup, meanwhile, is still shredding the first assailant's neck, even though the man has ceased scuffling and is now dead.

"That's enough, boy," I say, dragging Anup off the body.

The other stalkers, on witnessing this quick massacre, decide to end their pursuit and return instead to the security of their Temple and the depravity of their carnality.

~~~~~

6

Anup and I are hiking across a coastal path nestled in the top of rugged cliffs. The expanse of the Pacific Ocean lies to the right, and it is a long drop down to sea level—almost two hundred metres.

Lantana shrubs and banksia trees dot the cliff path, and tall grasses cling tenuously to the cracked and crumbling sandstone façade. But first impressions are deceiving, for many of the plants are either dead or dying. As I touch one of the banksias, the entire tree crumbles into dust—the wind whisking the remains away to be engulfed by the ocean. I nudge a lantana and it, too, disintegrates into a fine grey-black powder. A tuft of brown grass reacts in the same way. The once-lush vegetation is dying; the picodust is exterminating all life.

Although the destination lies just a few hundred metres to the north, the obstructive flora and unstable rocky ground slow our passage. Few people know about this hidden trail, however. So we have bumped into no one, and this helps to speed up the journey.

I stop, close my eyes, and inhale the clean crisp sea air.

The sound of the distant breaking waves lulls me into a natural stupor.

The soft sunlight, balanced by the cool ocean gust, toasts my skin perfectly.

After a few moments, I open my eyes and the sudden vastness of the sparkling turquoise ocean overwhelms me. What a numinous experience! Nature's majesty surrounds me. Life thrives in that ocean, with countless creatures settling in every niche—hostile and friendly. I weep. I shall miss the ocean. I shall miss nature. I shall miss life.

And then, in a panic, before it all vanishes, I try to absorb everything around me. I live in each moment, savouring each sensation. The sight of the Sun, the sky, the sea. The sound of tweeting birds and chirping insects and thrashing waves. The smell of dirt, grass, and ocean. The texture of the wind wandering over my skin. The sharp yet lingering taste of the salty air. I soak it all up. I have to clasp everything—every moment—for as long as I can. I must squeeze every drop of existence out of every instant. And though I yearn to freeze this moment, I cannot. For each instant inevitably merges with the next and then slips away. To my dismay, time passes and life inches away from me.

But why am I longing to preserve this moment? Why am I tormenting my soul with the impossible? For I shall only find peace and end my suffering, when I surrender to the moment and eliminate my desire to hold on to it. In desire, anguish; in release, peace.

I search for the Sun, which is now in the western sky. Today will probably be the last time I see this life-nurturing star—*my* life-nurturing star. So I stare at it, trying to discern any features on its surface, trying to sear its image on my memory. But within microseconds the Sun's brilliance blinds me, and I am forced to avert my gaze. The Sun has witnessed our entire history—life's entire history. For the Sun was burning when the first primordial single-celled organism evolved, and the Sun's rich nuclear energy has nourished all life since then. The Sun will also be shining when the last organism dies, and the Sun's rich nuclear energy will continue to flood the Earth long after this.

Perhaps the Sun will experience other miracles.

After soaking up the coastal scene for a few minutes, I decide to move on. Time, a scarcity I disparaged as a younger man, is now my most cherished resource.

Several steps later, I spot two pigeons camouflaged behind a clump of still-living kangaroo grass. Before he can react, I jump on Anup and leash him. And just in time—for the birds excite him and, snarling and snapping, he tugs on the leash trying to catch them. He cannot help his nature.

But something is wrong. The pigeons do not fly away. On closer inspection, I discover that one bird is dead and the other is distraughtly circling her lost partner. She can do nothing to bring him back; she probably cannot even grapple with the idea of his nonexistence, of his nonbeing. Yet here she is—shuffling back and forth and cooing her sorrowful song. Clueless, helpless, wretched. I imagine what she might be feeling and thinking: *why are you not moving, my love, my life, my raison d'être? I implore you—respond to me. Feel me.*

Ease my pain. Heal my hurt. Please, my love, acknowledge and accept me. Complete me. Make life relevant.

And right here, right now, I fully grasp the futility—the pathetic struggle—that is life. The hopelessness of this sad spectacle, of the absurdity of life, of the tragedy of existence, devastates me. So I fall to my knees and mourn. I weep for this innocent pigeon caught in the web of a pointless painful existence. I weep for all life and its undeserved misery. But, most of all, I weep for me.

I gaze at the sky, at nothing and no one in particular.

"*Why?*" I cry out, as tears stream down my cheeks and pool in a puddle of dirt in front of my knees. "Why have you done this to us? What is the point of all this suffering? *What?* Please, answer me! For once, *just answer me!*"

No response. Nothing. The sky remains blue. The ocean roils below me. And life continues its final forlorn struggle.

It is the nihilism that debilitates me.

~~~~~

The ancient cemetery rests in a recess carved into the cliffs, roughly one hundred and fifty metres above sea level. To the north, south, and west, a ninety-metre-high natural rocky ridge isolates the cemetery from the rest of the metropolis; to the east, the Pacific Ocean stretches until the horizon. The only way to reach the cocooned cemetery is via the concealed coastal path, which Anup and I have just taken. Few people know that this sanctuary exists, and even fewer have visited. And situated at the eastern-most point of the Occidental Union, this is the cemetery at the end of the world—the cemetery secluded from the rest of civilisation.

I survey the entire cemetery, which is roughly five hundred metres by five hundred metres. Although countless bushes, shrubs, and wildflowers pepper the cemetery, the majority are drying up and dying—desiccated dirty-grey tangles. However, a few mighty trees stand their ground, their foliage thick and rich and verdant. Near the cliff edge, at the northern-most tip of the cemetery, I glimpse my destination. No railing guards the edge, though, and to fall into the ocean from this height would be lethal. So I tread carefully.

I call to Anup, as he bounds over cracked graves and weaves his way through weathered Victorian and Edwardian monuments. Brushing me aside, he spots a dead black cockatoo lodged under a sickly bottle brush tree and rushes towards the carcass. Thousands of dead insects also coat the graveyard—and The Nightmare is among the casualties. Nothing is being spared.

The Sun now hangs low in the western sky; an hour more and it will set under the rocky ridge. Shadows are growing longer, and darkness is shrouding the isolated cemetery. I can sense the haunting presence of the thousands of souls buried here. And, on cue, the chilling caw of a crow shatters the peace. I take this as an inauspicious omen and hurry to finish my journey's final leg.

But as I near my destination I hear Anup snarl. He then barks, and I know from its tone and depth that he is about to attack something. So I stop and try to locate him.

Although I cannot see him, I deduce he is behind a barn-sized mausoleum, a hundred metres inland towards the cemetery's centre.

Seconds later a scream splits the silence. And then another. And then growling and the sounds of a tussle.

I pull the two machetes out of my backpack and sprint towards the kerfuffle. Moments afterwards, I reach the mausoleum. But I am too late: Anup has mauled and killed an Occidental Union Administrator and is just about to charge at a second unarmed Administrator.

"*No*, Anup!" I yell, while lunging at him.

I manage to grab the dog just before he reaches the second Administrator. But Anup resists me, and for the first time in my life he, my loyal Anup, sparks a flash of fear within me. My own dog—my friend, my family, my guardian—whom I have loved and cared for, lashes out at me. And before I realise it, I am sprawled across a tomb and a giant wolflike beast is standing over me, pinning me down. No hint of Anup resides in those black eyes—just untamed and untameable nature. His vicious breath suffocates me. His jaws are centimetres away from my neck, moments away from tearing my throat out and killing me. And even though Anup's physical assault overcomes me, it is his psychological betrayal that completely cripples me.

"Anup! Nupy!" I cry out, more in sadness and despair than fear. "It is I, your friend. Nups, please my old buddy, what are you doing? *Please.*"

Anup snarls in reply, those jaws inching closer to my neck—but I also detect a hint of uncertainty in his threat. A conflict within. He is battling against an unseen enemy.

"Yes, boy, that's it. Fight it!" I plead.

Shall I strike Anup while he is hesitating? *Can* I strike him?

A second later, a subtle yet concrete change surges through Anup. He remembers me! He recalls our loyal friendship and our ancient contract. Anup has returned. The beast dwelling within has been vanquished. I hug Anup, and he licks my face. He whimpers in delight and distress.

"It's okay, boy," I say, smiling, overjoyed at having my Anup back. "Everything is going to be fine. Just fine."

But everything will not be fine, I think to myself as I grapple with the meaning of Anup's betrayal. *How could he?* And what timing. Life has saved its cruellest and most devastating insult for the Final Act, when I am almost depleted. Or does life still have a few more perverse pranks left in its repertoire? In any event, nothing will be the same again. I am truly alone in this universe, and I can rely on no one but myself—perhaps not even myself.

Anup then jumps all over me, and I scratch his coat. Despite sustaining a deep and unhealable wound, I still rejoice in this bittersweet moment. After a few seconds of bonding, I tie Anup to a nearby monument and forcefully forget his betrayal. For it never happened: I must believe this. Life, as I know it, is deteriorating at a blistering pace, and I have many tasks to finish before *the* final moment arrives. I need to focus on the present.

So I glance over at the deathly-alabaster Administrator cowering under a flowering coast banksia tree. I shall finally meet an Occidental Union Administrator face-to-face.

~~~~~

I approach the Administrator with both my machetes raised. The Administrator cringing before me looks exactly like the other Administrator who Anup just killed. And both Administrators are identical to the one I saw in charge of food distribution at the Temple of the People a couple of days ago. They are all crop-haired effete-featured porcelain-skinned androgynous ectomorphs dressed in black robes, which are stamped with a red first on the front and an empty white circle on the back. Each of these Administrators also hosts, on the nape, a giant brown slug—again, just like the Administrator at the Temple.

As I draw nearer, the Administrator reaches quickly into its black robes. But before the Administrator can use what it has grasped, I slam my machete—blunt edge first, so as to avoid injury—into its upper arm. The Administrator shrieks and drops a medicine bottle.

"Don't you dare move!" I yell, while pointing a machete in the Administrator's face.

I retrieve the bottle and immediately recognise the contents: it contains the Tablet, the euthanasia drug.

"Well, you won't be needing this," I say, before hurling the bottle over the cliff edge. "Now stand up and strip! I don't want anymore surprises from you."

The frightened Administrator ponders my order for a few seconds before deciding to comply. It strips off its black robes and undergarments and then throws them at my feet. A fragile, almost sickly, woman stands shivering before me.

Despite her skeletal appearance, I take no chances. "Sit down on that rock there," I order her, "and keep your hands on your thighs at all times."

She submits to my commands without any resistance and then begins to cry.

"Please, sir," she says, still sobbing, "we shall not harm you. We cannot harm you. We have never hurt anyone or anything. We are peaceful. We are even vegetarian. So please, we beg you, do not hurt us."

Her voice, even while sobbing, manifests the same unsettling gender-neutral quality displayed by the Administrator at the Temple. This Administrator also refers to herself in the same irritating way by using the first-person plural "we" instead of the first-person singular "I". But besides these peculiarities, she seems harmless.

"Okay, I believe you," I reassure the Administrator, not wanting to upset her any further. "Please calm down. I also won't hurt you. And to prove it, I shall drop my machetes. See?" I say, as I place the weapons on the ground.

My offer pacifies her, and she stops sobbing. I then sit down beside her, and we inspect each other.

I stare at the Administrator's features. If it were not for her sexual ambiguity, I would call her beautiful. Her ears and nose are delicately miniature, and her full-lipped mouth is seductively feminine. But her brown eyes, though sparkling with intelligence, lack warmth. Something else is missing from them, too, although I cannot pin it down.

Without thinking, and intrigued by her features, I reach out and touch her face. She does not flinch and, surprisingly, welcomes my intrusion. I caress her glowing skin and delight in its silky texture. Judging by its flawlessness, the Administrator must be young, probably in her early twenties. I then stroke her cropped white hair, while carefully avoiding the sickening slug sucking on her nape. Her hair's suppleness surprises me. It feels more like fine fur than human hair.

"I'm sorry about your friend dying," I say, "but I'm also not sorry. You are, after all, responsible for cursing all life to death."

The Administrator remains silent and begins to shiver. With her tiny frame, and lacking body fat, she must be feeling cold, despite the warm spring weather. So I pick up her robe, empty its pockets, and hand it to her.

"Thank you," she replies, while dressing, "but we're also not thankful. After all, your dog ripped our partner apart."

"That was your partner?" I enquire. "Well, if that were my partner, I would be devastated and hysterical. You sure aren't acting like someone who has lost a lover. You seem too calm and distant."

"We differ from you. We are enlightened and, thus, superior to you. Emotions and desires and physical attachments lead to slavery. For if one were to let one's impulses rule over one, then one would live as a slave, not a master. One's master would, therefore, be one's desires; one would live to satisfy one's desires. This is not true freedom. This is a false freedom—an activity that leads to bondage. So we try to reduce all physical attachments and desires. We avoid false freedoms and activities that lead to subjugation. For we seek true freedom, which is mastery over our impulses. This is the only path one can take to conquer life."

"Wow," I say, shaking my head in disbelief. "You're really that apathetic about your partner, who is lying dead in a pool of her blood?"

"Perhaps you were not listening to what we just said, to our words of wisdom. We are naturally displeased with this outcome—with losing our partner. And we would, of course, prefer our partner to be alive. But this is the nature of life: death must follow life. Nonetheless, it is how one responds to death that counts. Weeping and unleashing one's emotions change nothing. Such behaviour only subjugates one to one's impulses. Such behaviour weakens one. Such behaviour increases one's misery. Such behaviour shackles one to a master, and this master is one's wants. Hence, one becomes a slave. Yet we, the Occidental Union Administrators, are masters—not slaves. Administrators must first conquer themselves—their emotions—before they can conquer others. Without this crucial self-enhancement step, then we are not free. And if we are not free, then we are enslaved. For an Administrator, such a position leads to an obvious absurdity, because an Administrator—who is born to be a master—cannot be a slave. And one cannot be master and slave simultaneously. For, as we have already explained, such a contradiction cannot exist in reality. You are either master or slave, not both at the same time."

Perplexed by her spiel, I smile wryly at the Administrator, who displays an icy demeanour. It seems she has now conquered her fear of death—which had, ironically, "enslaved" her just a few moments ago.

"Okay," I say, "I accept your argument. So, contrary to appearances, true freedom emerges from self-restraint, self-discipline, or self-sacrifice, whereas false freedom is the pursuit of every whim and desire, which would eventually lead to slavery. Therefore, false freedom is the lack of self-restraint or self-discipline."

She nods her head and says, "Correct."

"But haven't you missed something crucial in your reasoning?"

"And what might that be?" she asks in an icy tone.

"You are, in fact, a slave, because the pursuit of power is your master. You want—*need*—to control other people. You have said it yourself: Administrators are masters, and Administrators exist to conquer others. So you are a slave to your desire for power. And if it's one thing I've learnt, power is insatiable. Once you taste a little power, you yearn for more. And once you control someone, then you need to subjugate someone else. Soon, you need to control more and more people just to maintain the same control. And, in the process, you make enemies of those you control. So you need to apply harsher and harsher rules over those you control, just to wield the same control. You are, without realising it, engaging in the Red Queen's race, which you cannot win. For no end point exists, and you need to continue chasing after more and more power just to stay in the same place, just to maintain your status quo, just to preserve your rule over others. So power is the cruellest overlord of all, and you are the most miserable slave of all."

The Administrator looks stunned. Troubled, she strokes her slug, which quivers in response to her touch. Moments later, the Administrator begins undulating euphorically. The slug appears to be releasing some sort of chemical to placate its host.

After a few seconds, the calmed Administrator says, "You have trapped us by employing a sophism—for we neither need nor desire power. You, the people, need us, the Administrators, to control and manage *you*. For without us, your existence would become short, nasty, and brutish—and you would revert to life as it would have been had you been living isolated in nature. Thus, we are doing you a favour. Our control over your lives improves your physical and mental wellbeing. We are gifting the masses with our expertise and sacrifice. We are administrating your interactions. We are legislating the law. We are managing your consumption and production. We are the ones preventing your extinction."

"Ha!" I reply. "*Preventing our extinction?* The nerve! You have just condemned all life to death. And you think you are improving our lives? How did you arrive at that conclusion or calculate that so-called improvement? My dear Administrator, *you* are the one employing a sophism. And you have dodged my original claim: that the pursuit of power has enslaved you. And by the looks of that slug, you are also a slave to the mind-altering chemicals that it releases into your body."

In response, the Administrator kneads her slug once again.

She then says, "This 'slug', as you call it, is connecting all the Administrators together. It floods our brains with information gathered from all our sisters. You are, in fact, looking at a worldwide biological network. For we, the Administrators, are *one* in mind. We share all our information and experiences instantly. There is no 'I' or 'me' or 'my'; there is only 'we' or 'us' or 'our'."

"So that slug is like an organic wireless internet connecting all the Administrators to each other? So it is sending information to and receiving information from each Administrator?"

"Correct," she replies.

"So that means you would know what is happening to every Administrator around the world?"

The Administrator studies my face. "We should not be sharing anymore information with you," she replies. "Who are *you* to be ordering *us*? *You* should be answering *our* questions, not the other way around."

I grab my machetes from the ground. "I've waited all my life to corner an Administrator," I say, brandishing the weapons. "I've got heaps of questions, and I want answers. Do you understand?"

She eyes the machetes and remembers the natural order of things. "Yes, we understand," she murmurs in defeat.

"Good," I say, "so let's start with the most basic question: who or what are you? I mean you're obviously not physically like me or any other human being. You're the same, yet you're also different. So what are you?"

After mulling over my question for several seconds, the Administrator replies, "We are allowed to answer your question, for civilisation and life are perishing. But if the world were not being consumed by those who have judged us unworthy, then we would, of course, refuse to answer you. *You* would be submitting to *our* demands! And *you* would be addressing *us* in the proper manner as 'The Honourable' or 'Your Honourable'. But, alas, the Colony is collapsing. The law no longer exists. All contracts are void. Sci–Coll is defunct. The Occidental Union has fallen. It is a dark, dark day. So we have nothing more to lose. And our time, in any event, is almost expired. Consequently, we shall submit to your demands and answer most of your questions. To respond to your first enquiry then, we are the *parthenogenetic* offspring of the original progenitor. We are clones of the Queen."

"Parthenogenetic offspring?" I repeat, while trying to recall my scientific studies. "Clones of the Queen? So does that mean you are produced by asexual reproduction?"

"Correct," the Administrator answers. Although she appears surprised by my knowledge, she refrains from asking any questions about my past. "The Queen, the original progenitor, reproduces without fertilisation, without the need for a human male to impregnate her. All her offspring are full clones, identical copies of her; however, one major difference exists between the Queen and her Administrator offspring. The Queen can reproduce by parthenogenesis, but we—the Administrators, her spawn—cannot reproduce at all. We are all sterile. In order for one of us to start reproducing parthenogenetically,

272

without fertilisation, the Queen would need to die. Then, and only then, would the metamorphosis of a single Administrator take place. This 'chosen' Administrator would thus become the new Queen and start reproducing parthenogenetically. Nonetheless, the original progenitor, our original Queen, has never died. So such a metamorphosis of an Administrator has never taken place."

"Fascinating," I say, though I am also partly repulsed. "So you partner up with each other? You engage in clone-on-clone sex? Is there even a word to describe such a bizarre sexual relationship?"

"We do not engage in sexual relations with each other— that would be disgusting. Rather, we form a platonic couple to support each other socially and mentally. Each Administrator pair consists of a lifelong friendship– partnership contract. And we shall answer no more questions about this topic."

"Okay," I say, as my toes start to go numb. I try to wiggle them, but they refuse to respond. The reality is sinking in. An instant's panic floods over me. I am infected. I am dying. Nothing can stop this process now.

"My toes are numb!" I shriek. "*Please*, what does this mean?" I ask, despite already knowing the answer.

"If you know about the picodust—and we presume you do, because most people have heard about it by now—then you should comprehend what this sign means. It means the invading agent is starting to overcome and disable you. You are the living dead. And soon, you will simply be *the dead*. Soon, we shall all be *the dead*."

Unsure of how to take the Administrator's statement, I ask, "So how long do I have left?"

"It depends," she answers. "Some individuals succumb after a couple of hours, whereas others succumb after a day. One thing is certain, however, and that is death."

Feeling weak, I sit on an unmarked rectangular tombstone. A date is chiselled, in tiny numerals, into the top right edge of the marble monument. It says "1798".

I then massage my toes, trying to encourage some sort of sensation. But they resist reviving.

"What is *it* exactly?" I ask the Administrator. "What in God's name is the picodust?"

The slug on her nape begins to squirm, and the Administrator stops moving. Several seconds later, she says, "We cannot answer that question."

"*Why?*"

"Because we don't know with certainty what the picodust is. Individually, the picodust is too small to be life—too simple to be life. An individual particle lacks the cellular machinery for life. We have, nevertheless, discovered that individual particles are composed of inorganic elements: a collection of hydrogen, silicon, and lithium atoms, with a sprinkling of other elements. We have also found out that individual particles lack a fixed structure and contain no carbon atoms—hence, the picodust's inorganic nature."

"That's it?" I ask. "That's all you know?"

"No, we know more than that. We know, for instance, that when picodust particles gather in large numbers, then novel phenomena emerge. And when carbon-based life—

such as Earth life—is added to the mixture, then things become very interesting."

"You call the complete destruction of all Earth life *very interesting*?"

"No," she replies, "what we find interesting is the picodust's ability to transform into a living entity upon amassing and coming into contact with carbon-based life. Can you not appreciate the magnitude of this discovery? One particle is inanimate, but a group of particles, upon reaching a tipping point, becomes animate—becomes life! The picodust changes into an agent, an intelligence, an information- and meaning-processing entity. Now, *that* is incredible."

"Yes, I guess that is incredible—but *why* is the picodust killing everything?"

The Administrator smiles, though her lips arch menacingly high. "The answer will upset you," she says.

"I want to know. Meaning is life, and the meaning of my life is seeking the truth. That's all I have now."

"We appreciate the way you think," she replies, "and we tend to concur with your sentiments. Seeking the truth is important. Therefore, we shall assist you with your search for truth."

"Thank you," I say.

The Administrator smiles again, though this time her lips arch lower in a genuine show of friendship. "We believe," she says, "that the picodust resides in remote pockets all over the universe. When an intelligent species becomes advanced enough to explore space, then such a species might chance on the hibernating picodust. This, we think, is a necessary part of the picodust's lifecycle. Now, if these astronauts bring the picodust back to their home planet, then the picodust awakens from its hibernation and begins to disseminate all over the astronauts' home planet. And once the picodust saturates the planet, then the picodust moves to phase two."

"Phase two?" I repeat.

"Yes, phase two: either the picodust enhances the native life or the picodust exterminates the native life. We saw the picodust accomplish both these outcomes in our controlled underground experiments here on Earth."

"Yet you still released the picodust into our environment!" I bark.

"Yes, for we had a dream, an ultimate goal. Our dream was to uncover the *one equation* connecting everything in the universe. The original equation that gave rise to reality. The single equation that would unlock the mysteries of the cosmos. Imagine discovering such a unifying equation. Imagine the potential! What other purpose exists for society? Is it not to discover the truth behind reality? For us, this was the ultimate aim of the Occidental Union. All society's consumption and production and administration was designed with this ultimate goal in mind. We were going to reduce all existence to that *one equation*—and, then, we would finally be able to grasp all life's answers. We would, at last, discover the meaning of life and the universe. And we would be able to figure out where we came from and why we came to be."

"But what the hell does any of this have to do with the picodust?" I ask.

"It has everything to do with the picodust!" she snaps back, as a crazed look sweeps over her. "For as the *one equation* would unify all the physical laws of the universe, so the picodust would unify all life. *One equation* and *one life*. Billions of years ago, there was only one life: the original cell, *the one*. But that one life began to splinter—to evolve by branching out into many species. That was the original great fall, the original great error. From the original *one*, today the many. Disunity! Conflict! Inefficiency! No! Never! The picodust was supposed to change all that. It was meant to unify all life, every species: one life, one species, one living entity. We, the Administrators, were going to mend the original splintering, the original error. After billions of years of evolutionary *divergence*, we were going to begin the process of evolutionary *convergence*. We were going to heal the drift and unleash the true potential of the *one* universal life. We were going to restore wholeness and oneness. All life was going to be *one*, once again. Unity, harmony, efficiency—these would be the result."

As the Administrator ends her rant, it becomes clear that I am talking to a deranged lunatic. All of them—all the Administrators—deranged lunatics. Standing before me is the pinnacle of thousands of years of human "progress" and billions of years of evolution. And with this culmination, the world is destined to end in madness, in an abstract delusion. Separated from reality, dwelling in the land of fantasies and ideologies and theoretical equations, disconnected from the real world—that world of touch and sight and sound and smell and taste, that world of action and interaction, that world of thinking and communicating, that world of experience and intuition, that messy world of living and loving—isolated from everything good and tangible, they have doomed all life to death. For they yearned to reduce the symphony of existence to one monotonous note. For they longed to whittle down life's flourishing nursery to one homogenised and inbred collective. For they desired to prune away all the subtleties of the material and mental worlds and replace everything with one crude equation. They banished the mind and idolised the physical. They eradicated reason and logic, sentience and morality, and replaced everything with naturalism, with reductionism, with the motion of molecules. They unbalanced life's delicately balanced formula. This was their sin—yet all life was to pay for it.

"You're crazy," I say to the Administrator. "You and all your fellow Administrators are insane. You've gone utterly mad. You lived a lie, and your minds couldn't hack it. For you denied the reality of mind and consciousness and reason, even though you experienced the world through mind and consciousness and reason. You know, deep down inside, that life is mind and matter—not matter and matter. So how did you think this deceitful and schizophrenic approach to life was going to end? Of course, such an experiment was going to end badly. And now you've cursed us all."

"*Cursed?*" she asks pleadingly, her mad look starting to fade away. "*Cursed* for wanting ultimate knowledge? *Cursed* for wanting to forge the perfect society?"

"Listen," I say, "it doesn't matter anymore. Nothing matters. The damage is done. It's over. No use arguing."

278

Having exhausted her mania, the Administrator drops her head and droops her shoulders. She remains motionless. Along with her mental health, her life is slowly slipping away from her.

"Okay," I say, hoping to uncover a few final facts before it is too late. "You mentioned earlier that the picodust either enhanced or exterminated native life. Why do you think the picodust chose the latter when it was exposed to our environment?"

The Administrator lifts her head with great effort. Her glazed eyes focus eastwards on an imaginary dot resting on the dimming distant horizon.

"No idea," she finally whispers. "Perhaps this mass extermination is not a random event and there is a purpose to it: maybe the picodust sees Earth life as a threat; maybe the picodust is acting as a cosmic guardian, allowing only certain life forms to thrive. Or perhaps this mass extermination is a random event without purpose. We do not know. In any case, such questions are pointless, since we cannot stop the picodust. It has decided life's collective fate—and we have nothing more to say about this subject."

All of a sudden, I feel depleted and deflated. A numbness is creeping up my legs. My feet and lower legs are heavy yet still responsive to my mind's commands. I can act but not feel; I can move but not sense.

"Alright," I say to the Administrator, "if you know nothing else about the picodust, then may I ask why you came here with your partner?"

"Yes, of course. We came here because we wanted to die in this special place. It is a very *special* place."

Her emphasis on "special" intrigues me. Although I have my personal reasons for coming here, I cannot imagine why two high-ranking Administrators would want to spend their last living moments in a secluded and decaying cemetery overlooking the Pacific Ocean.

"So what's so special about this place?" I ask her.

"You don't know why it is special? In that case, why are you here?"

"I asked you the question first. If you don't mind, I'd appreciate an answer."

"*That* is why we are here," she says, while pointing at the monument that I am resting on.

I inspect the unmarked tomb once again. It looks new, despite the surrounding Victorian and Edwardian monuments and despite the year "1798" being etched on its polished headstone.

"This grave?" I say. "You're here because of this anachronistic grave?"

"Yes, this grave holds much value for every Administrator. All our dead sisters' ashes are buried here, in this unmarked grave. Just as importantly, however, the idea behind Sci–Coll was born in 1798. So we honour both in this one unmarked grave. Wouldn't you agree, then, that this might be a suitable place for us to die? The isolated location and splendour of the Pacific Ocean also add to the allure, making this the perfect place to pass peacefully away."

"I agree—this is a good spot to die. But what happened in 1798? Why is that year so special?"

"This is all we shall tell you," she replies. "Auguste Comte was born in 1798, and we consider him to be the father of Sci–Coll. His work, *System of Positive Polity, or Treatise on Sociology, Instituting the Religion of Humanity*, holds the key to our philosophy. Without Comte, without his philosophical publication, we probably would not exist. So we owe him everything. Hence, his birthday is our birthday, and it is placed as the first date on this tombstone: 1798. You will note, though, that the date of death is missing. And this is the final reason for why we have come to die here, in this cemetery. Someone needs to add a date of death to this tombstone, to the Administrators' collective tombstone. This will be our final act of administration. We shall inscribe the date of death on this tombstone—and that date shall be this year: 2212."

~~~~~

Although Anup cautiously sniffs the Administrator, he no longer displays any viciousness. He has settled down.

"Are you sure he won't attack us?" the Administrator asks, her voice trembling and losing its smooth metallic timbre. "He did kill our partner, and he even tried to bite you."

"Don't worry," I reply, while unleashing Anup. "Whatever was driving him mad has now passed. I think it was the picodust, because Anup has never attacked me before—not once. I am pretty sure he is back to normal and won't harm you, or me."

The Administrator eyes Anup suspiciously as he circles her. After a few moments, he loses interest in her and bounds across the graves in search of more novel curiosities. Within seconds, he stumbles upon a possum hiding in a Port Jackson fig, the largest tree in the cemetery. He yaps playfully at the possum, who sleepily gazes down at Anup and dismisses him as nothing more than a noisy nuisance.

"Anup, you silly boy," I say, grinning, "you can't get that possum. He's five metres up the tree! But it's good to have you back to normal, boy."

Anup, ignoring me, continues to bark at the possum and to scratch at the tree. My dog is happy, and I am happy. Even the Administrator appears to be enjoying this picturesque setting. It is good.

The Sun's dying rays bathe my face. I block everything else out and focus on the gentle warmth. For this will probably be the last time I experience it.

Minutes later, the Sun sets behind the western rocky ridge, and an instant chill circulates throughout the cemetery. In an hour, darkness will cloak everything.

~~~~~

The Administrator collapses on top of the tomb that is now marked "1798–2212".

"Are you okay?" I ask her. "Is it the picodust?"

"Yes," she murmurs, "not long now."

I lift her up—she is so light—and prop her torso against the Administrators' tombstone. She seems paler than usual, even in the fading dusk light.

"Why is the infection progressing at different rates in you and me?" I ask.

"Well," she answers, "Administrators are genetically modified, so maybe that has hastened the infection's progress rate."

"Genetically modified?"

"Yes, the Queen is genetically modified. She had to be in order to reproduce by parthenogenesis. And we—being her parthenogenetic offspring, her clones—are therefore genetically modified also. You can consider us as your ruling caste: a hereditary group bred specifically to be your superiors and to administer you efficiently."

"Kind of like an ant colony," I say, "where there are four castes or classes: workers, soldiers, males, and queens."

"Correct—a decent analogy. Each caste contributes to the survival of the Colony; each caste has its role to play. And the members of each caste are materially equal."

"Materially equal? Ha! You really think so?"

"Yes," she replies, "each Administrator is materially equal to every other Administrator, although Administrators as a group live materially differently from workers as a group. Each worker, however, is materially equal to every other worker. This is what counts: material equality among one's *peers*. Numerous studies show that envy usually occurs among one's peers—those physically, economically, and socially similar to you—not between persons who are dissimilar in every way. So by introducing a caste system into our species, we are erecting rigid boundaries between each group: the workers, the State's Spawn, Worldwide Industries employees, and the Administrators. This differentiates each group from the other, thereby reducing envy within each group and making it possible to maintain different equality levels. To each caste, their own."

"So everyone is equal within each caste, yet some castes are entitled to more privileges than others."

"No," she says, her voice starting to break, "that, that, that is incorrect. We, the Administrators, are a dissimilar caste from you, the workers. We, the Administrators, differ genetically, biologically, mentally, and socially from you, the workers. And we, the Administrators, contribute much more to the Colony than you, the workers. S-so it, it, it would b-b-be unreasonable to expect that we endure life like you. We have different needs, so our material circumstances will not be equal. And, of course, we are neither equal legally nor politically to you. That would be obscene, f-f-for we deserve greater rewards and safeguards f-f-for our greater contribution to the g-g-greater good. To treat equally those who are not equal is an inequality, an injustice."

Although I am trying to follow her arguments, my mind is fogging up. It is becoming harder to think clearly now. Her logic is confusing me.

Encouraged by my silence, the Administrator continues her speech. "We wanted t-t-t-to, to, to—" she stammers, unable to finish her sentence.

Then, in a flash and without any warning, the slug slips off the Administrator's nape, tumbles to the ground, and bursts into dust on impact.

The Administrator slumps across the tomb.

"Please!" I say, as I support her. "Please, are you okay?"

She gawks at me. "I, I, I, I, I, I, I, I don't know what I was about to say," she replies in a fresh voice.

The Administrator is now using the first-person singular "I" instead of the first-person plural "we". The slug has ceased to control her mind.

"Friend, I think you are finally free." I say, smiling. "The slug is dead. Your mental prison has crumbled."

"I, I, I, I, I am free? The slug is dead?" she asks. "I feel mentally naked. I can't describe the sensations flooding my mind. So strange yet so—"

She gazes about the place with fresh eyes, like a child experiencing the wonders of the world for the first time. She is lucky. For she will die happy and innocent.

I sit next to the Administrator and place my arm around her shoulders.

"It is incredible!" she cries out. "The colours and texture of the world! So vivid! So alive! And my mind—I am free to explore places that were forbidden just a few minutes ago. I can't explain it, but I guess it was like having a guard patrolling your mind and telling you what you could and could not think about. What you could and could not question. It was an actual physical presence in my mind. But that black shapeless fiend has disappeared. I can explore any idea or thought that pops into my mind!"

Life has, as usual, played another dirty trick on another victim. For the Administrator probably has a few minutes to enjoy her newly won mental freedom, before the picodust enslaves her body and mind—and then kills her. From one form of bondage to another—true freedom is an illusion. But who am I to ruin her moment of perceived liberty?

"Yes," I say, deciding to be pleasant, "you are indeed free, my friend. The nightmare is now over. For the first time, you are free to experience life as an individual. Your mind is liberated. The shackles of Sci–Coll no longer bind you to either a conformist collectivism or a soul-crushing scientism. Let your thoughts, feelings, and emotions roam where they wish. Relish your moment of liberation. For life is good, if we can find and clasp on to just one instant of freedom."

The Administrator then hugs me forcefully, almost painfully, despite her toothpick-thin arms.

"The darkness fogging up my mind has completely vanished!" she says. "I, I, I just can't describe how good this feels! I am so very happy. Thank you."

"For what?"

"For being here to share this moment with me. For not detesting me for what I am—what I did."

"You were born into slavery like the rest of us," I say. "All life is unfree. You had no choice. You knew no better. Your actions were predetermined. I cannot blame you. I cannot despise you. I blame life. I despise life. I blame God. I hate God."

"No!" she screams in a surprising burst of strength. "Don't ever say that!"

"Why should you care?" I reply. "According to your ideology, God does not exist. Sci–Coll made it clear that we—all life and the universe—are the products of blind chance and physical laws. So why should you care if I insult life or even if I curse an imaginary God?"

"Because I don't know what to think anymore. I'm scared and confused. Please, n-n-no more hatred. N-n-no no more anger. No more despair. That's what got us into this mess. We are here. We exist right now. That's all that counts. Just let life be life. Let the mysteries be mysteries. Please, I, I, I beg you. Just hold me and be with me. I don't have long. I just w-w-want to feel w-w-w-w-wanted and loved, even if it w-w-were just for a moment—and even if you have to-to to pretend."

I stare at the pathetic creature resting in my arms. I then feel as if I had left my body. As if I were floating above a man and a woman who are embracing each other. And from this vantage point, I can see they are alone, terrified, bewildered. A vast ocean of nothingness surrounding them. A second later I return to my body.

"I'm sorry," I say to the Administrator. "I'm trying my best. I'm exhausted and scared, too. But I'm not pretending, because I do like you. And I do want to be here for you."

I hug the Administrator and feel her shrinking in my arms. Her heart beat is dying. Her breath is weakening. But her muscles are contracting, stiffening.

"Please," she whispers into my ear, her voice barely audible. "I don't want to die without a name. Please name me before I die."

I mull over her words. How does one respond to such a request? And then I blurt out, "*Ishsha*. Your name is Ishsha."

"*Ishsha*," she repeats. "My name is Ishsha. Thank you."

Ishsha's grip weakens.

"Please, friend," she says, "I don't know your name."

But before I can answer Ishsha, her arms slide down my body and land on the tomb with a thud. Her body and muscles are hardening into a final shape.

"I, I, I," Ishsha stutters, "I h-h-have one final request before I'm p-paralysed—before I die. I'm so s-s-scared. I, I, I, I d-d-don't want to die a horrible and prolonged death. Some A-A-Admin-Administrators have died slowly and horribly. P-p-please don't let this happen to me. Please kill me."

I ponder over Ishsha's final request. I have killed many people, so killing one more person will not make a difference. And if it will free her from a miserable death, then mercy-killing her would be the right action to take. But how should I do it? Then, I remember the two euthanasia Tablets in my pocket.

"You know, Ishsha," I say, "I have the Tablet. A scientific officer gave me two Tablets. I was going to give one to my dog and take the other. But if you like, I guess—well, I guess I can give you my Tablet."

"Thank you. You are a g-g-good man," she replies, while flashing a weak smile.

288

"But, Ishsha, I'm really not sure about this. What about me? How will I die? What if the picodust kills me slowly and horribly?"

"No," she says with a final mighty effort and while straining under the weight of an invisible and invincible force. "Keep the Tablet for yourself and give the other one to your dog. I deserve this death. I deserve whatever I get."

She then stops moving. She is paralysed. I look into her eyes but see a nothingness residing there instead of Ishsha.

I force her mouth open and place a Tablet on her tongue. I shut her eyes for her. Her body tenses. She exhales deeply. She trembles. And then she dies.

~~~~~

7

I reach my final destination, an alcove dug into the northern rock face of the cemetery, near the cliff edge. I crawl into the alcove and, in the remaining dusk light, barely make out two dirt mounds.

The memories, though distant and ancient, evoke vivid images, and I shudder in response. I close my eyes and picture a man and woman. Although their voices escape me, their faces remain frozen in my memory.

A young woman, with kind features, is stroking my hair. She smiles at me and kisses my forehead. Everything, except her face, is blurred. She removes her gold necklace. A tiny gold crucifix dangles from it. She then drops the necklace in a freshly dug hole. After covering the necklace and crucifix with dirt, she leaves me and joins a man who has suddenly appeared in the distance. He now approaches me, while the woman stays behind. He kneels down, and we face each other: he, a middle-aged man; me, a young child. He softly squeezes my hand, and a tear flows down his cheek. He hugs me. Sadness fills the atmosphere. He then hands me a frayed leather-bound book. It is thick and lacks a title. As I begin to flick through its yellowed pages, he stops me and retrieves the book. He presses it against my heart and then places it in a second freshly dug hole. He fills the hole with dirt. The woman calls out to the man, yet no sound emerges from her mouth. He hugs me once more, fiercely, before abandoning me to join the woman. They stare at me from afar. The woman is now sprinting towards me. Her face—it is pale, sad, desperate. I open my mouth to cry out that two-syllable word, but nothing surfaces. The woman stumbles and falls down. A black-clad figure has tackled her from behind. Within seconds, several other black-clad figures swamp her. The woman's partner lunges towards the struggle, but he is overwhelmed by dozens of dark apparitions, which materialise from nowhere. Suddenly, everything goes black. I feel a harshness snatch my tender hand. I am being dragged away.

~~~~~

Anup is licking the tears from my face.

"Thank you, boy," I say, as I rub his soft ears. "You're a good loyal friend. Yes, the best. I forgive you for what you did to me before. I know that was not you."

I focus, once again, on the two dirt mounds in front of me. After all these decades they remain undisturbed. Although I have often visited this spot to meditate and remember the past, I have never dared to uncover the past—to unearth the buried treasure. What secret does that book hold? Will it tell me about my family? About me? Or does the book house some other hidden knowledge? Something about our society, perhaps? Or the Occidental

Union and Sci–Coll? Or maybe the book will reveal something else.

No, I am deceiving myself: I know exactly what is written in that book. I have always known. That book helped shape the old system, the old world before Sci–Coll. That book—and its ancient wisdom—*was* the old system. But the new system loathes that book and its so-called antiquated ideas. To be more precise, the new system *fears* that book and its timeless truths and powerful influence over the people.

I gaze at the two dirt mounds. It is now too late for revelations. For the old system and new system have now passed. Whatever secret that book holds will perish with it. So I leave the alcove with its entombed treasures. And as I walk away from my past, I also discard a part of my soul.

I have so little left to lose. Bit by bit, I am being stripped of all that makes me human.

~~~~~

Although a numbness has spread throughout most of my body, I can feel a tingling sensation crawling up my spine. But it is not painful, and my muscles are still functioning.

As a bonus, the numbness is also deadening my body's various afflictions. My two lower-left molars have stopped throbbing. The countless parasite bites no longer itch. My wounds and scratches have ceased hurting. And my muscles do not ache.

~~~~~

I am sitting on a Victorian-era grave near the cliff edge. Cracked black-and-white tiles cover the burial plot, and the location gives me a panoramic view of the ocean. Yet night has almost fallen, and the ocean has lost its colour. A threatening blackness now faces me instead of a blue grandeur. I can, however, still detect a trace of clean saltiness in the sea spray. This comforts me.

The time has come. I unwrap my now-nonfunctioning tablet computer from around my forearm and toss the technology over the cliff edge. I then lob my backpack and two machetes into the waters below. All my material possessions are gone, except for the remaining euthanasia Tablet. For no earthly goods will help me during the coming journey.

A thud! then another! and another! Each deafening soundwave tears through me, winding me and jellifying my bowels. Thousands of dead crows and seagulls begin to drop from the sky, each bird striking the Earth with a thump. The rat-tat-tat of countless dead insects as they hit the tombs soon follows, whereas the dead butterflies, light and graceful, float gently to the Earth in a pendulumlike motion.

Anup is trembling with terror, so I hug him while the macabre show unfolds.

The dusk sky then turns blood red, as hundreds of crimson bolts, one after the other, light up the horizon. After several minutes of relentless strikes, the red lightning suddenly ceases. The birds and insects also stop falling from the sky. Silence. Peace. Calm.

Moments later, near the horizon, an eerie red glow begins to snake its way down from the sky. It touches the water and continues to penetrate the depths of the ocean and spread across its expanse. The water, seconds ago black, is now a shimmering scarlet.

Branching red tendrils, having conquered the waters, now start hunting for fresh conquests. They sniff out their next target, and in a coordinated assault the tendrils begin slithering their way towards the land. As the first invaders wash ashore, the shimmering scarlet tide transforms into a brilliant red mist. An instant later, a sickly-sweet metallic odour suffocates me. The scent reminds me of the Red Fog of Death's—though more concentrated.

The luminous red mist then sprouts thousands of embryonic tendrils, which immediately begin to feel their way throughout the land. Several seething tendrils reach the cliff and start swarming up the rocky face. After a couple of seconds, the first exploratory tendril reaches the cemetery and, in a brilliant flash of ruby-red light, shoots off into every direction. The lands, deep to the west, shudder from the violent alien invasion, and countless cherry-red plumes erupt from every square inch of soil. The Earth is bleeding.

And, then, the scarlet phosphorescence washes over Anup and me. It tickles my skin, and I giggle in response. Equally delighted, Anup wags his tail and lets out several yips.

I feel euphoric, alive! My tensed muscles unwind, and I begin to breathe more freely than I have ever breathed before. The land, air, and water are dancing with life: red glimmering life. A celebration of alien magnificence.

After several surreal seconds, the heightened awareness ends and the shimmering red mist vanishes. Yet it leaves glimmering red traces all over the sky, land, and ocean. An unearthly scarlet luminescence now lights up the sky and coats the entire Earth.

The picodust's conquest is almost complete.

~~~~~

It is the moment I have dreaded the most.

Anup is twitching violently. He loses control of his body and collapses on what is now a luminescent scarlet grave.

"My beautiful baby boy!" I cry out, while stroking his fur. "No! Please, don't go!"

Anup whimpers as he fights against the invading alien entity. A wormlike wave washes over his body and then freezes his muscles.

"Please, God, I beg you!" I scream at the red sky. "I beg you! I have never asked for anything! Why are you doing this? *Why?* What have I done? What have we done? *Please!* I beg you!"

Everywhere—sky, sea, and land—the alien redness looks like it is glowing brighter. Is it possible? Perhaps it is my watery eyes. Or perhaps my mind is playing tricks on me, in the depths of my despair.

With a great jolting effort, Anup positions his head across my lap and sighs. It is the sigh of defeat. I have heard it before, and I know it well. I pat his head and then massage his ears.

My jaw is aching; my heart is breaking.

"I think this is it, Nupy," I whisper in a quavering voice. "I think this is goodbye, my friend. You've been so good to me. But I can't save you. I am so sorry, *my beautiful baby boy*. I shall miss you, for I have no one and nothing but you."

Anup's movements diminish. Flickering consciousness now.

"Anup. Nupy. Nups," I murmur, while gasping for air between bouts of heavy sobbing.

I think he hears my voice. I think he is comforted by its familiarity and my loving caress, during those moments of flickering consciousness. But I cannot be sure. I can only hope that the years of friendship, of good times, of shared life, have left an indelible stamp on his soul. Does anything last? Do goodness and love transcend this vale of tears? Or does everything rot along with the flesh?

"*My precious, precious boy*," I say, as I fumble around my pocket. "I am so sorry for what I am about to do to you. But, you know, it is for your own good, because I don't want you to suffer. I love you. I want you to be happy, forever, my little Nups. I want you to experience peace. No pain. No more suffering."

I finally locate the Tablet.

I wrap my arms around my baby boy, my lifelong companion, and place a final kiss on his forehead. He reacts: his tail flicks weakly, pathetically, one last time. He is a ghost of his former self—the final essence of Anup. A last drop of life. And each dimming dub-dub of his heart mercilessly tears my soul apart.

"We have been through so much together, *my beautiful baby boy*. So much. I can't remember a life without you. It already hurts too much."

Again, my voice appears to comfort him; his flickering consciousness responds to its familiarity. Yes, I feel a connection—feeble yet strong enough to anchor him to reality, to me. His light is dying but not doused.

"Good bye, *my beautiful baby boy*," I say, with the wretched tears of a final farewell. "Perhaps we shall meet again, in green-green fields, some sunny day. Yes, some sunny day. I'd like that. So would you. But for now no more pain."

Despite the crippling spasms of anguish, I muster every ounce of awareness that I can to witness Anup's final moment on Earth. I must memorise his last instant in this heartless universe. I yearn to connect with his final flicker of "I"ness and sentience. For some unknown reason, an instinct compels me to complete this concluding task.

I slip the Tablet into Anup's mouth. It is my final Tablet, and I am sacrificing it to ease his suffering.

I shut Anup's once-expressive brown eyes. He exhales sharply, his final warm breath. His muscles tense. He stops struggling. His light has been extinguished. And one less flame burns brightly in this universe.

My beautiful baby boy is dead.

Flashes from our past. Our first encounter.

A puppy is scavenging through rubbish piles in the metropolis. His skin clings to his protruding bones. Fleas and mites have eaten away most of his fur, and the remaining tufts are matted with filth and dried blood. A gang of teenagers spots the helpless creature. One teenager ties a rope around the puppy's bony neck, while another sears his tender flesh with a flame. The pup yelps, a haunting cry that captures the misery of existence. He pleads for mercy. For what has he done to deserve such random cruelty? What did he do to be born into such a hell? Where is God in all this vileness? And, in its usually perverse way, the universe answers the puppy's plea for clemency with more pointless cruelty. The laughing teenagers kick and ridicule the puppy, while dragging him, by the rope tied around his neck, across the rubble-strewn streets. For the puppy's destiny lies at the end of the street, where a massive scar-pitted pitbull is pacing up and down a fenced enclosure. The puppy is to provide momentary entertainment for humans whose lives have been stripped of all meaning and empathy, goodness and responsibility—humans whose lives have been reduced to senseless nothingness. But these soulless teenagers are unaware that they are being stalked. And, in a primal rage, I ambush them. The following moments are hazy, however. And the next thing I remember the puppy is waddling towards me, his tail flicking and his abused face full of hope. I pick him up and cradle him. Bone, skin, grime—my fingers find little else. Yet he lives. The pup clings to me with raw paws and buries his tiny head in the folds of my shirt. We share the warmth of the living, the miracle of life. The universe has finally shown him something besides ceaseless torment. For I shall shower him with love.

~~~~~

8

I am alone.

The world has been whittled down to one. One individual whose grief and wretchedness are his only companions. One man who will witness the climax of billions of years of life and evolution, of thousands of years of human curiosity and civilisation. Yet with whom shall I share my thoughts and feelings, my fears and agony?

The alien numbness is spreading to every part of my body: my legs, my arms, my face. No tingling sensation now. Just numbness, nothingness. Soon, the picodust will also numb my mental pain and end my curse: the curse of life.

I stare *east* at the shimmering red ocean, the luminescent scarlet sky. But I dare not look back *west*. I can never face that past again. Behind, in the occident, lies death and sorrow; ahead, in the orient, emptiness and purposelessness. The universe has gifted me with these two choices.

I slide my eyes shut, and my body begins to stiffen. So I recline on the same grave where Anup now rests.

The coldness of the grave slowly saps me of my warmth, of my will to live. Each breath is becoming shallower, and I am finding it harder to breathe. The nothingness is pressing against my chest, compressing my body, squeezing the life out of me.

Panicked, I try to open my eyes and stand up. But I cannot. My muscles refuse to respond to my mind's commands. It is an alien mutiny—the picodust's final triumph. I have failed. I am defeated. I submit.

Please don't let me suffer, I think to myself. Or perhaps I am pleading with someone or something? *I beg you, kill me quickly and mercifully. Please end this misery, this nothingness.*

A vivid image then irrupts into my mind.

A brown-robed figure is sleeping on a plain wooden cot, in a cold stone-hard room. It appears to be a mediaeval monk's cell. Next to the cot, a single lit candle illuminates the dark windowless room. And on the harsh walls, sinuous shadows dance to the flame's rhythm. The robed figure shifts his head and exposes his face: the man is I—but older and bearded and sickly. What am I doing here? What is happening to me? A heavy timber door creaks open, and a black-robed figure shuffles into the room. His face, however, remains hidden behind the robe's hood. In his right hand, he holds a thick ancient book; in his left, a gnarled wooden cane. He sits on the cot's edge, and rests the book and cane on my chest. He then grasps my hand gently, reassuringly. "From nothing, nothing comes; from something, something comes," he says in a frail yet authoritative voice. "So why are you so scared of 'nothing', when 'nothing' does not exist? For 'nothing' is just a word, a meaningless idea. 'Nothing' simply means 'not something'—and there is always something. Reality is something, and all that exists is reality—is something. Even 'empty' space is something, not 'nothing', because it contains energy and force fields. And the birth of the observable universe at the Big Bang came from something, from energy and force fields, not from 'nothing'. So 'nothing' does not exist, cannot exist. 'Nothing' is an absurd idea. The real question is not, why is there something rather than nothing? The real question is, why does anything at all exist? Therefore, your fear of 'nothing', of 'nothingness', is misplaced and pointless. Since there is existence, then there will always be existence. And 'you' are part of that existence. 'You' are tapping into that rich tapestry of reality. 'You' are something, and something will always be something, even if it transforms into something else. So your fears, my beautiful baby boy, are just as misguided as the concept of 'nothing'." I try to respond to the man with the hidden face, but I cannot. Who is he? Is he just a projection of my mind, my fears, my desires? Or is he the picodust, trying to communicate with me? Or perhaps he is something else altogether. And why did he use that phrase "my beautiful baby boy"? That is the phrase I would use with Anup, my beautiful baby boy who is now dead. The hooded man then says, "Your pain, I feel. Your confusion, I feel. Your despair, I feel. But, again, they are all entangled with the 'nothingness' that you so desperately fear and dread—the 'nothingness' that you have been fleeing from all your life. Although I am unable to show you that 'nothing' cannot exist—for that would be even more absurd than talking about 'nothing'—the evidence is all around you that something does exist. And that something you have experienced. For without experience, without sentience, then how could you know that anything exists? My precious, precious boy, your experience is not an illusion: your experience is real. Experience is reality. Experience is the ultimate constituent of reality. *You know that the physical exists because you* experience *it. But if you were to deny your experience, then you would also have to deny the physical—since you can learn about the physical only through your experiences. So your mental experience is just as real as the physical thing it detects and pictures. Reality is the experience* and *the nonexperience—the mental* and *the material. And the ultimate constituent of reality must include* both. *But because something always exists, and that something, at its heart, is the experience and the nonexperience—or the mental and the material— then both will always exist. You,* my beautiful baby boy, *are more than just an abstract idea or a mathematical equation or molecules in motion. You are a real, unique, and* experiential *individual. And, yes, I can guess your next question. Yet I cannot answer it. For even though your journey—*this *journey—is coming to an end, you should realise by now that the journey never ends. Journeys change—they transform from something into something else—but the journey never ends.* My precious, precious boy, *something will* always *be something. From something, something comes. Be at peace."* The hooded man then strokes my hair, leaves the book and cane on my chest, and departs the room. But as he shuts the door, a gust extinguishes the candle's flame—and I am temporarily left alone in the darkness.

~~~~~

I desperately gasp for air. Some leaks into my lungs—but not enough.

All I have ever known and experienced is condensing into a speck in time. The Occidental Union, my family and friends, even my beloved Anup—every thought and emotion and experience is now parcelled up into one distant dot. And this brilliant white dot is floating away. It is sailing towards a shimmering red horizon. Yet my "I"ness is trapped inside that distant dot. My memories, my sentience, my soul—"I" am slipping away. "I" am drifting farther away from the physical here and now. And nothing can stop this process. Nor do I want anything to stop it. For I no longer fear the darkness or "nothingness".

I have been fleeing from shadows long enough.

~~~~~

ABOUT THE AUTHOR

Ramy Tadros completed degrees in medical science and political theory. Seduced by the world of words, he then focused on enhancing his writing and editing skills, before becoming a researcher and a writer for various Australian Commonwealth Government departments. He now writes and edits nonfiction for a living, and teaches writing and editing courses at Sydney Community College. *The Book of Death* is his debut novel.